# AS DARK AS MY FUR

*Recent Titles by Clea Simon from Severn House*

*Blackie and Care Mysteries*

THE NINTH LIFE
AS DARK AS MY FUR

*Dulcie Schwartz Mysteries*

SHADES OF GREY
GREY MATTERS
GREY ZONE
GREY EXPECTATIONS
TRUE GREY
GREY DAWN
GREY HOWL
STAGES OF GREY
CODE GREY

B119

# AS DARK AS MY FUR

*A Blackie and Care mystery*

# Clea Simon

This first world edition published 2016
in Great Britain and 2016 in the USA by
SEVERN HOUSE PUBLISHERS LTD of
19 Cedar Road, Sutton, Surrey, England, TW9 1DA.
Trade paperback edition first published
in Great Britain and the USA 2017 by
SEVERN HOUSE PUBLISHERS LTD.

British Library Cataloguing in Publication Data
A CIP catalogue record for this title is available from the British Library.

ISBN-13: 978-0-7278-8682-8 (cased)
ISBN-13: 978-1-84751-785-2 (trade paper)
ISBN-13: 978-1-78010-854-4 (e-book)

This is a work of fiction. Names, characters, places and incidents
are either the product of the author's imagination or are used fictitiously.
Except where actual historical events and characters are being described
for the storyline of this novel, all situations in this publication are
fictitious and any resemblance to actual persons, living or dead,
business establishments, events or locales is purely coincidental.

*All Severn House titles are printed on acid-free paper.*

Severn House Publishers support the Forest Stewardship Council™ [FSC™],
the leading international forest certification organisation.
All our titles that are printed on FSC certified paper carry the FSC logo.

MIX
Paper from
responsible sources
FSC® C013056
www.fsc.org

Typeset by Palimpsest Book Production Ltd.,
Falkirk, Stirlingshire, Scotland.
Printed and bound in Great Britain by
TJ International, Padstow, Cornwall.

# ONE

I watch the girl.

She is sitting at the desk, as she has since daylight, reading over the letter she has perused a dozen times or more, the page laid flat before her on the stained blotter. I have eaten and slept, but lightly, in the hours that have passed, aware at all times of her slim form dwarfed by that old oak desk and the tension that keeps her hunched over that one piece of paper. That has her murmuring, anxious, as if by repetition she will soothe what worries her.

'Tenant deceased,' she reads out loud, and I believe she would argue if she could. 'Vacate,' she adds, reading further. The words stir something in me. A memory and a regret. But the girl only sighs and shakes her head. 'I can't even make out the signature,' she says, and falls silent once more.

This one room has been our shelter for weeks now. Our home. A shabby office in a rundown area of town, rented by the month by the old man, who was her mentor and her friend. As much an efficiency as a workspace, with its kitchenette and the battered sofa, where I slept, yesterday, as the spring rains fell. As need drove her out, despite the cold and wet, to forage in our ruined city.

I woke as the paper slid beneath the door, which has been broken and must now be crudely barred. Guarded it until she returned, her worn cloth sack fragrant with broken fruits. Already, I had examined the notice, cataloguing the scent of the hand that brought it, the ink that forms the words as well as the strange imprint at its top. Markers I may once have known, but which now mean nothing.

The girl took her time with it as well, upon her return, staring at the imprint before putting it aside. With deliberate focus she then parceled out the contents of her sack onto the larder counter. Apples already darkened by decay, but which she separated into piles: wrinkled and sweet, bitter. Gone. She'd looked over as she did this, turning toward me, the question clear in her large green eyes, and I did my best to respond, settling myself comfortably on the windowsill and turning away to signal my disinterest in such vegetable matter, fresh or rotten. Only then did she eat, devouring one small fruit, sweet with rot, and sucking each finger clean. She is hungry, this girl, to the point of weakness, and yet she would share her food with me, a cat.

She owes me nothing, this child, burgeoning on womanhood. Despite the time I spend here, my predilection for this sill and for a certain worn spot on that sofa, I am sufficient unto myself, a creature of the streets, and I have no need of her meager provisions. I appreciate her generosity, however. Few of her kind would choose to share – shelter or food – with such a beast as I, ragged and undomesticated. But I have little taste for what she consumes, the fruit of plants halfway to fermentation. Not in this form. In this life, and what came before is fading.

Even if I did feel such yearning, hunger burning beneath my coal-black hide, I would not take from her. My green eyes may seem distant, focused on other matters, but I see the blue tinge of her skin, the fraying lips. She is hungrier than I, as well as cold, and I – I would remedy both, if I could. For although I am a beast, I am not without heart. Indeed, I have tried to feed her, bringing her the choicest of my prey on several occasions only to see her turn aside, much as I did earlier. And as I cannot will her out of such dainty habits, I have taken to dining in private, sharing her company only once I have fed, before I return to sit and brood on lives past and the possibilities that remain.

I sit now on the windowsill, aware of how I must appear: a large, black cat at rest, my paws tucked neatly beneath me. As ruminative as any pet to the undiscerning eye, but what I brew upon is not fit for most to hear. My thoughts are dark. Although my eyes may seem to close, I remain alert. On a vigil. Waiting for what may come. For now, I watch the girl.

'It's no use, Blackie.' She doesn't look up as she shakes her head, her mop of pink hair falling over her eyes. She is addressing herself more than me, although she goes by the name

Care – a ridiculous name, as bad as that hair – and mine is not Blackie. 'We have until the end of the week.'

I jump from the windowsill at this to join her by the desk. I have no reply to offer – what I wait for is not hope, nor will it ease her hunger – but I lean against her in support. Her leg is warm through her thin jeans, and her skin smells clean.

'At least you don't seem too desperate.' Her hands grasp my middle, and I let her haul me to her lap. 'You're plumping out,' she says, one hand smoothing my midnight fur. 'If I didn't know better, I'd say you were getting younger.'

I can't help myself. I purr. It's not the compliment, although I take some pride in my coat, which has indeed grown lush and thick in the weeks we have been together. Since she pulled me, drowning, from the storm drain where I was overwhelmed. Where I faced three men – two lackeys and a leader both fearless and cruel. And where I woke to awareness in this feline form. No, it's the rhythmic stroking that evokes this involuntary response, a purely animal reaction beyond my conscious control. No matter, the low rumble relaxes the girl, and for that I am grateful, happy to share my pleasure as well as the warmth of our bodies in this dim, chill room.

I would sleep. The sun has passed its peak, leaving the sill, my accustomed perch, in shadow. And although there are hours yet before the light will fully fade, I would rest for hunting. I may appear younger, once again, having taken renewed vigor from the girl, but even as I stretch and sigh, I feel my age.

And something more. My acute senses aid me even as the skills honed in my former life – the one I have begun to recall – recede.

'What is it?' The girl sits up, her hand still, as she feels me tense. I jump to the floor, unsure myself of what had startled me, and then I know. A noise – footfall, quick and quiet – a man, but a careful one, is coming up the stairs.

'The landlord?' The girl has noted how stiff I stand, facing the closed door, and has the wit to whisper. The messenger did not arrive like this, with stealth and care, but I lack the means to tell her, to appease her trepidation. Nor is it the one I fear – the leader of my tormentors, a fiend who still haunts my dreams. She rolls back the chair and starts to rise, as quiet as she can.

She has not barred the entrance and would remedy that lack. But even as she approaches it, the door squeaks and opens. I hunch down, readying myself to leap.

'Hullo?' A low voice, soft and tentative, is followed by a brown felt cap pulled low over the ears of a small man with large eyes, which blink in at us. 'May I?'

'Of course.' Care stands to greet her visitor, assuming a posture of ease. 'Please, come in.'

The little man does, and she ushers him to the old sofa before wheeling the desk chair up to face him. I keep watch, but at a distance. No, this is not the one I fear, but his minions may appear just so innocuous when they make their inevitable approach.

She does not know this. Indeed, her anxiety is apparent as she wipes her palms on her thighs, eager to present a firm handshake. A good impression. That he appears more solicitous than patronizing, more mole than man, matters not. Although he has removed that soft cap and now holds it before him, with both hands, she is the eager one. Uneasy, not for fear of possible harm but for what he may bring. The visitor is a potential client. The girl is starving. The stakes are high.

'How may I help you?' she asks, holding her voice steady with an effort that I, at least, can hear.

'You are – you have taken over the agency?' His voice suggests some other doubt, a questioning.

Care hears it too, and immediately begins to recite the catchphrase of her mentor, the private investigator whose office she now occupies. 'I do the needful. Find the missing. Locate the wrongdoer. Retrieve what has been lost, and—'

'That's it,' he interrupts. 'Retrieval. Not – the others.'

She nods and waits. He has begun to talk, and her silence will do the rest.

'I recently ran into some – some trouble.' His hands tighten on the cap, turning it slightly. 'I do not – it is all in the line of business.'

The cap continues its silent rotation, but the man holding it is still. Finally, she prompts him. 'And what is your line of business, Mr—'

'Quirty. Just – Quirty,' says the little man. 'I am a keeper. A keeper and a scribe.'

Care nods again. In this city, the trades often go hand in hand. A man who can write, an educated man, is often the repository of papers. It is a good living for the small and weak, as I can still recall, but not without its risks.

'I am good at my job,' the little man says now. 'People know me, and I do not ask for much. But my eyes—' He waves a hand, as if to emphasize the near blindness of the large and bloodshot orbs. 'I use a lens. A magnifier. It would mean nothing to most. Certainly not to the men who came, but to me . . .' He falls silent, his eyes cast down as if to study the floor.

Care nods. That look explains it all. 'I'll take your case,' she says, as moved by his apparent frailty as by the injustice of the theft. It is not a wise choice, I would warn her. She too is one of the smaller creatures out there and may well be set upon as this man clearly has been. But her offer springs as much from a generous heart as from the need for clients. Besides, keepers – scribes – are trusted. His word may bring more custom.

'I will need to visit your office,' she says, her voice grown soft. From somewhere, she has learned how private such men may be, unless her time with me has heightened her awareness of the prey mentality.

'Of course.' He jumps up from the sofa, energized by her assent. But as he leads her from the building and down into the warren of streets down, I cannot help but be reminded of the scurry of a mouse. This man was born a victim, and I would not have the girl drawn too close.

Although he leads us swiftly – for surely I would not leave the girl alone – he does not appear to take a direct path to anywhere. Instead, he ducks through alleys, scuttling around the edge of first one vacant lot and then another, crossing narrow streets shadowed by the buildings that loom above. The street names come to me, as if from a distant dream, and I recognize the printer's district. Along Leading, as some wag had named this narrow road, the buildings nearly touch. Kern Lane, and then – yes – Ink Square, a pitted plaza where few of the cobblestones remain. Half ruined, this place is quiet, and has not enjoyed the seamy resurgence of the harbor so nearby. The block-like towers here, most now piles of rubble plundered like those cobblestones, are more the home of quiet squatters and small businessmen, such as this Quirty, where they are occupied at all.

The little man skirts the open space, like some frightened rodent, and ducks into a muddy alley fragrant with a scent like that of fermentation, sharp and slightly sweet. I follow, lingering over one pile of rubbish, but there is no carcass beneath. It is ink that I have sensed, a surfacing memory informs me, a fragrance I now associate with Care and with that pile of papers. I am not surprised, therefore, when with one last look at the open square behind, the small man ducks around a mound of crumbling brick to a set of stairs. Nearly hidden behind the rubble, it descends to a metal door. There is no lock, not anymore. Perhaps there never was: a keeper relies on secrecy rather than such devices. But still he opens the door, holding it wide for her to enter, a gesture that recalls another, older time.

For myself, I am leery of such portals, whether they latch or no, and instead make my way around the corner from where that same sweet, fruity scent emanates. I am rewarded by a window, long bereft of glass, although a flap of waxed paper must keep out the worst of the rains. It is easy for me to brush aside, and I have jumped down while the scribe is showing Care to a seat. It is a small room and private; its walls still hold. Wherever he keeps his stash of documents, it is not immediately apparent.

Which may be just as well. That the thieves wrecked his place is evident, using more force than most would deem necessary. Although the little man appears to have wrestled his large desk back upright, marks upon it and upon the plain stone floor show where it had been thrown. The shattered remains of an inkpot have been swept into a corner, a chipped mug pressed into service in its place, although the pen that rests within is bent. This man, this keeper, has done his best to restore order, but my senses are attuned to other clues than sight. I can hear the whistle of the wind. A lack of solidity in this office, in his life.

'I don't ask—' he starts and then catches himself. A hesitation based on fear, perhaps? 'I hold my secrets, that is my stock in trade.' A small smile as he sneaks a glance at her. Even amid this ruination, he is relaxed here. A creature in his den. The men were not successful in their quest. 'Of course, that's easier when I don't have what is being sought. It doesn't matter.'

In his new volubility, he confirms my first conclusion but hastens to preempt any further lines of inquiry. 'This world runs as it must, and I'll not stand in anyone's way. But my glasses – they're magnifiers, like a giant lens. I need them for my livelihood and to take them . . .' He shakes his head. 'I need them.'

'I can look for them,' Care says with more alacrity than I'd expected. The job is small, and I cannot imagine this poor scribe can pay. She has been desperate, however, and more than that, I believe she feels a kinship with this little half-blind man. 'If I can retrieve them, I will. And in return . . .' She pauses. Bites her lip. 'In return, you'll owe me a favor. You can spread the word that I'm in business. That I can find things.'

'Maybe I'll be able to do more than that.' The little mole man smiles, the first sign of joy I've seen on him. It transforms his visage, even to his tired eyes. 'I knew your old man, you know. He'd be proud of you.'

They shake on it, the bond of business, as I leap once more to the window and then out.

'Did you hear that, Blackie?' she whispers when I find her on the street. She is not surprised to see me, I believe, but neither does she expect me to comprehend her words. I walk a tightrope with this girl, each unsure of what the other can grasp. She stares at me, as if waiting for an answer. Unable to provide one, I sniff the curb. A dog has been here, as well as other men.

'He knew the old man. If I can help him . . .' She shakes her head, the remainder of the thought unspoken as she begins to walk.

Despite my silence, my thoughts teem as I keep pace by her side. I have no memory of the man, which troubles me. I should, if he knew her mentor. For although I do not yet understand how such a change occurred, that means he knew *me*, as I was in another life. A human life, before this feline incarnation. An existence I have only recently – and imperfectly – begun to recall. Perhaps this is merely another gap. Perhaps something more. Yet whether it be by feline instinct or some deep-buried recollection, I believe this man an honest sort, for one who survives as needs must, and I can tell that for her the reward may come in many forms.

# TWO

C are pounces on the assignment as a kitten on prey, working it as if the effort alone will yield sustenance. She seeks distraction, that I know, but also hope. She cannot have caught, as I have, the foul male reek of the two who did this. Who waited by that curb to catch the little man and force him to reveal his secrets. And her client, through some remnant of decorum, did not reveal the intimate and insulting nature of the puddle in the corner, which he has worked so hard to clean. But she has taken their descriptions, unwilling as he was to give them despite her promise not to interfere – not to seek the offending thugs directly.

'I only want my magnifier,' he repeats, after describing two men: one large and thuggish, the other, smaller, with a blade. Still, she knows her trade, or well enough. Knows to inquire about even the smallest details. The factors that do not seem to matter – and to record as well the manner in which her queries are received. She had been learning when the old man, her mentor, was taken from her. When he – when *I* – was ambushed and summarily killed.

'The question,' she says, more to herself than to me, 'is what those bully boys would do with a set of lenses, once they left. That they took them just to be awful to Quirty is obvious.'

We are sitting side by side on a block of granite on the edge of that pockmarked square. The sun has penetrated both the morning clouds and the shadows that overhang the narrow lane behind us. It is warm, and I listen, content, as she counts off her reasons on fingers bitten to the quick. 'They trashed his place, but I don't think they found what they were looking for.' The keeper was silent on this point, but the girl has picked up the signs – his calm, despite the attack. His continuing allegiance to his office, to his craft.

'They probably can't read and might resent him because he could.' She stops at that, as if to question her own logic – another

crucial skill. 'But if they were here, they must have been looking
for something on paper. Something written. I wonder if there
was an insignia or letterhead they were made to memorize?'
she asks, her voice grown soft. 'Why would someone send
illiterate thugs to find a document?'

The sun is glorious, and I stretch to take it in. There is
something in her questions, a rattle and a scramble like small
feet heard down a passage. But before I can follow them to the
kill, she has already moved on.

'Well, they weren't sent for their learning,' she says at last.
'And since I doubt their boss would care for a magnifier . . .'

She stands. 'I've got it,' she says, and sets off again, darting
around the open square toward a small passageway opposite.
Although she sticks to the side streets, down alleys and across
deserted lots, darkened by shadows even at daylight's peak, she
is not headed back toward the little man's lair, not this time. I
smell her destination in the salt tang, in the particular fetor of
rot and commerce. She is leaving behind the quiet of the printer's
district and heading toward the harbor.

I follow, discreetly, making my own more circuitous way
along the lower rooftops and behind the piles of trash. I do not
like this area, a warren of abandoned and disused warehouses
most of which have been repurposed for functions unsuitable
to a young girl. I do not trust those who gather here. Down
farther, by the water's edge, the district assumes more of its
original purpose. Goods for trade fill the featureless brick buildings, signs of commerce that continues despite the failure of
laws and boundaries. The rutted streets rumble with the traffic
of large vehicles, the shouts of the men who load and unload
them for their daily pay.

Struggles of a different sort occur here as well. The rotted
piers and the creeping damp, which corrodes even the brick
and mortar of those huge structures, swarms with life on a
smaller scale, including those of my own kind. It is here that
the girl and I met. Here where she saved me, pulling me as I
hissed and spat from a storm drain that would have taken me.
Would have swept my lifeless carcass to the harbor. Where my
life began again.

But the strange ill feeling that sets the fur of my ruff to rise is not mere memory. Nor, I hope, presentiment. This district, with its rough labor, is unsafe for a young female such as Care, and I do not like the way she strides along the main thoroughfare, toward the train tracks and the no man's land beyond. If I were larger, my animosity would serve some purpose. As it is, I am a cat, and so I make my way at a distance, watching. I have skills I may be pressed to use, and I will be ready.

She does not, I am glad to see, keep up her pace as she approaches the intersection where the trucks and men congregate. Instead, she pauses in an open area that I know best from nighttime traffic. After dark, it draws those men and others, workers in the uptown offices who seek companionship or entertainment of another sort. I have accompanied Care across this plaza before, witnessing the drunkenness and debauch, and observe with relief the composition of the daytime congregants. Older and more ragged, they are less aggressive than those nocturnal celebrants, their interest more geared toward what one young female may seek to spend than sell.

'Just looking,' says the girl, when one of the small crowd glances up. Of indeterminate age – only scent identifies her as female – the creature started as Care reached her patch: a block of stone, a pedestal once or stoop, spread with small and broken things: a dented metal cup, a basket, torn, and a nib-less pen. The creature eyes Care's bag. 'Nothing to barter,' she says, hugging the faded sack of canvas slung over her shoulder. 'Not today.'

She steps back, but lingers as if reconsidering her words. As I follow her gaze, I see why. Here, in the shade by the plaza's poorest vendor, she can surveil those at its center. A baker – or the baker's man, more likely – has a table, where broken husks and misshapen loaves are displayed. A fruit vendor, her basket full of bruised and broken apples, beside him. Hard by them, a rag man has set up shop, the open sides of his cart hung with gaudy strips of green and yellow. He plucks one of these for a passerby, and I see it forms a shirt. The shopper – a thin man in grease-stained jeans – pulls the bright top over his head, ripping it in the process and provoking the laughter of several larger types who stand nearby. The rag man is less amused and begins to argue as the thin man pushes the ruined piece back.

He would have payment for it, despite its shoddy quality, that much is clear, but the would-be customer stands firm.

The little drama, meanwhile, has drawn attention away from the other vendors, at least in part. On the sidelines, something moves, small and fast. A child emerges from the shadows by the baker's table to grab a hunk of bread. The cry is raised too late: the child is fast, and in the hubbub the grease-stained man makes his move as well. I watch the girl, attending her interest and reaction both. The child, it is clear, has support. The ragged creature by the stone steps sideways as he runs, putting herself in the way of the pursuit. She gets slammed – hard – into the block for her trouble, but the child is gone. The thin man, meanwhile, has made his own escape, for now, the ruined garment left behind.

The girl notes their passing and how the crowd responds, but only after the ragged woman pulls herself up does she move on. She walks slowly, as if without a purpose, but I see her eyes. Another table, hard by, piled with better wares than those of the ragged woman at the edge has gained her interest. The sun is still high above and, even through the overcast sky, reflects off the blades of knives and silver lying on the dealer's cloth. A pair of boots, good leather, stands next to candlesticks, three different sets.

'Nice wares,' says Care. She saunters close, and I follow, concerned that her assumed nonchalance will be questioned. Will be exposed.

The man behind the table sizes her up with one good eye. The patch over the other does little to hide the scar across his face. He nods, as if she's worth the effort. 'What do you want?'

'What else you got?' she asks. She reaches for a serving spoon, its handle heavy and ornate. Glances up to see if he is watching, then lifts it anyway to turn it over before replacing it on the grimy cloth. 'I think I've seen all this before.'

His eyes narrow. 'I get new wares daily,' he says, a hint of defensiveness tightening his voice. 'My boys comb the city for the best.'

Care shrugs, her thin shoulders eloquent in their dismissal. That's when he shuffles, pushing the silver spoons over toward the boots to clear a space. And from beneath the trestle that supports his table, he pulls a sack. From it, he withdraws a fist-sized lump of something solid and clear. *Crystal.* The word comes to me. Its heft is apparent from the vendor's grasp. Then a book, its pages frayed and feathering. Last, an awkward fist-sized object. A box of some sort, it would seem, only with legs at either end.

I am close enough, my hearing acute enough, to hear Care's breathing catch, but to the vendor standing by she is silent. Indeed, when she reaches once again, it is for the book. With an indifference I know to be studied, she flips through its pages before replacing it once more. The crystal she cups with more interest, as if weighing it in her hand. And when she sees the flap on top – a small piece of metal that opens to reveal the reservoir within – she makes a cooing sound, reminiscent of a pigeon come to roost.

'Make an offer,' says the vendor, a little too fast.

'For a toy like this?' She holds it still. Turns it so it catches the light. 'When the toff who lost it might come by at any moment?'

'There's no—' The one-eyed man catches himself. 'I bought it fair and square. I've got a regular distributor. He comes by once a week.'

Care makes a face as if she's considering. As if the inkwell might appeal. 'I think your distributor ripped you off,' she says. Her voice is quiet. 'I hear the rozzers are looking for a toy like this, or someone bigger. And that—' One finger, a gesture, nothing more, toward the box-like thing, which I now see has a clear panel between its edges. 'That's broken, too.'

'Someone bigger . . .' He reaches for the inkwell, but she holds firm. 'You wouldn't,' he says, his voice growing softer still.

'Two guys, one bruiser, one with a face like a hatchet?' She repeats the mole man's description of his assailants, the one he was so unwilling to give. 'I hear they've been doing a little business on the side. Business the boss doesn't know about.'

'No, no way.' The vendor looks around, as if expecting to see uniforms approaching. Or worse. 'Not my old mates. Look.' He steps back, hands in pockets, and gestures toward the inkwell with his chin. 'You take that. You take that and go, all right? Just – go.'

'This? No.' She places the cut crystal back on the table, where its polished facets catch the light. 'But a token. Just so we know we understand each other.'

The magnifier, for that is what that last item must be, she picks up lightly, as if she might toss it back too. But with a smile that she keeps cool and guarded, she slips it into her bag and, with a nod, turns to go.

'That bastard.' Her voice is bitter, with an anger I do not understand. 'He's got stolen goods from all over the city. From people who can't afford it, either.' She stops and shakes her head. 'But he's as scared as anyone. I wonder if there really is something going on?' We have walked away from the market square, slowly at first, and then with speed once the vendors are out of sight. Four blocks away, she stops to examine her prize, sitting in the shadow of a dumpster.

I sniff the middle part. What I thought a box is filled instead with glass, which concentrates the sun onto the ground below. The side pieces, of some hard plastic, are of more interest, smelling as they do of that fruity ink and of the warmth of the mole-like man.

# THREE

He had already told her he could not pay, an admission made in shame, his eyes upon the floor. Care didn't ask, but I could hear the unstated question in the air – a question of what else the thieves had taken. What the little man had considered vital, and what only a further humiliation.

He did find other ways of showing his gratitude, and the next morning, we share the hard cheese he pressed on Care, along with some soft words of advice. *Don't pursue those men*, he had said. *Don't ask why they came to see me or what they came for.*

She must be thinking of these words as she eats, scraping thin curls off the small block with her knife. I lick at the slice she has offered me, enjoying its salt if not its waxy consistency. I have hunted, while she slept, and much prefer the fresh and juicy taste of prey. Still, it seems churlish to refuse her offer, made in generosity and in celebration of success.

'Next gig, I'll get us tuna,' she says as she savors her own slice, nibbling at the edge like a mouse. 'Quirty couldn't – or, no, wouldn't – tell me why he'd been targeted. I wonder . . .' She pauses to chew over more than the cheese. 'No.' She shakes off her own conclusion without sharing it. 'But he did tell me that the city's cut back again. More jobbing out, he said. But that's good for us, Blackie. People still need things found. Need things done.'

She hums to herself after that, a sound I take to have the same function as a purr, both as an expression of contentment and a form of self-soothing. I wonder at the latter, if perhaps her optimism is less hearty than she would have it. The little man had sounded tentative to me, a quaver in his voice betraying a new anxiety when she returned with his magnifier and her tale. I find myself joining her, as I mull this over, the vibration facilitating thought. But both our inner serenades are interrupted as a loud rap shakes the door in its battered frame.

'Yes?' Care calls as she stows the cheese in the desk drawer. The knife, I am pleased to see, she tucks in her pocket as she stands.

Another rap. The door will not withstand many such. 'You open?'

'Of course.' The girl sets her shoulders back, breathes deep and goes to lift the bar. 'Come in.'

A man steps in, short and rounded, a balding head on a stout form. From slack, wet lips hangs a matchstick, which moves around as he chews. It buys him time, letting him stand and take in the room: a desk, a tattered sofa, bare bookshelves along the wall. Something here confuses him. He does not regard me, seated in the shadow behind that broken door. Perhaps it is the lack of light, or else he didn't expect the girl. It may be her hair, pink but for a darker line at her scalp. He blinks again, but she's waiting.

'May I help you?' She has pitched her voice low, using a courtesy not common in this part of town.

'You the new girl? His helper?' The matchstick moves to the corner of his mouth as the man steps forward. He keeps one hand on the door and tilts his head, as if other questions are pending.

'This is my office,' she says. It's not exactly an answer but he nods. 'Are you looking for some assistance?'

'Yeah,' he says, and rubs his chin, callus rasping on bristle. 'Maybe.'

She waits. She has learned that much from me, in one form or another. Silence elicits speech.

'I heard someone was working here. Taking jobs like the old man did.' He looks at her, waiting, and she urges him on with a nod. 'I've got a job like that. Like he used to do.'

'I do those jobs now,' she says, pride swelling in her voice. 'Find that which needs locating. Solve what puzzles you may have.'

'Yeah, well.' As she finishes her patter, he tilts his head again, his small eyes dark and bright. 'Maybe. Just – you work alone?'

'What's the case, Mr—' She has turned away, as if to resume her paperwork. As if his question – his custom – were of no concern. I can hear the desperation in her tone. He sees only her back, as she intends.

'Gravitch,' he says, to fill the void. 'Teddy Gravitch. Folks call me Gravy.'

She rewards him with her face – and more waiting.

'It's not a big deal. It's a guy. One of my crew. He's got something going. Something outside, if you get my drift. And I don't like it.' He grunts like a pig, three quick snorts in rapid succession. No, it's a laugh, humorless and cold. The fur on my back starts to rise.

'And what is your line of work, Mr Gravitch?' The girl keeps her voice level. I doubt he can detect the effort involved. He does, however, release the door and steps into the room to look at her, a different kind of appraisal in his stare.

'All inquiries are confidential,' she says, her tone cool. Emotions now controlled. 'But different fields require different methods, and I believe you would like me to be both efficient and unobtrusive.'

'Efficient, yeah,' he says. He works his mouth around the word as if he does not understand it. 'I'm in fashion.' Maybe he sees her reaction, although she tries to hide it. Maybe he hears the absurdity himself. 'Manufacturing,' he explains. 'And distribution.'

'I see,' says the girl. Something in her tone makes me believe she does, more than the visitor would want. 'And I gather you've had some losses?'

'Someone's shorting me, I know that.' His eyes move quickly, side to side, avoiding hers. 'One of my crew, I'm pretty sure.'

'And you would like me to find out who?'

'No, no.' His eyes again, those sideways glances, making him look more rat-like than before. He twitches like a prey animal. Could he be afraid? 'I think I know who it is. Only I want to be sure, see? I need to be sure before I face him.'

'And you want me to follow this man,' says the girl. Her voice is calm and businesslike. 'To find out what he is doing and with whom, and report what I find to you.'

'Yeah, that's it.' Gravitch nods a little too enthusiastically,

his lips clamping down on the match. I narrow my eyes, the
better to take in his scent. His sweat has a bitter edge – fear
and something more. A chemical smell, dusty and sharp, more
than can be explained by the sulfur of that matchstick, and also,
strangely, soap. 'I need you to follow him.'

'And you can pay?' Somehow she has sensed the weakness
of the man as well, has drawn the same conclusion. 'For a
shadow job, I get forty a day. Half of that up front.'

'Sure, sure.' He digs into a trouser pocket and comes up with
a roll of bills. I hear her intake of breath as he peels off six.
He holds them out, an offering. 'Will three days be enough?'

'It should be,' she says, returning to the desk. 'Now, Mr
Gravitch, if I can have some information?

He steps forward awkwardly, placing the money on the
scarred wood before him, and shies slightly as she pulls a sheet
of paper loose and retrieves her pen. It's the writing, I believe
at first. The presence of such formal documentation unnerves
him. Still as he answers her questions, I catch him leaning
forward. Watching as she writes.

'This is the standard contract,' she says, noting his unease.
'I'll need the subject's name and habits.'

'Dingo,' the man before her says. 'Everyone calls him Dingo,'
he repeats when she pauses in her writing. 'His real name's
Paul Dingett, or something like.'

She takes it all down, then enquires about his hours, the
location of his workplace and where this Dingo spends his
time. He relaxes as she does so, one purpose of the ritual, as
if the form, the pen and ink, give her authority beyond her age.

'And how may I contact you?' She raises her eyes at last,
and I will her to study him. To note how he stiffens again and
withdraws. 'Do you have a phone? Should I come to your
office?'

'No, no.' The matchstick moves as he chews. 'I'll come back,'
he says, nodding as if to seal the deal. 'In three days, I will.'

She nods too and studies him. The money is on the desktop.
'Good,' she says.

He steps back and exhales, the tension he's been concealing
released at last. I strain to catch the tang of something under-
lying, but it will not come to me before he backs again, and

turning, makes for the door. I watch him go, but flick my ears. Care, behind me, has grabbed up the money with a soft sob. She is counting it, placing some of it in an envelope, some in her pocket as she leans heavily on the desk, her last reserve exhausted.

The outer door of the building has opened and swung shut. The footsteps, lighter, fading, as I turn toward the girl – toward Care.

'We're saved, Blackie,' she says, a smile playing around her pale lips. 'I'll find us another place. Get us some proper food. I have a job.'

I look up at her but do not purr. My tail, ever my betrayer, lashes behind me.

This is why my thoughts turn dark, my ragged ears begin to flatten back. I cannot tell her what I sense. Cannot explain myself. This man – this client – who would deliver us? He has resources, more certainly than that mole man does. No doubt, he has a purpose, too, a reason for employing her. Employing *us*. But there is more here: I feel the truth of that in every bristle of my whiskers. I am an animal, unable to communicate as I would, but this I know. This man? This Gravitch? Whatever his motivation, it is not the one that he disclosed.

# FOUR

There is another reason for my discontent, for the impotent rage that makes me stalk about and lash my tail. I was not always as I am now, black of fur, acute of nose and eye. In my dreams, I find the truth. Once I was such as Gravitch or that mole creature, Quirty, or nearly so. I was a man, an old man. This girl's mentor, but how I came to be as I am now, I cannot tell. That she rescued me, pulling me from the icy flood, is the first true memory I have, from soaking tail to bedraggled whiskers. Before that, though, all is shadow, and my inability to understand, as well as to fully recall, infuriates me. Perhaps if I were, as I once was, a contemplative man. Rational, deductive . . . then I would understand. But I am not.

I whip around, leather paw pads silent on the bare wood floor, and begin another circuit of the room. This I know: I was a hunter, such as this girl aims to be. Only I was snared. Entrapped and shot, and left to die. The image comes to me in sleep. Three men, their eyes more cold than mine could ever be, who watch me as I sink, as life recedes. I know them now, or feel I do. Those eyes, those forms – a memory in nightmare form. And more than that. Those who wish me harm are still at large; I sense this as I can the rats beneath the street, the roaches in the wall. They seek to hurt the girl now too – for her ties with me, for work that she has done that has cost their criminal enterprise dear – this is what I believe, and this is the root of my frustration. The one true thing that I am unable to share.

I am, I know, a cat. And while I have come to terms with many aspects of my animal nature – am more than amply recompensed for many of its drawbacks, in fact, by the finely tuned senses that I now enjoy – there are others that discomfort me. That remind me of another life, before my mind – my conscious self – assumed this form. In my former life, I vaguely remember, I was taciturn. Were I now capable of speech – intelligible speech – with even a fraction of the articulation and precision I have so long admired – my words would flow freely. I would be voluble. Verbose, even, and content.

As it is, I am confined to mews and chirps and must make myself understood through gestures, like the one I now make. Ceasing my endless pacing, I brush against the girl's shin to get her attention and then stare up at her. My eyes, I know, appear cold. Their green, reflective surface not softened, as hers are, by the subtleties of brow and smile. Often, this frustrates me, but at this moment it may serve my purpose. I want to disconcert her. She must question. She has to be aware and on her guard.

'What is it, Blackie?' I blink in acknowledgment. I have long ago given up any hope of communicating my name. We have started a new life together, this girl – Care   and I, and what came before would have little bearing on the present, were it not for the arrival of this man. This Gravitch. For her sake, now, I would have her trust me. Would have her regard my warning as more than brute instinct or, worse, the panic of a small and vulnerable beast. 'Do you want my lap?'

She sits again and pats her thin thighs, encouraging me. I hesitate a moment, and then I jump. A simple matter, really, although the physics of springing more than my height straight up sparks a quick, fevered calculation in some fading part of my brain. It is not the girl's hand I want, although she lays it gently on my back. It is that envelope. Ignoring her gentle touch, I push my wet nose toward it, eager to discover on the bills within what traces I may of the stranger's hand, his origins. The real impetus for his visit to our lair.

Closing my eyes enhances my other senses, and I do so, leaning in. In the fibers, I taste the salt of sweat. The stubby fingers of the man, and many others, held this note tight, fear and desire making them averse to let it go. I get traces of those emotions – the pheromones that leak from the grasping hands. Fear, again, and longing. And, that astringent scent of soap, as well as other, harsher cleaning agents of a kind I would not associate with such a grubby man. That scent – with its bite of lye, the overlay of cheap perfume – almost obscures another odor, more deeply ingrained, and with a bite reminiscent not of nature but of industry. A chemical tang, the scent of rainbow slicks on puddles. It is the same odd scent I got from the rat-like man, despite his attempts to wash, only stronger. Wherever this envelope and the bills that it contains were stored, it is near the source of this strange smell. I would know more.

'Is it the glue?' Care's voice interrupts my thought and I realize I am licking the envelope. I have progressed from diagnostics to savoring the glossy inside, redolent of some animal in a sun-soaked field. I sit back up and blink, somewhat abashed and troubled, frankly, that she will regard me as simpler than I am. And as I do, she tucks the envelope into a drawer, which she then closes shut. It is times like this that cause me to despair of my current form.

'You must be hungry.' Her voice is soft, and I do not believe she expects an answer. She simply speaks to me in lieu of other company. Were I to read anything else in her occasional appraising glances, I would surely go mad. 'I am, that's for sure.'

She makes to stand, and I jump down. She fishes the remaining bills from her jeans. Her face is pale and so young. This girl is barely in her teens, but her brows come together in a way that ages her as she examines the well-worn notes. I stretch. Even up on my haunches, I cannot reach them as she turns them over in her hand, but my sense of smell is acute, and I pick up once again the tang of sweat, the dulling overlay of dust – and something more – before a rumble startles me out of my reverie. She has opened the drawer again and tucked all but one note inside.

She looks at me now with a trace of a smile, the apology in her voice. 'Did I scare you? I'm sorry, Blackie.'

I sit back and begin to groom. Bad enough to be a beast, but to be judged a coward as well is infuriating.

'I'll lay in some provisions. I promise.' She has read my mood aright, but misinterpreted the cause. 'It's only, well, if we have to find another place . . .'

I cease my washing and regard her once again, unable to respond. My lack of language maddens me, but at this time I still my tail and keep my ears erect. Although I do not under-stand the means of such a transformation, or why it has come to be, I have returned – both to this life and to this girl, this

Care. I stare at her, a mere child hungry and alone, as she peruses the pages before her. She's planning, this one, jotting memorandum, and I strengthen my resolve. I have my limits, specific to this form and which I have only begun to learn. Still, I am here with her. I am trusted, and I will merit that faith. Whatever I can do to keep her safe, I will.

# FIVE

I curl upon the couch, my resolve, at least, at rest. But soon drowsiness takes over, and the dreams begin once more. Three men, silhouettes against the sun, looming over me . . .

In my dream, I welcome them, as terrifying as they may be, and seek in them the answer to my state. But when the girl leaves some time later, following our visitor's path out the door and down the worn steps of our building, I turn from them and rouse. It may be that all she seeks is nourishment, to forage as she has before. And yet I watch her from the window, a nagging fear goading me from resuming my rest. Instinct, perhaps, one of the few benefits of this form, has pricked me. Troubled me, although I know not why.

And then I see it – the flutter that has weighed on me. A line of movement, dark and spare. A trick of the light, perhaps, that shimmers a half breath later than her passing. I pause and sniff the air, but I am stymied by the distance. By the aromas in this room, and by – perhaps – my age. A shadow, but it shrinks into the greater shade cast by the building rather than stretching out.

I make my move. For although I am aged – much older than my newly glossy coat suggests – I do not believe I am mistaken. I will not take that chance and leave the girl unattended. The door is shut, but the window remains ajar and I use that as my path, maneuvering beneath the raised sill and with two successive leaps attaining first the brick ledge that protrudes above the ground-floor window and then the alley.

The girl had shouldered her sack, empty now but for two of the better apples and the few small essentials she always carries. Whatever else this Gravitch brings us, he has brought her ease. Not only food but light has been lacking in her life. The loss of artificial power does not bother me. I prefer the softness of her candle, the play of flame upon her face as she leans over her few books. It has hurt her to part with any of these, I could tell. She went between them many times before packing up the largest, those covered with the freshest hides and hammered leaf. Still, it has been several nights since she has had such stock to sell, or the means to heat even the small kettle she keeps in the alcove off the office proper.

I do not have the skill to foretell where she goes now, whether on the hunt or drawn forth on some mundane errand. But if I have seen her venture forth then, so too may others. That fleeting shade, perchance, or those for which it scouts. And so I wait by the alley's mouth until she passes by. It is a simple matter then to follow her, and I dart from one shadow to another, taking full advantage of the graying sky, of the dimming afternoon.

When she turns from our rutted street and from the center of this blighted city, I yearn for my first guess to be correct. Although I dread her interacting with that one-eyed man, I would have her continue on in this direction – to the market and its offerings. Other vendors gather there, with trade of a more honest kind. It was there she brought the books, swapping them for tins with dents in lieu of labels, apples, and once, for newer footwear, only slightly worn. She's growing fast, is Care, despite a diet that would be well supplemented by what I could provide. But, no, with this strange split awareness, I can almost comprehend the disgust my offerings evoke and shudder from it as I would a flea. I do not need this additional reminder of my animal state, bestial and crude.

Perhaps, were I other than I am, I would understand. My hope would not be in vain, but as I track her turning path, as she turns off toward the setting sun, I face the truth. She is not heading toward the market now. Nor, as I had wished, does she intend to use those bills to treat herself, perhaps to another of those books she so admires, at any of the city's more refined vendors on this evening sojourn. No, I gather that she is on one of two paths. The reasonable one relates to her new commission. I heard what that man Gravitch told her, and so it is possible that she makes her way toward the district run by his crew; the harbor, even would be preferable, in search of that suspect employee. But I fear her steps lead elsewhere. When she takes another turn, leaving behind the missing cobbles for the smoothness of asphalt and concrete, I feel a heaviness come upon me. I know where she is heading. And I cannot say a word.

'Tick, they call him.' She is talking softly, only the tightness in her voice betrays the import of her words. 'Thomas – Thomas Sears.' She gestures with her hand to indicate a height below her shoulder. 'Brown hair. Little, he's maybe ten?'

'I've not seen him.' The gruff voice is new to me and startles me back into focus. As much as I dislike admitting it, I have allowed myself to become distracted. A rat has died, its body settling into the refuse-filled well of a basement window. Not by my actions, but its fragrance proved alluring, and I had been studying it while we waited. We are in an alley, the girl and I. I followed her here as I have before, almost daily these past few weeks. She had been leaning back against the brick when I first became aware of the decaying rodent, close enough for me to ascertain the girl's movement, or so I thought. She has crossed over, while I explored, to press against the iron fence that rises opposite. She waits now, grasping the bars. The man on the other side steps forward quickly, with a furtive glance to either side. He's tall, although the coarse shirt hangs loose on his gaunt frame.

'What you got?' His voice is hoarse.

A dirty hand reaches through the spikes, and Care fishes in her bag, bringing out an apple – a better fruit than the one she gave herself. The big man takes it with surprising delicacy and then devours it, core and all, in four bites. Even as his jaw still works, he looks around, those sunken eyes as jittery as a spooked horse.

'Thanks.' The voice is unexpectedly soft, and Care manages a smile of acknowledgment. Just then, a whistle blows, and I know we will not be long. Her routine varies only in her confederate, as each visit seems to match up with arrival of a different shift. It matters not. None of these men have any news for her. None of them have seen the boy she regards as a brother, the little one who was taken away by men in uniforms, like those who watch over this yard.

'You'll keep looking, won't you?' Care sounds near tears.

'I'll pass it on,' says the man, glancing back at those uniforms now. 'To the next crew. I'm due for a work duty soon.'

There comes the sound of feet, a hoarse voice calling. 'Tell him Care is looking for him.'

The man's head whips back. 'Care? You're Vic's kid?'

'You knew my father?' She grabs the bars, leans in. Her voice drops as she looks around. 'At the Dunstan?'

'What?' He turns again. Those feet are getting closer. 'No. I don't know nothing about that. Nor do you.' A yell hastens him, and he turns to run. A loud smack. The sound of leather on flesh.

I stay by the basement well, though I give up the temptation below me for the raised ledge of a bricked-up window. I do not need to see the yard to know what has just transpired. I examined it the first time we came, its dark paved space echoing with the steps of booted feet. Have seen the inmates lining up and the reluctant march back to the hulking building, its shadow growing in the fading day. A metal grid covers the windows, as small and deeply recessed as the well beneath me, but the girl strains forward anyway. In vain, she tries to make out faces in the pale shapes that file past, but they fade away into darkness.

'Who's the boy?'

Care spins around. She sees the woman coming up the alley; she must. It would be hard to miss the blowsy blonde tottering toward her, unsteady on absurd heels, heavy legs bound close by a skirt too short for the early spring chill, a dirty purse in hand. But the girl did not notice the rat either, and now cranes her head, as if expecting someone other to appear from the shadows.

'The boy you're looking for,' the newcomer says to clarify. It serves to still Care's desperate searching. The woman nods toward the fence, although she has stopped short of it. Maybe it's those heels, but I suspect she prefers to remain in the shadow of the building. 'I've seen you here before.'

'You have?' Care may have been caught off guard, but she knows better than to volunteer information.

'Uh-huh.' The woman crosses her arms, tucking her bag beneath them. This has the effect of pushing her breasts up, but the dimpled flesh suggests she does it more for warmth. 'They took my Billy, last time I went inside.' She turns away, blinking. 'Truancy, they said.'

'Here.' Care reaches into her pack. 'Would you like an apple?' She's pulled the other fruit from the bag. Another bribe she didn't get to use. The woman forces a smile and shakes her head. Then she speaks. 'What the hell,' she says. 'Thanks, kid. I'll take half.'

Care breaks the apple and hands the woman the bigger piece. They eat in companionable silence, finishing it down to the core.

'So, this Tick.' The woman licks her fingers, looks at them as if more apple might be hiding in between. 'He your boy?'

Care shakes her head. 'My friend,' she says. 'I was looking after him, only . . .'

'Yeah,' the woman responds, when it becomes clear that Care isn't going to say more. She peers down the alley, as if uniformed officials waited, just out of sight. 'They're like that. Said I couldn't care for Billy properly, as if they could.'

'Mmm.' One wordless syllable conveys it all: sympathy, support. The woman takes a small flask from the bag. Drinks and then offers it to the girl.

'No, thanks.' Care watches as her companion tucks the bottle away. 'Do you know where they took him?'

A shake of the head. 'I can tell you they don't stay here, though. Not the young ones.' She looks toward the building, the empty yard now darkened with shadow. 'Process them and then move them out. They say some go to families, still—'

'That's how we met,' Care interrupts, the force of memory overcoming her reticence. 'We were in a foster together, and we ran away.'

The woman nods, her greasy curls bobbing. Care doesn't have to explain. 'Hey, there's someone else I'm looking for.' Care tilts her head. It's a gesture I recognize. The stranger does too. She waits for the question. 'Dingo?' Care asks. 'Paul Dingett?'

A pause, and then the blonde lifts her chin, questioning. 'Is he a friend, too?'

'No,' says Care, and then realizes her mistake. 'I mean, I don't really know him.'

The woman eyes her, cautious. Asking about someone she doesn't really know.

'It's about a job,' says Care. The truth gives weight to her words. Enough so that the woman nods.

'You from the bureau then?' Her make-up masks any emotion.

'The bureau?' Care keeps her voice level. She's not sure what question the blonde is really asking. Mirroring the words back is the smart move.

'You know.' The woman wipes her mouth with the back of her hand. Looks down at the lipstick smear she has made. 'The Dunstan. Where they keep the papers and all.'

'No,' says Care. It costs her, but it's true. 'You think someone there might know where he is?'

A shrug. 'You said a job, not me.' She licks her lips, as if the taste makes her remember, and begins to rummage through her bag. 'But that's where they're all divvied up, like so many playing cards, they say. More souls are bought and sold out of that old tomb—'

'I know it,' Care barks, cutting her off with a tone that causes the other woman to flinch. She eyes the girl, waiting for an explanation. None comes.

'You have family in the system,' she says at last, her dark eyes looking for a response. 'Someone who went in.'

'Something like that,' answers the girl, her voice low. Now it is my turn to appraise her. The girl has no family. No brothers who would have been sent to such a place. Even Tick is only an adoptive charge, an acquaintance of months before she went on her own, leaving behind the foster home where she was placed on her parents' death.

The woman gives her a look I can't decipher. A question in her eyes. In response, Care juts her jaw out. She's not giving any more.

The woman relents and reaches once more into the bag. 'I thought you might be a runner for them. They keep some poor souls there, I hear,' she says at last, fishing out a lipstick. She reapplies it and exhales, her body sagging. 'Those that can't do other jobs. They don't have my Billy, though.'

She falls silent then, retreating into her own sorrow. From her ready first response, I had thought she would say more.

But pain – fading bruises show still on her bare arms – and, perhaps, the substances taken to dull it have pulled her back from any awareness of companionship, or the obligation of a gift.

After an extended silence, I decide to act. I jump down from my perch and walk toward Care, in full view of the other woman.

'What?' The blonde steps back, but I ignore her. The girl may be surprised – I've noticed her start ever so slightly, and then smile – but she is not displeased.

'Blackie,' she says as she squats, holding out her arms. It's not my way, not how I would prefer to collect information. But there's more at stake here than my curiosity, and so I jump into her arms and rub my face against hers. The woman beside us coos, her reaction almost involuntary. Me, I'm interested in what Care didn't say. From her scent, I pick up that she has had a slight shock, more than my appearance would warrant, one that she hid. A fresh coat of sweat – as if from a blow – is already drying in the cool of the fading day, and from the way she holds me, I sense that whatever triggered that moment of discomfort also aroused an awareness of loneliness and loss. I lean in and purr. I am not a machine.

Nor is Care. 'This is my cat,' she says. Unnecessary, but her words serve to bridge the gap created by her rebuke. 'I'm Care,' she continues, when the woman doesn't respond. 'You know, I can find your boy for you. That's what I do. Investigate.' She pauses, waiting to see if the woman understands the word. Her would-be trade.

'Yeah, I heard about you.' A flicker of a smile tweaks the edges of that painted mouth. 'You were with the old man.'

Care nods once. She's proud, but she has the sense to wait. It is a form of interrogation, to see what the woman offers. To hear what exactly the stranger has heard.

'Maybe I'd hire you. I make decent coin, you know.' The woman says it like a dare. Like she expects an argument, but Care holds back. She has entered a negotiation, and waits to let the client make her own decision. 'Only, I've got something else going on. My own lead on things. And you can't find your own friend, can you?'

The challenge is unmistakable.

'I will.' Even my ears can catch no quaver of doubt. 'And then I'll look for your Billy, if your lead doesn't work out. That is, if you want.'

'Maybe,' says the woman. 'Maybe I will.'

The girl shifts and I resist the urge to hold on with my claws as she extends her hand.

'I'm Gina,' says the woman as she takes it. 'Good luck.'

Care watches as the woman makes her way back to the other end of the alley, ever more unsteady after the drink, on those ridiculous heels. She releases me to jump down, and I wonder if she'll pursue her, the unspoken questions clear on her pale face. But before she can decide to do so a car pulls up – it would be white, were it not for the rime of dirt or the streak of rust dulled to brown – and Gina is gone.

I, for one, am grateful. This detour served no purpose for either warmth or food, and I am glad to see how the big woman's departure seems to free Care. Straightening her spine, she runs a hand over the ridiculous mop of hair and looks around. I follow her lead and stretch, extending first one claw and then another out to catch the last of the fading light.

'Oh, Blackie!' She laughs at my contortions, seeing in them, perhaps, the echo of her own. While the warmth in the girl's voice is flattering, I would that she had kept her voice low, her greeting softer. We are small creatures in a dangerous city, and it is not wise to advertise our presence.

'I should have known you'd follow me.' Care's voice has fallen to a more moderate level, and I let her approach. I do not care to be lifted again – on the street, I rely on my ability to run and turn and jump – and she seems to understand, crouching to stroke my sleek black back. 'Sometimes I think . . .' She pauses, and I look at her. Meet her gaze with my own. 'You must miss him, too,' she says.

I pull away, frustrated by my lack of language. I do not miss the boy she seeks: Tick, or Thomas, as he is sometimes called. He is well named, however he came by that unfortunate sobriquet. Not only because he is small and dependent. A sickly creature who drew predators that we can ill afford. But because he feeds off the girl, I do not trust him. Do not share Care's conviction that he returned her complete allegiance. The boy was weak, having been taken too young from his kind to comprehend the benefits of cooperation, not to mention the loyalty due an ally. I am aware that she did not see this, but as a cat I lack the flaw of sentiment. Were he a furred creature, he would have fallen prey already. Under the girl's protection, he had survived only to be taken up by the city, by this system from which they had both previously fled. For her sake, I would that he remain in that system.

I cannot tell her this. Cannot impart the simplest of lessons anymore, but at least my thwarted desire represses my purr. Such involuntary reactions are only part of the indignity I suffer, in this life as a cat. I pull away from her hand and glare, my cool stare meeting hers. If she is hurt – shocked – she does not show it, and that is something. She is learning, this girl, if not as quickly as I would choose.

'Well,' she says, standing. 'Might as well get to work.'

# SIX

The girl moves like a cat. She has been taught well. Her mentor was not with her long, not in human form, but he did what he could and among her lessons were those in how to progress unnoticed. How to commingle with her environs, until and unless she should choose otherwise. And now I assume – *resume* – her tutelage, as best I can. I hang back to observe and find that I am soothed by her progress. By the heedful way she takes in her surroundings, turning her head up to scan above as well as along the street. Waiting before crossing open spaces, alert all the while for signs of others. Signs of life.

She gives away as little of her own presence as she can. Now that the light is nearly gone, even the wider thoroughfares offer shade and the girl makes use of these, darting from one patch of shadow to the next, as silent as she can be. Although she is growing – has grown, even, since I have known her – she remains small for her age, and slender. With minimal caution she can progress undetected by her own kind, and on these streets it is her own kind that presents the danger. The smaller beasts about us, and as night draws near, I hear the scurrying and squeal of many, consider her presence only as a precursor to my own. She is on the move, however, and therefore my hunt is postponed. I may no longer be her teacher, not in this form, in this life. But I will do my best to guide her, in my way.

'There you are.' She has come to a halt at a corner, where a brick monolith comes out nearly to the curb. I join her there, rubbing gently against her shin to announce myself without a sound. It's a large building, almost as oppressive as the hulking mass we have left, and may even be as old. But it does not have the care or usage of that other place. I smell rot and moisture, a mustiness familiar from those folded bills. The wall she has pressed herself against is crumbling, and as she peers around it, her fingers dig into the surface, releasing the faintest fall of red clay – but not the dust that I have smelled. For all the drawbacks of my feline form, I have learned to trust my senses. In particular scent and hearing, which serve better in this failing light.

Care, however, does not have these advantages, and I see her squint as she peers around the wall toward the building opposite, its darkened forecourt enclosed by a tall, iron gate. Almost, she seems to be waiting, although the area appears void of her own kind. If I could ask her, maybe I would, although I have never been the type to inquire when instead I could observe. Instead, I take the air, opening my mouth slightly as if my fangs – still sharp – could draw her knowledge to me. I sniff, I taste. There is – something. Anticipation? I am picking up her own awareness of time. Her heart is beating faster. Her breathing, too. She—

A howl from a nightmare splits the night and I leap, instinct compelling me to safety. But it is too loud. It surrounds me, surrounds us both, and pressed behind her, against the wall, I find I cannot run. I cower, a dumb beast clinging to the hope that my midnight fur will hide me here. The thunderous howl is ceaseless, and soon it is joined by the noise of men. Of feet and the swing and creak of metal. It is deafening, monstrous, and even the flattening of my ears against my head cannot block the sound of men as they flee. Shod in leather or in board, their feet add to the thunder. The wall beside me vibrates, the pavement quakes as they churn down the street, moving swiftly away from the infernal cry. From the howl—

Which stops, as suddenly as it began. I open my eyes and let my ears reassert themselves. I am panting, my heart is racing. And Care has disappeared.

I creep to the edge of the building, vigilant and alert. The herd of men is thinning out, the rumble of their footsteps quieting, but I am wary, waiting for another assault.

'Hey, look!' A figure in the blue uniform of a rozzer turns. A truncheon points toward me. I snarl and back up. Even as my fur rises, expanding my size, I know I am no match for this man, for that nightstick or his hobnailed boots. I bare my fangs and spit. 'That's bad luck for you.'

'Don't talk about luck,' his companion growls, eyes darting left and right. 'Someone's gotten sloppy, everyone's saying. Things are getting lost, and one of Gravy's own crew gone missing. They'll be looking at us next. And then . . .' He gestures toward the shabbily dressed men who have gone before.

'You're the one getting spooked now, aren't you?' The first man lowers his arm. Pokes his companion with his stick. 'Thinking above your pay grade. No one goes missing, but the big guys want them to. You know that; you just need a drink. Let's get this group back to their bins – and this time, you're buying.'

I watch as they move on, unwilling shepherds to their shabby sheep, but I hug the wall more closely. I am stronger for my size and more lithe than these stumbling, brutish men, but I am small. Only as the last straggler passes, his eyes on that baton, do I dare step out, searching the air for any sign of the girl. Sifting through the dust and sweat and – yes! – I catch her scent and follow, daring the open space to cross the street.

She's waiting there, in the mouth of an alley. From the shadow within, she watches the gate, which has closed again now that those it contained have been disgorged. She is quiet, as befits a watcher. But she is not calm.

'That must be it,' she says, as much to herself as to me, although I have made my presence known to her, rubbing against her shin as she crouches, peering toward the building's front. Of more interest to me is the gutter she shelters behind. Although it has been repaired recently – the smell of men's hands still on it – it is old and rusted, and the brick behind it soft with rot. As I lean in, I hear the rustling of small creatures within. The susurration picks up the fading echoes of those marching feet, but they are busy about their own business and do not heed our presence. I take in their perfume, which intrigues me, although I do not believe that is why she has chosen this spot. For her, this alley is a source of cover, but for me it holds more promise. I try my claw on the brick and find it soft as the clay from which it came. If I had time – no, if I had the use of hands – I could easily gain entry.

'Not in there . . .' I pause, but, no, she is not commenting on my situation. Still crouched behind the hanging gutter, she is watching that gate. Clearly, she expected someone in that rush of men. Tick, I realize. The boy. We are at the house of records, the place of which that slovenly woman spoke. The girl had hoped to find him in the rush of bodies that emptied out.

Tearing myself away from my own deliberations, I consider. That strange aroma – a mix of the chemical and more mundane. The traces of the man who hired us. For a moment, I had caught a whiff. And yet . . .

I take in the air, searching for that odd scent – and for other signs. For while Care took down the information the client provided, I was busy cataloguing my own information on the man. A less voluntary and more accurate means of identification. I close my eyes now to make the memory more vivid. He had been sweaty, more so than the short flight of stairs to our office should have brought forth. For humans, with their autonomic systems, this could connote tension or fear. But that laugh . . . no, that greasy man did not fear the girl. Did not fear me. Excitement, then, which had increased upon finding her alone in the office. And yet there was more propelling him than lust or greed. One such as that would have tried to take what he wanted, seeing the girl as weaker, being smaller than himself. And so . . .

'Maybe they don't let the runners out,' she says, thinking aloud, her words disrupting my deliberations. 'They probably wouldn't, a boy his age.'

It does not matter. Whatever traces I may have discerned have been lost, overrun by the sweat of the men marching past and the dust they raised. Abandoning my post by that softened brick, I lean in, eager to pick up what I can of her reasoning from her body as well as her words. What she is saying has a certain rationale. It is possible that her charge – I hesitate to call him friend – remains in the building, behind those closed gates. It is also possible that he never entered.

Our waiting here is pointless. The light has all but faded. It is the hour of the hunt.

She seems to reach the same conclusion and pulls a sheet of paper from her bag. The contract. Once again, I regret the liabilities of my feline form. I reach to brush my jaw against the paper, but it has been in her bag for hours now and carries only traces of the fruit she gave away.

'T.G. Fashions,' she reads. 'Harborside,' and I feel her tense. It is a sensible reaction. Where we are now is cold and paved, but there is an order here. A kind of quiet imposed on these wide streets, these lofty structures. I have been by the harbor and know it to be a very different place. The hunting is better there, in among the empty buildings, the rotten shells of industry and commerce. And while that can have its benefits – I cannot help myself, I lick my chops at the thought of fat water rats, of sea creatures grounded and left to die – it can mean danger. We are not the only ones who hunt, the girl and I, and both age and size mark us as quarry. I should have known that man, the client, came from the water. Like those rats, his type tend to gather there, their activities fostered by the decay and the damp.

Without another word, the girl stands and peers around. She is learning, this girl, and it is with some pride that I see her take the measure of the alley, of the street before us. I hang back as she crosses, walking openly to that big gate, but when her goal is clear, I make my move, dashing across the open space to the cover of one large post. I watch as she grasps the gate and shakes it and let myself feel the flood of relief as it stays shut.

It is not merely the cage aspect of those gates that concerns me. It is the way they clamped shut. The wail of the siren as they opened to release the workers and their keepers. Everything about this place signals danger, sparking in me something more than instinct – some buried memory. I watch and concentrate. My ears go back as I take in the air, trying to read its scents and movements. No, I cannot remember, if memory it was. All I know is this place means something to the girl. Something beyond my ken. I would not have her go inside.

When she returns to the alley, my concern lessens. This is the sensible approach, the one I would make were I seeking prey. But as she examines the alley, following it through to its dead brick end, I feel my hackles rise. It is not simply that this place has no apparent outlet. I am familiar with its type, the remnant of a more civilized era, designed to let air or light into the hulking building that surrounds it. No, as the dust settles, I catch a whiff of something sweet and sickly. A smell of rot, and of death, emanating from the closed end.

I see no corpse, no shreds of fur or flesh. Instead, the passage appears to the eye to be well traveled and clean. Washed, I believe, by more than the rain. There is a sheen on the stone paving as well as a lack of even the usual debris common to such a cul-de-sac. More telling still is the bite of cleaning agents, the bitter burn of bleach. People come here, people who matter, or such initiatives would not be taken, and neither of us is surprised when we find a doorway recessed into the brick.

My ears do prick up as I hear her exhalation of recognition. In that breath, a word, so soft even I barely catch it – could it be 'father'? Of course, this could mean nothing and I trust more to scent than any thought she may voice. Rot – and the attempt to erase it. Not knowing what creature left such foul traces, what sought to cleanse this passage of them, I cannot tell if the one we seek has come this way. Care, however, acts as if the conclusion has been reached. Another sigh follows as she tries the catch and fails to open it, and then turns to take in the view before her.

The light is fading, and though her eyes are good, both strong and young, she has not my capacity for sensing shapes, for sensing movement in the dimming of the day. For surely she must perceive the bin at the end of the alley, and it is from this the odor emanates. She heads toward it now. Even her limited perception must detect the unmistakable reek of rot within. But to my surprise, she pulls it, its inset wheels rumbling over the stone. She sets it against the wall. Above her, a high-set window leaks a dim but steady light.

She clambers to the top of the bin's lid and, balancing with caution, stands. I settle on my haunches, readying myself to leap beside her – and then I pause. She does not seek to explore inside the bin, availing herself of the illumination from above. Instead, she would use it as a prop. Standing on it, her pose is precarious, and I sit back to wait. I would not startle her into falling or into making any undue sound. If she succeeds in making entry, it will be short work for me to follow, now that she has provided an intermediary step along the way. If need be, I will return to the gutter. My nose told me that more than insects have used its vulnerability for egress.

As I watch, she reaches for the window, revealing skin as white as a snail's. My ears tell me there is no one near, but still I am concerned. In the twilight, her belly looks more exposed, more vulnerable than I would like.

No matter. She cannot force the window. She pushes, but each effort causes the bin to roll further from the wall, and after several attempts, she gives up. Only as she would dismount she slips, catching herself on the basin as she tumbles to the ground.

'Sorry, Blackie.' I have jumped back as she landed, on her feet and hands, as I would advise. 'You startled me,' she says, and stands, brushing one palm against the other. 'Here.' She reaches for the bin. Pulls it on those rattling wheels to replace it in its original position, I see. The girl, as I have noted, is well trained. No good will come of revealing our presence here, and it is a moment's work to obscure our passage.

'Wait.' She stops. As she has maneuvered the bin, its lid has come loose in her hand. 'Rule number one,' she says. 'Look everywhere for information, because you never know.'

She pulls the lid off, releasing a wave of the stench so powerful that even she should gag. But, no, her response is one of surprise, not disgust. And as I steel myself, forcing myself not to back away from the foulness, she reaches in, one foot rising as she stretches. I hunker down, gauging my leap. But before I can join her, she stands up, steps back and pulls. It's not easy, but as she leans her full weight away from it, the bin begins to tip, its edge to scrape the stone beneath. I jump back, alarmed, and just in time she does as well. The bin falls to the stone with a crash that pins my ears flat and freezes me some feet distant.

The girl holds back, too. Though not, I suspect, because of the noise. Her ears lack the sensitivity of mine, a deficit that turns blessing at times like this. No, I realize, as the echoes of the crash begins to recede, she has been watching the door and the head of the alley. Waiting to see if the tumult would serve to raise an alarm or even a curious onlooker. But we are alone, the smaller creatures stilled to silence by the terror of the crash, or fled already to some safer locale. And as I begin to inch toward the toppled form, my body low to the ground

– ready to spring or to flee – she, too, crouches low on all fours and I watch in horror as she crawls inside.

No! I do not like this. She cannot see, cannot hear, inside that thing. And if she is so truly oblivious to the stink within, as this foolish action implies, I cannot count on any of her senses alerting her to what may be inside. Although I have no direct memory of being caught, I recall traps – the pain and panic of creatures seeking food or shelter, who crawled within such enclosures, and so shaking off the shiver that would set my fur back on end, I push in beside her.

The scent is overwhelming. The alley has been kept clean and the bin emptied, but no amount of washing could remove its trace. Refuse and rot, foodstuffs of some kind, as well as something other – the biting tang of machine oil, an acrid streak of which stripes the bin that I avoid as I would a snake. And something worse, thick and heavy. Blood, but not fresh. Not from a rat. And not from a clean kill, either. The tang that breaks through the musty sweetness of rot came from the chemicals that course through a body as it attempts escape, the scent of panic. Its headiness masks all else, leaving me as helpless as the girl. I do not like it. Whatever bled here had some consciousness. Something died in fear.

I would back out. Some deaths are not to be fed upon, but the girl is still inside. Scrabbling about beside me, as helpless as a mole, and so I remain. Scent dazed, but less handicapped than she. At least what limited light exists will avail me should danger materialize.

'What?' She jerks back from the touch of fur. But my coat is softer than a rat's. Smoother than a possum's, as if those creatures would risk proximity. And as I squeeze ahead of her, to explore what has aroused her interest, I see it – a scrap that even here reflects the light. Metallic and yet, not. Fabric, I realize as I put my nose up to it.

'Blackie!' She has seen it too and reaches for it. I begin to back out, happy to leave it to her and to seek the cleaner air outside of this enclosure. But, finally, the fug has gotten to her, and she begins to cough. My movement, I suspect, has raised whatever foul residue has settled here, and I will have much bathing to do to rid my coat of its putrid essence. I inch backwards, unwilling now to turn, to brush against the sides of our enclosure. The girl's body heaves as she retches and, for a moment, I am thrown to the side – the noise and smell disorienting me. I feel trapped. I am about to be overcome.

With effort I free myself, my claws connecting with the girl as I kick loose. I hear her cry. Too loud for safety, and yet I am relieved. Grateful to get out of that enclosed and noxious space, I do not pause to check my surroundings. I do not stop to take the air.

'Oi! What's that?' A man's voice, harsh and cut short by a spike of fear. 'Who's there?'

Belatedly, I hear their footsteps, the approach the girl's coughing had obscured. Smell the sweat that I could not in the bin. They are moving slowly, trying to decipher the murky movement that must be all that they can make out.

'Yo, Dingo? That you?' Care's breath catches at the name. She makes no other sound as they approach. 'We missed you last night. You with someone?'

I am – we are – lucky that these hunters are even less aware than we. I leap silently to the side, as they come forward, the better to assess the situation even as it unfolds. Care hears their approach, too – or perhaps has felt me move – and crawls backward out of the bin. She is not yet on her feet, however, as they draw near. Two men, large at least by my standards, though one looms over the other. Taller, broader, too. They must have paused near the head of the alley – this bought us time – but now they are striding down its course, arms swinging. As they walk, they separate, each seeming to expand to fill the narrow passage. It's a technique I know well: they use their limbs as I do my fur, creating volume. Filling space. Only in their case, the threat is real. They are both larger than we two. The smaller one has a knife, its blade catches the dim light from above, a light that also shows his evil features – scarred and sharp. I glance behind us. The wall, brick, is worn here and pitted. I do not see any gaps, such as the one behind the gutter, but there are craters that would offer some small footholds, uneven places where my claws could seek out purchase. But even if I could scale it – a venture I would be ill disposed to try even in my youth – the girl could not.

'It's a girl,' says the bigger man. The one nearest Care. In the space of three syllables, the fear melts from his voice, replaced by something worse. His companion glances at him in surprise, the alteration has been fast and he has not caught up. But then his hawk-like face splits in a grin of confirmation.

'Well, so it is.'

Care has seen them now. Still crouching, she eyes them both, and I can feel her tense, readying to leap and run. But she cannot move as I can, and the men are large. Their spread arms block the alley, and they begin to call to her.

'Hey, girly,' says the first man, the big one, his voice unnaturally high. As if his tone would tame Care. As if she would believe it. 'Aren't you cold out here, all alone?' To his companion, his language is more blunt. 'I saw her first.'

Care gasps, and the men chuckle. It's an evil sound, with little of humor in it. But it serves to put them, ever so slightly, off their guard. This is my chance. I am black, and in the dusk I have been invisible to them. Still, they will realize soon that I am a smaller creature than they are. I can only hope that Care is ready, too. That all her training will propel her forward, on to safety as I lunge at the nearest man.

Although he has begun to lean forward – preparing to grab Care and throw her down – I cannot hope to reach his face. Instead, I leap and, spitting, land, all claws distended, on his outstretched arm. What light there is reflects on my eyes, and his stare back in horror. A green-eyed demon, I must appear. He lets loose a wordless cry as his partner turns to look.

'Yo, George—'

I hiss fiercely, waiting for the movement behind me that tells me Care is on her feet. That she is running. I will her to elude this brute while he stares down at me.

She doesn't, and I feel his hand clamp down on my back. I cling tight even as he pulls and then lets go, stumbling to his side.

'Stop that!' It is Care. She holds the bin lid in her hand, its metal ringing still from the blow she has dealt. 'Don't you dare!'

The big man steps backward, the surprise as much as the reality has shaken him. I free myself and hit the pavement, hissing as I land. In a moment, these men will recover. The one she hit was startled more than hurt, I see. He pushes himself up to his feet. His friend is taking in the scene. But as he steps toward Care, she throws the lid, causing him to hesitate. Then she bolts, and I dash after her, following as she turns the corner and then another, slipping into the shadows of the night.

# SEVEN

I am winded by the time we stop, ducking for cover behind a wall. Fear has driven the girl to run long and hard, and I feel my age. The wounds of violence and time. In particular, my left hind leg, which twinges with the effort of my exertion. Still, I did not dare risk losing her, and I endeavored to pant and lean to the right, favoring that aching limb, as we ran. In part, that is because I saw her trajectory. From habit, if not intent, she has led us toward the waterfront, dashing as she did down deserted streets, taking the turns more shadowed and empty, the roads increasingly rough. She lived down here, when she first struck out on her own, and it has a familiarity for her. She has also known great loss and violence down among the wharfs, and I would not have her fall prey to such again, even if panic drives her to her former haunts. To places no longer safe.

In part, I fear what is within her. The way she snapped at that woman was not like the girl whom I have come to know. Also, I now realize belatedly, I have missed something I should not have. The girl's venture into that alley – her attempt on that window – these were not as random as I had previously surmised. Something about the way she moved, the way she immediately went for that window, as opposed to continuing her perambulation, speaks of prior knowledge. I know this girl as well as any now alive, and yet this nearly escaped me. The two are linked – her knowledge and her whiplash withdrawal – both to that building, the Dunstan. Combined, they make her vulnerable, and I would understand what meaning they hold and why she reacts as she does.

I would ask outright, if language still served me as it once did. As I am, I will follow and observe. For this at least, my feline form serves me well. As we rest, I press into her thin side, and she drapes an arm around me in a gesture of affection. Her ribs are heaving from the run, and she is warm. I am content to lend my softness to her comfort. I am content to purr.

I do not intend to nap. It is a characteristic of my kind, abetted, I suspect, by age, which allows me to conserve my energies till needed. An hour, perhaps more, has passed, a respite for us both. In my dreams, I had believed myself observing – three men, their voices too low for me to hear, a replay of some bygone time. That alone should have alerted me: my hearing now is more acute. Still, I am taken aback when the girl begins to speak, recalling me to that dream image. Her voice is soft, as theirs were, too low for her to be addressing another of her kind. No, she is murmuring her thoughts aloud. I would do well to listen.

'I don't get it,' she is saying, as she shakes her head. With one hand, she brushes back her bangs. That absurd pink mop is growing out and falls into her eyes. This is my cue to sit up and to blink. I would appear a willing audience, although she cannot grasp how much I understand.

'It doesn't make sense, Blackie,' she says to me. Were it not for that silly name, I might have almost forgotten how she sees me. Who I am to her. 'The Dunstan was where he worked. Where they sent him. My dad, I mean, after we came to the city.' She shakes her head. 'But he did books. Numbers and accounting. I knew there were other men – other prisoners – working in the building, but he never said anything about kids.'

She falls silent, but it is enough. I never knew her parents. Never knew her as other than an urchin – whip-smart but not worldly. Too likely to fall prey to the predators on these streets and too promising to let go. In another life, another form, I tutored her, after a fashion. And then – well, now we are companions again. That past life – a father? A family? – has no resonance for me.

They do explain her reaction, however. The reason she rebuffed that woman, the memory that led her to a particular window. And that horrid bin? No, that was motivated by something less. I regard the scrap of fabric she looks at now, its silvery threads catching the last of the twilight. Then stretch forward to examine it again. It stinks, still, of carrion. But beneath that now I pick up something else – dust and sweat and . . .

'Hang on.' The girl drops the scrap to rummage through her bag, and I step up. Although I am normally fastidious, much more so than the girl, I reach for the disgusting scrap with my mouth. Unlike the girl, I do not eat rotten meats. I do not eat plants, either, as a rule, not that there are many in this grim and concrete world. However, my acute perceptions would inundate a child like her – or any human, really, caught unprepared – and while that makes me careful of my food, it also allows me to read the traces contacts leave.

I mouth the filthy strip of cloth, feeling the loose threads along its side. I close my eyes, willing myself to ignore the sweet foul taste of rot for what is older. Deeper. I get the warm salt of the girl and of others, too. They, too, were tired. Scared?

'Blackie!' The scrap is pulled away, and I mew in dismay, a foolish, little sound. Another indignity of this form, but she ignores it. Instead, she examines her finding, holding it close in the fading light. In her other hand, she has the contract her new client signed. Although it is nearly overwhelmed by the stench of the alley, on the paper I recognize the stink of the man, the strange mix of chemicals and perfume. As I watch her face turns from one to the other and back again, and I wait. Clearly, she has seen something, and, unlike me, she does not trust her senses.

'It's a label,' she says at last, biting at her lip. 'T.G. Fashions.' She is talking to me, and although I suspect I am simply a mirror – a reason for her to voice and then to weigh her conclusions – I blink slowly to encourage her. 'That's Gravitch's business,' she says, conviction growing in her voice. 'This could be a coincidence, but my old mentor? The old man? He would say that wasn't likely.'

I am silent, barred from responding as I would see fit. Although I would like to make myself understood, would choose to warn this girl, I cannot. Even had I the language, I am not sure what I would say. She has drawn a reasonable conclusion, and I cannot fault her logic. She has learned well, this girl, and at the feet of a master, assimilating the skills of observation and deduction. Seeking out the bits of detritus and unattended scraps of refuse and debris that may reveal a greater whole. It is good work for the careful, and she has become adept.

That this master, her mentor, is gone is nothing either of us can help. That his reasoning, if not his very soul, has moved on is more than I can communicate, at least in this form. I am as dumb as any beast, and worse, for I have now my feline sensitivity. The trace left there – old blood, spilled cruelly – is more than I would have once been able to discern. Now, it can only add to my frustration. Add in a nagging worry that the girl has been distracted, has not considered all the options, and I am disquieted. The girl is following a trail, and she is doing it with skill and spirit. Only she has not considered the possibility that this trail has been set, rather than laid by chance. That it may lead to more than answers. And I, in this feral feline form, am unable to help her, despite what gifts I now possess.

There is no point in regret. Its sorry pull is only a remnant of what I have left behind, and so I dismiss it with a flick of my tail. What matters now is this girl. Her hunt and my role in it are all I need focus on. And so when she starts off again, her worn sneakers nearly silent on the asphalt, I follow. We have gone some paces when she stops and turns toward me. I have been staying close. My inability to read even that paper which she consults has stymied me, and although my nose tells me we are near the docks, I do not know this street nor what path she will take. I am aware that the two men we left behind are not alone in their appetites or in their inclination toward violence. Aware as well that other dangers wait, and while my bulk may be small, I have little doubt that I can hear and scent what she cannot, and I can raise an alarm.

'You're still here.' She states the obvious. I blink to reassure her, but it seems to have the opposite effect. 'I don't know.' She shakes her head. I see sadness there and something more. Could she be worried about me? 'It's not safe for you down here.'

She is remembering how she found me. How she pulled a half-drowned cat from a storm drain and shared her food and the warmth of her body until he revived. That is what she knows of me, of my past. To this, I have no doubt, she attributes the allegiance I now show. That I had another life – a previous bond – she cannot suspect. How could she, when I have only recently discovered it myself?

I have no response. I know that to her my eyes appear cold, but I continue to stare into hers. Surely, something of what I would will her to understand must get through. Surely, some scrap of memory or resemblance . . .

But no. The girl sighs and shakes her head again and then she looks back – toward the city. Toward the office where we two have lived these past few weeks. She steps toward me.

And I bolt. I would not have her grab me, even if she thinks it is for my own safekeeping. I would not have her abandon her trail to ferry me to safety. I skid to a halt only yards away and yet, to her inferior senses, out of sight. Thus, the die is cast, and as she turns and continues on, I remain beyond her limited vision, following her easily as she slowly makes her way down this dark street. I may no longer be her mentor – the old man whose methods she would make her own – but I am a cat.

It is not long before we reach our destination. I cannot read maps or signs – but I can make out the features of the girl as she looks down at the scrap again and up at a rundown ware-house, one of a series of squat buildings on this dank and ill-lit street. Like its neighbors, it has no signage, and all but one of its windows have been blackened by paint or dirt, but there are markings on the door and a rumbling within, a vibration I sense as much as hear. It seems to growl, almost, as if some fiendish beast were stirring inside, as if the building itself lived. It is a sign of life – of industry even – I suspect, but it disquiets me. There is something ominous about that deep and throbbing sound, that ceaseless reverberation, particularly at an hour when the offices in more frequented areas have been shuttered and stand dark.

The vibrations change as we move from the rutted road to an unexpected smoothness, hard and cool. Flagstone, my claws tell me as they extend by reflex, gripping all the harder for the lack of purchase. A remnant of another age, and barely here at that. Only an attenuated strip of the wide, flat stones remains, bridging the gap between the road and the low brick building hard on it. Whatever commanding edifice was once heralded by such monumental paving is long gone. The low structure that now sits here, squatting like a toad, is undistinguished.

Blind, except for that one window. Faceless, except for that metal door, distinguished only by three small markings of a kind I can no longer read.

It is the markings she looks at, checking them against the sheet in her hand. Once she has confirmed her hunch, she steps back off the stone apron, and retreats to the building next door. Unlike its neighbor, it stands quiet, empty at least at this hour of industry or trade. A rusted fire escape hangs from its side, but its platform – one story up – is long gone. Still, I see the girl appraising it, and wonder as well at its utility as a means of observation if not egress.

The faint sigh of metal – the squeak of a door nearby – and a slight elevation in the machine noise draws her away. Skirting the cool stone, she crosses the front of the rumbling building with a stealth I admire, and peers down the alley at its other side. Unlike its neighbor, there are no safety features here, nor signs that there ever were. However, this alley seems more traveled, illustrated as it is by a covering of graffiti. At its far end, a streetlight's yellow glow highlights these scrawls – symbols even I can tell serve as cries of frustration, impotent and angry. There are other signs as well, which I, if not the girl, may read.

I smell the air. Another tom has been here. It is spring, despite the chill, and he is young and on the prowl. My fur begins to rise as I take in his rank, assertive scent not unlike the bite of bleach, and I must recall myself to who I am – to what my purpose now must be.

Was this my territory, at one point? A place that I – this feline form – knew before my transformation? A shift in the air brings me the aroma of a female as well. A queen whose early litter was endangered by that reckless male. She chased him off – the air holds traces of their spit and blood – and for a scant moment, my heart races as well. Could that female, those kittens, have been mine? I came aware as an adult male. Aged even, but this body must have lived before . . . It is no use. My understanding of time has become an animal's, all fades back from the present, and yet . . .

'Gina!' It's the girl. She calls out softly as a figure stumbles from a door into the alley. Like its partner, at the building's front, it is grey metal. Windowless. Unlike its mate, it has opened, expelling the woman from earlier, now the worse for wear. Her face is smudged, the paint has run, and even the girl must see how she favors one leg, one side, as she steps away.

'It's me,' Care tries again, her voice a little louder, 'Care.'

The woman pauses. She must hear the girl, and for a moment I believe she will turn. But then that moment passes, and she hurries away toward the other end of the alley. Limping, she turns the corner and is gone.

Care is standing at the alley's mouth. Oblivious, I fear, to the creak and shimmy of the door as it begins to open once again. To me, the movement is plain to see, and I crouch down, ready to do all in my power to alert her – and to lead off those who might emerge. But the light within highlights the movement, and as it spills out, she steps aside. She is not hidden, there is no time for that as two men lumber laughing from the portal, toward the building's rear. I hear the intake of her breath as she presses against the wall. Stillness, as well as shadow may serve her yet.

'Goddamn Dingo,' says one, and I see Care start at the name. 'He was going soft, he was.'

The speaker looks up – the movement has caught his eye – but then he turns away. Night blind from the illumination within they continue on their way. This close even she must smell him, as well as see his ill-featured face. He is one of the brutes we encountered in the alley, smaller than his colleague, though neither would I have Care confront.

'He never liked it rough. Not like you, George.' The bigger man slaps his friend in play.

'Ah, you just don't want to have to clean up again,' the smaller man responds.

'Not my job,' his colleague laughs. 'Let's get some beers.'

'You don't want to—' The other man's question is lost as his voice drops and a hand gesture finishes his thought.

'No, no,' his colleague replies. 'He's home safe, all right. He's sulking.' It seems a non sequitur, but I have been distracted by my concern. The girl is moving. She is keeping to the shadow, but still this is rash. She crosses the alley that the men have left. She would follow them, I believe. Only, as she steps into the street, the sound of an engine urges her back against the wall. A car, its engine rough and noisy, has turned the corner. In the sulfurous light, it is yellow, the long stain on its side darkened almost to black. It pauses for a moment, and then it drives away.

# EIGHT

cannot tell her that I am uneasy. The girl is set on her mission, and the brief reappearance of her earlier acquaintance has heightened her mood in ways I cannot decipher.

'Brutes,' she mutters, her voice a rumbling growl beneath her breath. I too have seen the woman, and I understand her response. Mating spurs rivalries, as I have so recently noted. And the violence can spread to the offspring, especially when resources are limited. These men, however, seem to be the kind who take pleasure in the pain of the other, who see the act of mating as a form of subjugation. What I do not understand is why the girl has allied herself with the blowsy woman. She is weak, the blonde, and as such, poses a danger.

I take comfort in one fact: Care does not go after her. Instead, once the men stride off, she follows as far as the streetlight, though I am pleased to observe how she surveys both the corner and the buildings opposite before she approaches. Stepping into the yellow light, she pulls the paper from her bag again, holding it close as she reads. Of course, the reference to her quarry – the 'home' mentioned might well be the known locations she had asked her client about. Except . . .

The fixture buzzes like a trapped fly, and I long to snap it down. I am watching this girl, this Care, go about her hunt. Witnessing her use of the procedures she has learned both from her mentor and, more recently, through her own experience of crime and of the streets. And yet I am not easy, and it is not only that high-pitch whine above, or the building's rumbling drone, that sets my ears back against my skull. I am a cat, and as such, I am practical. We live in the real world, we beasts, and have no time nor use for the fancies that preoccupy humans. I do not believe in hunches or magic, or even spirits, although my own continued existence remains a mystery to me. However, I am aware that my senses are acute and that my instincts may be picking up on factors that I have not yet consciously acknowledged. The memory of movement, a shadow that reacts, comes to mind. No, I am not easy.

The girl leaves me no time to consider, however. As I pause to ponder, one paw raised to smooth my harried fur, she takes off, ducking from the sickly light back to the shadows as she makes her way up the avenue. To one of her own, she would be difficult to trace. Her movements are stealthy, and she is small for her kind. For me, to follow is but child's play. Kitten's play, perhaps, not that I recall a feline youth. An image of a day-blind vole surfaces, one that stumbled and darted, too dimwitted and confused to recognize its peril or seek cover. It should be a pleasurable recollection – that creature was a fat find on a particularly cold morning – but it isn't. The memory of vulnerability sits poorly on me. I am a hunter. It is how I live. But others are hunters, too, and I would not have Care become their prey.

I follow in her wake, with double precaution in mind. I am alert to the city. Down here, by the water's side, it is never truly quiet. Hunters of many types make their way both before and behind us. If I were not watching Care, I would join them. The taste of that vole is fresh again in my memory. But I ignore it to keep myself engaged, alert to signs of passage by others on the prowl. At the same time, I remove myself from the range of her sight and hearing. I would not have her distracted as she makes her way across this wilderness. Nor do I want her attempting to remove me again, through affection or concern. Better she should suspect me gone – on the hunt or to the makeshift home that we both share. She will not worry overmuch, I do not believe, if I disappear until the morning, until some other place.

Still, I cannot avoid a frisson of fear. The girl has turned into an unlit street, but the moon has made its passage while I slept and her shadow stretches long before her in the cold. She stays close to the buildings here, crouching as she runs to shrink her profile. Still, her shadow precedes her, clocking her progress on the broken pavement. It is a route I know, a passage to the wharfs. And while here the pavement reaches to the cracked concrete that once served as a walk, we are not far from where even this rutted surface will falter and fall short. Where the gutter that runs alongside will widen to catch the outflow and effluvia of a working city. A roaring torrent after a storm, funneled into a corrugated pipe that leads to the harbor, that drain was where my old life ended, where the girl I follow found me. Where she saved me.

My hide ripples involuntarily, as if some unseen flea has irked me. For sure, it is no accident that draws her – draws us – to this area, but my discomfort may stem from nothing more than memory. The harbor has long been the home of commerce, both open and illicit. The low brick buildings here do not draw the same attention as the larger warehouses by the train tracks and the water, but they remain standing, more or less, and there are good reasons why a business such as Gravitch's would be located here. His workers, perforce, dwell nearby.

Besides, I have seen no trace of that shadow, the one that eluded me before. I have not forgotten it. I forget little, one remnant of my earlier training that has survived. But I do not worry overmuch about that which is not present, and tonight holds troubles of its own. That drainage ditch will not be one.

Before we reach it, the girl pauses. Has turned from the wider avenue into a lane that leads her to an open space. We have passed beyond the commerce district, as paltry as it may be. Whatever stood here once was gone, leaving an open lot, now washed in moonlight that plays up the sole heap of rubble rising in its center.

Not mere rubble, I see. It is a shack of sorts, assembled from that refuse and the findings of the piers. Warped wood, worn by water or by age, makes for patchwork walls. Rusted tin rests at an awkward angle as a roof. The torn grating of a fence propped alongside seems to serve as support. There is no cover. No plants grow here. Nothing that would be green, even were it not bleached by that fulsome moon.

She waits and I hear my own breathing settle along with hers, till we are in quiet synchrony. The moon moves overhead, sending shadows out to meet the little shack, but still no sign of life appears. No life beyond what I would expect, that is. I hear the scrambling of rodents in the dark. An opossum who has made her way in search of grubs or something sweeter. I watch the girl. Such as these are not to her interest, but if she chooses to wait . . .

She does not. I am thinking of the hunt, of the iron tang of fresh blood in my mouth, as she steps forward, moving quickly through the elongated shadow. She has made it almost to the end before I recover, those thoughts of eating and the kill distracting me from her fast and silent progress. But I am made for moving unnoticed through the dark and so I follow, darting ahead even as she pauses to glance back at the street. I reach the hovel before she does, my advance over the last lit lap only a flicker, a dark shade low to the ground.

The shelter, such as it is, is open: darkness has concealed the unlocked door, which hangs broken from a hinge. I sidle by it. I do not need such obvious portals, and the makeshift wall sports several less obvious means of entrée. I size up one set further toward the back. The marks of teeth around the edges reveal how it was enlarged, but they are weathered and old. The rat who made these has found other egress, or is gone, but even as I rub against it, marking it as my own, I hesitate.

I had intended to pass ahead, to scope out this place before the girl, but now I pause. There is more than darkness within. An odor, as thick and powerful as a wall, stops me in my tracks. I would not go into this ruin. I would not have her enter either.

I am too late. Too late and powerless in my concern. Care makes her move, pushing the door before her. I hear the sigh and creak of it before I realize she has passed within. I catch the sharp intake of her breath before I can will myself to move, to follow via my own entrance into the dark and fetid hut.

I find myself beside her. We are in the hut's main room, a square space toward the front. She does not see me. She cannot. Although the light seeps through the rotted walls, I know that I am invisible to her, my black fur blending with the dark within. It matters not. She has illumination enough to see what lies before her, before us. There is little furniture in the room – a cot, its thin, stained mattress raised but inches from the floor. A peg on which some rags are hung. A far door, still in shadow, and that is all. And on that bed, the source of my dismay. A body, far from fresh, lies stinking in the night.

'I guess we know why Dingo went missing,' she says. She's talking out loud, but not to me. It's a reflex I recognize, a way of forcing herself to breath. To breathe and not gag on the putridity. Still, her words alarm me. She is looking around when she should be leaving. Seeking some clue, some trace or trail, when her instincts – like those of any living creature – should urge her to flee this place of death.

She forces herself to regard the corpse. Shivers as she makes herself turn toward it. Makes herself take in the body, the cot with its faded stains. A small wound to the throat – its edges already blackened – reveals the likely cause of death, but two days or more have passed, and fluids have leaked from the body's orifices as well. Although it has not begun to bloat, its stench is horrid. When she turns away, to examine a sheet of linoleum, a makeshift bit of flooring, I cannot find it in my heart to fault her.

'I wonder if he killed this guy,' she says, kicking at the curling edge. I see her doing the math regarding Gravitch's contract. What the rat-like man suspected, and what his employee may have feared. 'Or if he just found him and took off. He's been dead for a while, I think.'

It's incomplete, her thought process. She has missed a point. Not considered all the options before her. I feel my tail lash with frustration. If I could simply speak in a way she would comprehend, I could guide her. Direct her thought processes, as her onetime mentor did. She is smart, this girl, but she is still a novice in this field, which she would master. And it is a dangerous profession, as the corpse upon the cot makes clear.

My reaction, involuntary as it may be, does not help. Instead, it raises dust and fans the foul miasma. I back slowly, wishing to remove myself – to remain unseen.

But as I retreat, my perspective on the room changes. I am watching the girl, attempting not to alert her. Hoping that she will make her observations and leave this benighted place. She has lifted the sheet of flooring and is examining its underside, peeling something free and disturbing a centipede that hastens off to join its mates. Only it is not simply the girl's movement or that retreat that alters the border of the room. I creep forward again, my tail now stilled through force of will. A shadow – the edge of a door left ajar? No, it moves and shifts – and not with the light.

I advance with a hiss, ears pinned back and ready to attack. It is not often that I, a cat, experience regret. No, I am a creature of the now. But I have been fooled, allowed myself to be misled by those very instincts that I have come to trust. I knew that this was a dangerous place – a place of death – but I let myself believe that Care's response was what was wrong, that she was missing some crucial point. I did not dream that I had, too. My concern over the girl has blinded me.

But my advance now – spitting, fur blown up to double my size – does not undo my fault. Instead, I realize with horror, as I press toward where the shadow falls, it amplifies it. The girl has turned toward me, rather than the doorway. A paper folder – filthy from its hiding place – hangs from her hand, disregarded. It is me she looks at.

'Blackie!' she calls out. Distracted, she does not even lower her voice. I look up at her and feel my fighting stance begin to fade. I am confused. I have failed.

'Care?' I whirl again toward the shadow, as at last she looks up. Only the rapid steps she takes toward the darkness – toward that voice – are not the preliminary of an attack. Her arms, spread wide, are not in imitation of my fighting stance, designed to startle and scare. No, she has dropped the file, instead of wielding it as a weapon. Her hands are open, rather than in fists, and as she steps forward, she falls to her knees. A figure has emerged from the shadow. The source of that one word. Tick – the boy she has sought all these weeks – steps forward, and she folds him in her embrace.

'Tick.' Her face is buried in his hair, but I can hear the sob in her voice. 'I thought I lost you,' she says. I approach gingerly. He is small, this boy, even for his age, and thin. It is difficult to scent anything properly in this room, but without much effort I can sniff his hand and see his large dark eyes looking down at me.

'It's okay,' she says. She has felt him stiffen and misread the cause. He is staring at me, as I am at him, but I do not believe it is my appearance that makes him draw back now. 'What?' she asks. 'It's just Blackie. You remember him?'

'Care, you can't be here.' He has turned from me at last and looks up at the girl, his foster sister. 'Me neither. It's not safe.'

'What?' Care looks over her shoulder. She could not have forgotten the stinking corpse behind us, but what with the papers she has found and the appearance of the boy, it almost seems as if she has. 'I'm on a case, Tick. Don't worry – whatever happened here, it was days ago.'

He shakes his head, dark hair falls over his eyes. 'You don't know, Care—'

He would say more. I see it in his face as he brushes that hair back, as he looks up at her. Only even as I watch, his too pale features are flooded, his eyes shut by blinding light. Care turns toward it. They both do, arms raised to shield themselves from the glare that comes not just through window and door but through the rickety wall itself.

'Come out!' A male voice, unnaturally loud, follows hard on that light. 'Come out with your hands raised.'

'Care!' The boy recovers first, grabbing the girl's hand as if he could pull her from that house, out of that searing light. 'We've got to run. It's the rozzers!'

# NINE

There is no escape. The shadow that had shielded our entry has been banished; the bare ground around the hovel flooded with light. Squinting, I see the refuse – a bottle, a worn shoe – that litters the yard. None of it is large enough to provide cover for the girl, and although I could make use of it – darting from tussock to trash, my midnight fur making me one more frenetic shadow cast by that searching light – I will not leave her.

'Come on.' She glances at me as she snatches up the tile and grabs the boy, dragging him back to the door. It swings inward, at least, and thus does not reveal her location, but one look suffices to stop her. The blue-white of the moon has been bleached out by the floodlights. The neighboring building, with its welcoming façade of crumbling brick, impossibly distant.

'Come on out.' The voice, male, sounds bored yet confident. This is a game the speaker has played before, and the amplification does nothing to soften its tone or its intent. 'You don't want us to have to extract you.'

Extract. The word suggests the surgical, but there is nothing in that voice that is healthy or clean. Care whips around in response but does not attempt a reply. None is expected. The volume – the light – they are both designed to evoke panic. To provoke flight and easy capture. But although I see the girl's mouth has opened, hear how her breathing accelerated, I am gratified to also see that she is taking the measure of this shoddy hut. Having turned from the door, she glances up at the roof and down at the floor. Neither will suffice: the roof is accessible, its corrugated metal sits on the tilted pilings that hold up the walls, but it is exposed. The floor mere dirt, except for that patch of lino, which she has let fall back into place.

'Come on, girly.' That voice again. This time, the amplification picks up the laughter of those gathered around the speaker. 'We're not going to wait all night.'

At that, Care freezes, her pale face taking on a focus that makes her look older than her years. 'Girly?' she asks of no one in particular.

'Care, come on!' It's Tick. He's not responding to the question in her voice. He is staring at that front window, as if he could make out anything in the harsh white light. But he tugs her hand, and she looks down. I bristle even as she does, knowing that she will overlook the timing of his appearance here. His apparent lack of concern over the dead body that lies nearby. 'I know a way,' he says.

I do not like her choices. There is nothing about this boy I trust, and while I understand that the girl feels an allegiance toward him, I would woo her from it as I would from the habit of drugs that has ensnared so many of her peers. Despite my feline form, I have done my best to make my opinion known. If the boy were to look over toward me now, he would see my fangs are bared. The fur of my ruff stands tall and menacing.

But he does not, and with the clamor outside, my low growl goes unremarked. Instead, he pulls at the girl, and nods his head toward the far side of the hovel, toward the doorway where I first spied him, a shadow in the dark. 'Come on!' he says again, his voice climbing higher with urgency.

She hesitates, the question in her eyes. She takes a step back as he leans toward that door. I will her to voice that query. I would stop her, would put myself under her feet if it would make her reconsider. Only just then the tumult from outside is broken by another, a deeper, roar. An engine, revving. It is enough like a growl to convey its threat. She lets go of the boy's arm, letting him turn and make for the door, and she follows. With only a moment to decide as the machine roars outside, I dash after them, and out into the night.

For a moment, I am blind. After the harsh brightness of the artificial light, the brief patch of shadow immediately behind the hovel is too dark – too black. But my eyes are made for such darkness and recover more quickly than those of the two children, who stand against the hut, blinking and sightless.

'We've got to run for it,' says the boy. He reaches for her and as he does, his sleeve falls back, revealing bruises. 'Come on!'

I wait for her rebuttal. It is too neat, his appearance, and I trust she has the intelligence to recognize this. She has been shown a body, for reasons I cannot yet decipher, and now she is being herded from it. I wait. But she only nods wordlessly. He does not see it, he cannot, but he must feel the movement, or else he simply knows she has few options left.

'Where are we going?' Her one question gives me hope. She may be committed to this boy and the course of action he has plotted – but she is looking ahead. She is gathering information.

'A straight shot to the back of the lot, then into the basement. It goes through. You can make it.' The boy peers from side to side. He is, I see, watching for the shadows of approaching men. 'Then I'll go back.'

'Wait, Tick?' The girl turns toward him, her hands on his shoulders. 'Go back? Where?'

He shakes her off but at the same time grabs her hand. He has seen something – heard something – or he has knowledge of this type of attack. The machine roar starts up, the noise augmented by the laughter of men, and the ground begins to tremble. It is this, I see, that he has anticipated. The turmoil of movement, the excitement of the attack. The laughter has gotten louder, punctuated by shouts. On each side of the hovel, shadows become visible, stretching ahead of us as the attackers grow closer. The volume rises. The wall behind us shakes, and a piece of the roofing falls to the ground, the metallic clang only adding to the tumult as it crashes to the hard dirt. The laughter has a frenzied edge. Dust fills the air.

'Now!' Tick darts forward and Care follows. I too run, fast and low, crossing the shadows that converge on our path. Behind us, the screams of men and machines. I do not turn to see when, to see if, they stop. I can no longer distinguish between their hideous shrieks. The volume is painful. Ears flat, I follow the boy, watching to see if he will lead the girl to safety or if I will need to intercede. He has made it to the building behind the bare lot, and he throws himself down and disappears.

'Care! Here.' A voice like a hiss, and I see her dive, as well. A low opening – a vent for some machinery or to load in fuel

– appears in the brick. I eye it, wary of traps. But when I hear their whispered conversation, several feet away, I too slip in.

The room inside is dark, and they have crossed to the corner, where another opening – half filled with fallen brick – lets in some light.

'I have to.' Tick is insistent. 'The enforcers. If they catch me out, they'll know.' He rubs his wrist.

'Oh, Tick.' The gesture draws her eyes. She sees the welts. 'No. Come with me. We'll be okay.'

He shakes his head. 'You don't get it. It's not just the services anymore.'

That stops her. He licks his lips, and his eyes dance, darting as if to scan for enemies – or as if wishing to avoid detection in a lie. It's a reflex. Only my eyes can see them here.

'Look, I'm working, Care,' he says. His voice is steady, despite his lack of breath. 'I've got a job. Only, it's complicated.'

'Tick.' She imbues years of sadness in that one syllable. I know what she fears – this city is not kind to its young, and there are few good options for such as this boy. But she has made her offer. Outside, the shouts are growing louder. The hunters are no longer laughing.

'Go this way!' He shoves her toward the pile of brick and waits while she finds her way through, then follows. I too jump free and join them on the broken pavement outside where the moon can still be seen, low between the buildings. She takes a few steps and stops, hidden for the moment in the shade. He has paused as well, only in the blue-white light that reveals how gaunt he has become.

'Over here!' One of the men has found the vent, has found the room, and the opening on its other side. Tick turns away – toward the harbor – and runs. 'There he is!'

I hear Care sob, one hand stifling the sound as the men pass by. But then she too takes off, back into the shadow, into the path of the sinking moon.

# TEN

I should be able to lap the girl back, having routes open to me that are not available to her. I wait, of course, to make sure she is safe – to see that the thugs have followed the boy, have lost her trail as she ducks into an alley and then vaults over a fence, a move easier for a girl her size than for the heavy brutes who follow. But then I make my own way – a more direct course – from ditches to rooftops, where the last of that moonlight bleaches the dirty tar, stretching the shadows into tiger stripes. I become that tiger, some instinct surging in me as I take in the night.

A rustle in a sheltered corner – an early nest – distracts me, and I pause to imbibe the scent of the quarry within. Young, still blind and helpless. Tender – a female. And I stop. Care. I have eaten recently and to sufficiency; while she, too, is hunted, I will abstain.

Still, she is not at the office when I reach the building. I do not need to attempt the pitted brick wall to sense how still and dark the room inside lies. No light, no movement, no fresh scent of the girl reaches me in the alley alongside. I consider the building's front door, propped open by the vagrant who makes his home beneath the stairs. I could slip in, glide up the worn linoleum to the entrance that Care must use. But although I do not like such obvious approaches – they are too easily turned into traps – I do not reject this option out of fear. No, even from the pavement below, I can tell. The emptiness is complete; the dust undisturbed. The girl has not returned to her base, and that is the cause of my concern, the reason my fur rises along my spine.

I will not panic. I am not some heedless prey animal that darts and skitters without sense. She was not pursued upon leaving the basement, of that I am sure. And she has learned much of how this city works. As I return to the street, I take in what the cool night air has to tell me, all the while mulling over what I have heard – what I know of this young woman and her goals. If she has not returned to this, her base, it must be because she has another destination. Another approach she means to try.

Not, I fear, in her search for the missing Dingo – or even to decipher the mystery of that corpse, foul thing that that was – but in pursuit of the boy.

Slowly, more slowly than I made my own return, I find her scent and retrace her path back to the harborside lot. It is not a quick journey, and it tires me. Although my fur has grown thick, my hide beneath is marked with the fights of many years, and as the night fades I feel those scars pull and tighten, the muscles beneath crying out. It is not without reason that I chose another route. On the ground, in the girl's footsteps, I become more vulnerable, and I do not want to test my tired limbs against what else stalks these streets.

It is an odd emotion, to be worried so, but one I have often known. In this form, I have been beaten. Have fought and at times lost, incurring wounds that still, now, cry out as cold and overuse awaken them. My left hind leg knit badly from a kick not so long ago, and as I step forward onto a slick cobblestone, I feel it slide out from under me, a moment's reminder of my age. In response, I leap ahead, claws finding purchase in the gravel just beyond, but it makes me wary. I do not fool myself that I am alone out here, or that my misstep was not observed. A fox has passed this way not long before. In my prime, I could have met her tooth to claw, but if her ears picked up that slip, she will know to wait. To corner, and attack.

I would do well to keep such vulnerability in mind for other reasons, as well, for there are other hunters here and dangers beyond my limited scope. Although I do not understand the entirety of it, I know I have had another life before this one. A life in which I watched over this young girl, as her mentor and her friend. And while my concern was with her youth and green experience, I misread the symptoms of my own advancing years and allowed myself to become vulnerable. I believe now that my concern distracted me, as it plagues me now, unable as I am to communicate my fears directly to the girl. But I also know that I may still do her some service. If, that is, I have the wherewithal to survive such nights as this, to preserve what is left of my failing strength.

I stop. The sense of my own thoughts has caught up with me. That and the throbbing of my leg. I lift a paw, the pad grown rough and sore from city streets, and consider my surroundings. Halfway between the dull and sleepy district where Care has made her home and the harbor, this is a border zone. The fox whose scent had caught me up has moved on, I now perceive; her hunt has yielded food enough to feed her kits. What other life remains is hunkered down, as perhaps the girl is too. The trail grows faint. This is the coldest time of night, and here in the quiet, I should seek my rest.

A light, and the quiet rumble of human conversation. These should not draw me, but I am weak. I seek the warmth that humans bring with them, and I do not catch the sounds of threat or anger among the murmured talk, not for such as I am now. I see the door, outlined faintly in its tilting frame. The bottom corner brighter, where both wear and weather – and an industrious wharf rat – have eaten the wood away. I sniff it with both care and interest: wood beetles burrow in the soft rot. I have dined on worse. But another, more welcome scent entices me to bypass such easy prey and, instead, duck down to my belly and squeeze through to the room within.

It is a tavern, of a sort. If such a low room could be deemed the site of commerce and of refuge. At any rate, it is a public place: two old-timers lean against the plank serving as a bar. The barkeep glances up at my entrance. His eyes are good to catch my passing shadow, but he quickly turns away. I am neither trouble nor a paying client, except in as much as I may help keep the vermin down. Still, I am alert as I make my way along the wall. The few chairs – backless, broken – are empty, and the two drinkers look incapable of standing without the aid of that raw plank. But I am tired and am not at my quickest, and there are those who would do a creature such as I harm, simply for the diversion.

I settle into a corner by what once must have been a noble hearth: soot-darkened stones as large as my body reaching up nearly to the sagging beams. Here, I am in shadow and yet within sight of the door, and although the fire smokes and sputters, it has burned for long enough to take the chill from these stones. On one side, near the door, a pile of rags stirs at my approach, but briefly. Rheumy eyes glance toward me, their focus disconcerting despite their filmy nature, and then down. The woman underneath has come seeking shelter too, I surmise, her position on the floor a plea for sufferance. I return the gesture, the slow blink a courtesy among my kind, before I turn away.

From here, I can make out the far corner, beyond the makeshift bar and its two clients. A row of crates on end, their empty, splintered sides set back against the wall. On one of these, sits Care, whose warm scent drew me in. As I watch, she places a dirty glass on the crate beside her, its murky contents still untouched, and surveys the room. The flames reflected seem to glow within her eyes.

'Hey, you. You gonna drink that?' The barman stirs. 'I'm not running an inn, you know.'

He has not rousted the two now leaning on his plank. Care is unknown here, has no custom. She does not drink. Instead, she raises her head to stare at him, the flames replaced by sullen fury, and with a shrug he turns away. Now that I have found her, I am content to wait. As, apparently, is the girl.

Perhaps I doze. It is the gift of my kind, to sleep whenever life permits. Besides, the hearth area is warm. But then a change in the air rouses me. The door has been pushed open. I hear the echo of it scraping on the floor and glance up to see a woman stumble in. She pauses, blinking even in the dimness of the hovel, and takes a moment to pull her garment up above her shoulder, to tug down her hem, before stepping to the bar with exaggerated care. This is whom the girl has waited for, the reason for that untouched drink. A movement at my side earns a glance. The rag woman has roused, as well. I catch her looking down. She too avoids the direct gaze.

'Gina.' Care's voice is low, but in this small room it carries. The woman jerks as if stung, pausing in her progress, mouth and eyes wide.

'Oh, it's you.' Her body slumps in recognition. The girl is not a threat. Indeed, as Care holds up the dirty glass, the woman smiles and shuffles forward. 'Don't mind if I do,' she says, and takes the offering. She looks around, but Care anticipates her, dragging another crate from against the wall.

'Take a load off.' I hear the flatness in Care's voice. The woman, however, does not – or dares not question an apparent act of friendship – and with a placatory grin, tucks her short skirt beneath her as she sits, holding tight to the glass all the while. She downs the drink in a shot and looks over at Care. But the girl's face has gone stony and so, after a pause that says more of desperation than of hope, the woman reaches over to place her empty on the bar. The barkeep's expression isn't any more giving, and so with a sigh that appears to deflate her, the woman pulls a coin from her bag and pushes it toward him. She downs the resulting refill in another long pull, her eyes closed in something like ecstasy. When she opens them, she turns toward Care, ready, now, to pay for that first, much needed shot.

'What brings you here?' She punctuates the question with a smile. This, it is obvious, is her modus operandi. Never mind that Care is far from her usual clientele. 'Looking for a bit of fun?'

'I'm looking for Tick.' Care stops herself from saying more. Her hands are in her pocket, balled into fists. The effort is obvious, even to the woman, who nods slowly.

'Yeah, your boy,' she says. She has confused Care's story with her own. I settle down again, waiting to see what the girl intends. 'I was a good mother, you know.'

She addresses the room, as if expecting an argument. The barman has moved away, unwilling to deal with the sodden woman, and so she turns to Care. When the girl doesn't respond, she grows more maudlin. 'He was my baby. My youngest.'

Care starts slightly, a movement too modest for the other woman to notice, even were she less inebriated. She is taken aback, perhaps, by this admission, as if the woman were not simply another beast, breeding and releasing her young upon the world. Perhaps she isn't. I know I cannot remember any offspring, kittens I may have begotten in an earlier life, when I was young. I doubt the females of my kind do, either, once they have weaned. We are, as I have noted, solitary hunters, and such pointless reminiscences serve no purpose in our world.

I look to Care, expecting a similar reaction. The girl is fastidious, almost as much as I, despite inferior capabilities. But she is not withdrawing. Although she turns away, I can see sorrow in her face, her features so much more mutable than my own. And I recall, again, how young she is. That she has survived thus far is testament to her spirit, as well as to what skills I have shared with her, in one form or the next. She is of a different mettle than the woman who now sniffs back tears, melancholy with the drink if not memory. Still, for her kind she is too young to be on her own.

And she desires something from this woman. Not guidance, but a lead. With a barely audible sigh, Care shifts back now to regard the blowsy blonde anew. Not with the disdain of one both clean and young, I suspect. Some other thought – some strain – is at work. 'Do you know where else – where they keep them?' She makes an effort to keep her voice steady.

'You got to check out the Dunstan, I tol' you.' The woman digs another coin out, and the barman appears, bottle in hand.

'I went to the Dunstan. He wasn't in the crew,' Care says, but the woman is focused on her drink. 'Anyplace else? Gina?'

The woman wipes her mouth with the back of her hand and sucks on her lips. 'They've got hidey-holes all over.'

'No.' Care isn't letting go. 'I know the Dunstan. My father—' She stops. Catches herself. I see her blink back tears.

'So you did have someone there.' The woman – Gina – seems to focus now, as if shared grief makes the girl more real to her.

'My father worked there.' Care is talking to the table, her voice low. 'His last job. Before he – before the accident.'

'Your father was a screw?' Gina sits up straight, her voice shrill. One of the drinkers rouses and grumbles.

'No.' Care keeps her voice low, but her tone is insistent. She looks up at the barman, but he has turned his back. All kinds come in here. As long as they have coin to pay. 'He did the books.' Her voice has grown soft. 'He was a good man.'

A grunt that passes for a laugh. 'If he worked at the Dunstan, he wasn't no good man.'

Care's eyes flick toward the other woman, and I crouch, prepared to leap. I hunt alone, but when this girl fights, this Care, I will fight with her. But she doesn't. I see the skin around her mouth grow tight, her lips pale with the pressure, and yet she keeps her silence. When she does speak, it is on a different topic.

'So how much did you tell them?' Now her voice has that sing-song quality. My ears prick forward, curious as to what this signifies. A rustle to my right lets me know that the rag woman has shifted too.

'Tell who?' Gina is examining the glass. In different circumstances, I believe she would lick it.

'The men – whoever picked you up.' Care has kept her voice even, but Gina glances up at her. Despite the drink, she is alert. 'What did you tell them about me?'

Now it's the woman's turn to fall silent, though her mouth is open and slack with shock.

'I saw you,' says Care. 'You were at Gravitch's place. It was Gravitch who sent me to Dingo's squat.' She doesn't mention Tick this time. The boy who also appeared unexpectedly in that foul hovel. Instead, she pulls her hands out of her pocket, one hand balled into a fist. I wait, as does the girl, for a reaction.

But the woman doesn't respond. Instead, she glances at the door. Either she is thinking of bolting, or she is expecting someone to enter. Care reaches out with her empty hand and takes the woman's. It won't hold her, if she wants to run. The other woman may be drunk, but she is bigger than Care, and I have seen how cornered creatures can fight back.

Still habit, or perhaps the thought of the cold outside, have an effect. After a moment, the big woman shrugs, her sad face sagging with fatigue. And then she nods. 'They asked,' she says at last. 'I didn't offer.'

'Besides,' she says after a moment's pause, 'they knew.' Her voice is so quiet even I must pitch my ears forward. 'There wasn't nothing they didn't know.'

'They knew . . .' Care leans forward, willing the woman to finish the thought.

'About Dingo. That you're looking for him.' Gina looks up, her face drawn. 'Look, I had to – those toughs are my bread and butter.'

Care sits back, pocketing her closed fist and whatever it may have concealed, but her eyes are sharp. I can tell she is working through the woman's speech. That she is confused by the woman's words. I am alert, my ears up. I wait, whiskers forward. 'What, exactly, did they know?'

I could purr. This girl – this Care – has chosen her words well. Would that I could speak, but I have other ways of following a trail, and I wait my turn.

'Nothing else.' She looks away and, with one hand, reaches for her hip to rub it, surreptitiously, as if to soothe or groom. I remember her limp as she exited the alley. I would know more.

I amble toward them and rub myself against her bare leg, aware as I do of the heat and swelling of contusions. She starts, but only slightly, and then lets out her own purr of pleasure. She has no recollection of me, I believe. But I am soft and I am warm, and this woman knows little enough of either.

'Jicks,' she calls over to the barman, confirming my impression. 'I didn't know you had a cat.'

Jicks grunts and turns toward Care. She nods, and he refills the dirty glass. Care keeps her eyes on Gina as he pours the murky liquor, and I feel a tug of grief. She must grasp my purpose – to ease the rough woman's fear, her urge to run. And yet I would not have the girl believe my affections tended this way.

'I have my own methods,' Care says, watching the woman as she downs the drink. 'My ways of uncovering the truth, and that can help you, too. Gina.'

She pauses, and what passes for calm settles over the make-shift table. My actions have bought the girl time, and I am therefore recompensed.

'But first, you need to help me,' says the girl, her voice even and soft. 'Help me, and maybe I can help you. For starters, Gina, who was the stiff they left for me in Dingo's place?'

# ELEVEN

As I have noted, I am a cat. And while I may be frustrated by my inability to communicate directly, at least with the girl with whom I have forged a bond, I do enjoy my superior senses. Scent, for example, tells me that this woman does not panic when Care asks her about the corpse in the hovel. Fear gives a sour edge to human sweat, a tang made more bitter when the anxious creature cannot or does not allow her or himself to flee, as any sensible creature would. Nor does she relax unduly, giving one of the great unwitting exhalations that follow a revelation that has long been expected and comes as no surprise. Instead, she leans in, a blank expression on her face that is mirrored in her widened eyes.

'A stiff at Dingo's?' She tilts her head. 'No. You sure?'

'I'm sure.' A bitter laugh cuts through Care's words, fracturing them with its exhalations. But she retains her focus, despite the involuntary response. I discern how her eyes fix on the woman's slack mouth, on the way she leans forward, rather than what she says.

'What happened?' There's an urgency to the woman's question. And to the next one. 'Who was it?

It is Care's turn to fall silent, and as she considers her reply I can see the play of emotions across her face. Sorrow, perhaps. Disgust. 'I don't know,' she says at last. 'Some – guy. He was stabbed, I think. At least, that's what it looked like. I had to get out of there and it was – it happened a few days ago.'

The woman sighs, expelling the mild tension of her curiosity. 'Dingo's on a job, I heard Gravy say. Could be a friend dropped by. Could be someone needed a place to crash.'

'So you did talk to Gravy?' The girl doesn't miss much, but the woman only shrugs.

'I hear stuff.' She looks away, distracted. 'I'm in his office a lot. It's – convenient.'

Care digs her hands in her pockets. It's a gesture of

frustration, but almost immediately she draws one out again. 'What do you know about this?' This time, she opens her fist, and the wrinkled scrap unfolds on her palm. It has her scent on it, now, her warmth. But I know that if I were to put my nose to it, I would still get the stench of death and of decay.

The woman lacks my acuity, her senses dulled by drink. She looks it over without flinching. 'What of it?' Her voice reveals no distress, only – yes, a little tension. 'It's a label.'

'I can see that.' Care's voice has gone cold as the woman turns away. She gestures to the barkeep, raising her glass. 'Gina?'

Avoiding the girl's stare, she addresses the barkeep. Her glass. The whiskey. 'A label, the kind they sew in the clothes,' she says. Her voice is unnaturally even. 'You're probably wearing some of Gravy's duds yourself.'

With that, she turns to the two drunks with something very like a purr. One of them mutters and digs out two more coins. The barkeep scoops them up, but the woman has seen them, too. She stands with a wobble, steadying herself by reaching for the bar and steps toward them.

'We're not done yet.' Care keeps her voice low.

'You want some too?' The drunk leers, revealing missing teeth. 'I know a place that's nice and warm. Private, too. Eh, Gina?'

The girl looks away, and he laughs. I glance up at her. I trust her to have observed what I have – that the woman is distracted by more than drink. By more than the promise of custom before the night ends. There's an uneasiness to her, a worry that she is not ready yet to name. Her discomfort is contagious and makes my hide twitch, as if I had contracted mange.

I have not, having retained a certain fastidious self-regimen that carries over well to my current form. But the instinct to scratch and then to bathe is difficult to suppress until a grumble and the scrape of raw wood make me freeze. The other drunk at the bar has roused. And while his friend is preoccupied with Gina, he has taken notice of me. I cannot hear what he mumbles to his colleague. I doubt he retains the ability to form coherent words. But the dumb malice in his eyes is clear to see, and I have lived long enough to know it is better to

avoid a battle than to fight one, no matter how incapacitated
the opponent may be.

Whiskers alert, I scan the room. No other seems to mark my
presence any longer, none but the ragged woman by the door,
who still sits, watching, from the hearth. I envy her now that
cozy berth, but the time has come to act. Using the rough
furniture as cover, I move silently, running low to the ground.

The drunk has shoved the makeshift stool aside but stumbles,
cursing, the ragged woman somehow in his way. I do not pause.
Any acknowledgment on my part would render her gesture
futile, if in fact the move was generously meant. Besides, I am
at the door. I push myself through the rat-gnawed corner and
back into the night.

Where I hesitate. The girl remains inside, and that drunk is
spoiling for trouble. I flick my ears back. She would make
noise, if accosted. It's a sound strategy, a means of putting an
assailant on edge. What I hear, though, suggests another option.
A high-pitched squeal – a woman's voice – rises and then
falls within. I envision the pile of rags. But, no – the squeal
becomes a laugh before it climbs again. I pause, waiting, but
there is nothing of fear in it. Nothing of pain. It is a practiced
sound, with all the spontaneity of that factory whistle and serving
much the same purpose. Gina, plying her trade, summons both
the men toward her, and when Care appears moments later, I
assume she has succeeded, reaching some accord as to coins
or to liquor.

Now that the girl has emerged, I experience a faint regret.
I should have hunted while I had the opportunity. The nagging
fear that kept me beside the makeshift bar has lifted somewhat,
and I am aware of my hunger. Of the pain in my belly and my
left hind leg. But I have larger concerns than these simple
animal needs. I am glad to see the girl emerge unharmed and
I make myself known, coming from the darkness to twine
around her ankles.

'Blackie.' She reaches down for me, and I let her lift me and
hold me in her arms. I am tired and in pain, and her embrace
speaks of her own trials. 'I should have known you'd be here,'
she says. 'That you'd wait for me.'

For a moment I wonder. Is there any chance that this girl

understands? That she has comprehended who I am, and why I dog – yes, that is the word – her steps? Can she?

'Good kitty.' She nuzzles the thick fur of my ruff, which keeps me from turning in her arms. From looking into those green eyes, not so different from my own. If I could, perhaps I would be able to gauge what she comprehends. If she sees in me her former mentor and her friend, or if she has any understanding of how I came into this form. But I cannot. She holds me tight, and her breath is warm. And I am an animal, and for the moment at least, such questions are kept at bay by the comfort of another. By her scent and the warm pressure of her hands.

Indeed, this time I let myself be lifted into the girl's canvas bag. I am tired. It is late, and I have learned to trust her, feral creature though I am, and it is pleasant to be carried. To be heading back to a place of safety and of warmth. Once I am safely stowed, she begins the long walk home, using a more measured pace than earlier. And as she walks, she cogitates upon the events of the night, murmuring beneath her breath. The bag rocks at her side as she makes her way, a gentle rhythm, and I slip in and out of sleep, cradled on the papers she has also stowed within. But my hearing is acute and I catch her quiet musings. She has questions still that the woman did not answer. About the boy whose brief appearance saved her. About the body we discovered, and the man who called that hovel home.

Dozing, I believe myself on the hunt and consider the young tom whose path I crossed. His raw, masculine scent haunts me, and my paws twitch as I drift, as if I were readying for a fight. In my dream state I perceive my adversary turning. Growing into a thing most large and dangerous. Caught as I leap, as I judge myself about to land, I twist, desperate to escape, and I do, in that I wake to find myself still hungry. Still aching, but still safe as well, for now, tucked inside canvas thin enough to convey the warmth of the girl beside me.

'I wonder who he is,' she is saying. 'Or was. Someone must miss him, surely. Poor guy, left there like that.'

It's a fate I know well, as does the girl. She must be remembering another such – the old man, her mentor – left to die alone. The ragged edge of the dream begins to pull me under, but I resist. Adjust my position to stretch my sore leg, aware as I do that my movement may disrupt Care's train of thought. I would not sleep with these thoughts in mind, and stretch again, this time flexing my hind claws against the papers she has also stowed within. She kept them, despite their stink. But her sense of smell is not as keen as mine. She can tell, she has said, that the man was not newly killed. That the corpse in the hovel had been dead before she took Gravitch's commission by hours at least, if not by days. But did she have time to discern that it had been moved? The cot beneath it, while dirty, had not been soaked in the natural outflow of death.

I recall the poor room now and wonder at the papers curled beneath me. A nest they've made, an added cushion to my aching form. But now I twist to face them, to take their edges in my mouth. The taint of death, yes, much as anything in that room would carry. The old, dried husks of insects, discarded beneath the flooring. But there is more. Blood and sweat, both infused with the sharp bite of pheromones. Of fear, and another scent, familiar as my dream and yet—

It is too much, my movement. The girl has stopped. The bag opens as she peers in. I blink up at her, but she does not meet my gaze. Instead, she reaches past me, grabbing for the papers that have been my bed.

'Excuse me, Blackie.' With a disconcerted mew I let them go as she pulls them forth. I would have had more time with them, but I have only my own foolishness to blame. Fatigue or, more likely, age, have robbed me of the opportunity. And as she settled on the curb to read them, I extract myself as well to draw close and rub my head against the gathered pages.

'It's numbers, Blackie.' She reaches for me, one hand gentle on my back. She has misread my interest.

'One three-digit number and then this list of longer ones. One, two . . . nine digits, all of them. I don't know what they mean.' She looks from one page to the next, and as she does, I seize the opportunity, brushing up against them once again. Death and dirt, for sure. The fragrant sheddings of that centipede. But something sharper as well, something beyond the sour scent of fear. A trace of that young tom? Is it the pungent alkali of spunk that irritates the wet leather of my nose? Not feline, though—

'Deliveries? Payments?' She pulls the page from me. Brushes it off, as if the faint spatter on its surface were so much soil, easy to flick away. 'Payoffs? Is this why he was killed?'

She falls silent as she examines the page and then turns to stare at its reverse, and once again I regret my mute state. She is adept at reading the symbols written there. The obvious signs made by men on paper. But can she sense the remnants of violence there, which are so obvious to me? Is she aware of their age, which pre-dates the demise of the unfortunate in that hovel? I will her to remember those lessons long ago. That she must know better than to assume a connection she cannot prove. That those who live by the harbor kill each other for little reason, or for none. I mew softly in protest, but she does not hear. My mute state, the inequality between us – in terms of perception, in terms of communication – more troubling than any lingering pain.

'He was left there purposefully, Blackie.' She talks to me still, although she has no knowledge of how much I comprehend. I find this realization comforting, despite everything, and with the soft burr of her voice, allow it to lull me back into the half-awake dream state I have so recently left. 'Left for Dingo. Or for me.' The words have fear behind them, but the voice is calm and thoughtful. 'The question is, who was he? And maybe more important, why was he killed?'

# TWELVE

*T*he dream is of shadows. Three men, tall and cruel. Two are silent as they bend over me. Silent as they recede and fade, as my dying body sinks. I know them now, and even in sleep I can fill in their faces: one piggish and thick, the other a slight, rat-faced man. It is the third who remains unclear to me. He is taller than the others and looms larger in my dream. Almost, I can hear him speak . . .

'What?' Not a man's voice. A girl's. Care, startled from sleep beside me. And I, who pride myself on my keen senses, am taken unaware. The sound of pounding: fists. No, boots, making the office door shake. Despite the hour of our arrival back here, in the office. Despite fatigue, the girl has taken precautions. Barred the door. The piece of lumber, salvaged during a midnight stroll, makes a sturdy barricade. It bounces in the metal brackets, souvenirs of the same construction site. But it holds, as do the nails the girl drove in with swift, strong strikes.

'Police!' A gruff voice barks. 'Open up.'

I am up and onto the windowsill before the girl can respond, the night's stiffness forgotten as I leap. She glances toward me, then back toward the door, half rising from the sofa where we – where I – have slept since our return. She stayed up till dawn, I know from dreamy memory. The candle by her face. Searching for meaning, I gathered from the soft utterances that she made. The lists of numbers have proved as opaque to her as they are to me.

'Police!' The word itself a threat, sounded with a volume that would pin my ears flat to my skull even if the tone did not. The girl is not as sensitive as I, but as she stands to face the door, I experience a moment of dismay. Surely, she will not obey such a harsh command. Surely, if the assaultive sound has not alarmed her, she will have noticed the sequence of events. It is no accident that the pummeling woke us. If the door had given way, those on the other side would not have bothered to announce themselves.

My earlier dream comes back to me. The impression of the hunt turning, the quarry looming to attack. If she should continue to stand there, like some fear-blind rabbit. If she should open the door . . .

'Come on, girly.' The voice a brusque command. 'We know you're in there.'

Another blow makes the portal vibrate, and I can hear the board begin to crack. I do not know if the men outside are as perceptive, or if they bother to mark the way the door itself has begun to sag, its hinges giving way. The repeated word – that appellation 'girly' – has roused Care from her stupor, though, achieving what the violence did not. She runs silently to the desk and grabs up the papers scattered there, shoving them once more into her carryall.

Another blow. The door shudders but it holds, and the thud of boots retreating down the stairs offers the promise of relief. The speaker has not left, however, although his tone now moderates. 'We just want to talk to you. We have some questions.' If the words are meant to reassure, they are undercut by those that follow. 'We need to know about that stiff in the wreckage, girly. About why you killed Paul Dingett.'

At the name, the girl freezes once more, and I hunker down, hindquarters quivering, prepared to jump. I could be out of this room, away from the violence those men intend, with a leap. The ledge below offers me safe passage to the street and beyond. But the girl cannot move as I can. Cannot launch herself to safety, and so I turn back toward the more wonted entry to where footsteps rush the steps once more. I will have one chance to distract them, to claw at exposed flesh and to howl. If, in that moment, she can make her escape, my sacrifice will have been worthwhile.

Another crash, louder this time. The men have returned with some kind of a tool. We hear them count – 'one, two' – and we both recoil as their battering ram, makeshift or not, rattles the door, sending splinters flying. I store the tension like a spring, ready to pounce. But the girl moves before I need to. Throwing the bag over one shoulder, she grabs the old overcoat she has slept under in one hand and the chair in the other, pulling them both toward me, toward the window. I sit up in surprise as she pushes the sash up and clambers up beside me on the sill. As I watch, she takes the arms of the overcoat and ties them together, around and under the back of the chair. Then, using the body of the overcoat as a rope, she lowers herself out the window,

The chair rises up as she descends, crashing with a ferocious bang against the window. I freeze at the noise, as it holds and totters – nearly filling the open space. Beyond it, I can see her, hanging there. Her feet are swinging free, too clumsy to find footing on the concrete ledge. She looks up at me, her eyes wide with fright. Behind me, I hear a final thud – a crack and a bellow, as the men break into our sanctuary.

'Blackie!' Her voice is a harsh whisper. Imploring. But the chair still sways, like a thing alive, the echo of its crash ringing in my ears.

'Blackie,' she calls again, though softer, and her voice brings me back to myself. My better self. For despite my limitations, I am no mere animal. And while I would flee the noise both before me and behind, and the violence it is sure to herald, I answer to a stronger allegiance.

I turn. I hiss. 'It's that cat.' The leader, he now wears some kind of uniform, points me out. His troops understand this as a command. Two step forward and I react, arching my back in my own display.

'Blackie!' Her voice is louder now, but it is too late. And then – yes! – I hear a thud, and I turn to see the girl has dropped to the ground below. She pulls herself to her feet and stares up, her face drawn and bloodless, despite her own escape.

She fears for me, I realize, just as the danger that she dreads descends. A hand larger than my head has grabbed my tail, and I look up to see cold death in my assailant's eyes. But I am lucky. Had he grabbed my ruff, I would have been unable to turn as I do. To twist and lash out, spitting, with all four claws bared for the fight. I am smaller than he, by far, and should be easy prey. But my speed and fury, as much as the thin lines of blood now welling along the back of that hand, cause him to

draw back. Make him momentarily loosen his grasp as he cries
out in startled dismay.

And in that moment, I am gone. I jump toward that hideous
chair and squeeze through the window, scrambling for purchase
on the ledge below. Before I have even fully righted myself, I
launch myself again to the alley floor below. Toward Care, who
is waiting, and together we head for the street, leaving the
shouts of the men behind us.

# THIRTEEN

'**G**ravitch knew.' The girl is talking to herself, and I flick my ear to listen. 'He must've known that Dingo was dead. He didn't need me to find that out. So why hire me?'

I can't fault her logic, but she has been repeating herself. Unable to move her thought process forward, instead she worries this one deduction like a kitten with a wounded vole. 'He told me where Dingo lived,' she says. 'He has all those guys working for him. He could've found him. He must have.'

It is as well that we both slept before we were forced to flee. The girl is too wrought up to rest now, and while I pass in and out of a doze, I keep my focus on her. It's not that I doubt her ability to reason. Unlike so many in this world, she thinks before she acts and takes in factors beyond her simple appetites. Only she has had a shock.

'He had to have known I'd go—' She stops, and I open my eyes. From the look of concentration, I can see that she has pieced the parts together. That not only is the man she sought dead, that he was, apparently, the corpse that we found, but that he was laid out like a trophy. Like a mouse or bird, ready for her to find.

She must, I trust, have noticed the other salient fact. Her sense of smell is not as keen as mine. But surely the other signs – the appearance of that wound, the lack of blood and of those who live on blood – must have informed her: that corpse was neither freshly dead nor killed in that place. No, that scene was staged, and our discovery was simply the trigger for the arrival of the authorities, or whoever these enforcers may be. This is what the girl has spent the last hour piecing together. What she has been chewing over, when she could have been resting.

We have, after all, found shelter of a sort. As does any scared animal, the girl ran toward the area she knows – toward the harbor – and I followed. I do not fret about the future. It is not the way of my kind, even less so now that I have met what is deemed the one irrevocable end. But as I made my own way down those rutted streets, darting ahead into shadows to avoid the workaday traffic, I did find myself wondering what I could do for this girl. How I could rein her in when she seemed so intent on seeking out danger, when we had so recently gotten free? Inchoate and vaguely anxious thoughts – remnants of another life, really – that I calmed by watching for the traffic ahead. For the trudge of workers making their rounds. For the rumble of tires on the hard stones.

It was full light by the time we went to ground in the basement of an abandoned building. It was a place I remembered, retaining as I do the memory of scent and taste – of dampness and nights huddled around hoarded food. The boy had found this hideaway. It was he who hid his stores behind the loose bricks. A crust of bread and some cheese too hard and dry to offer much even to my rasping tongue. He and the girl had spent a night here, back before the boy was taken.

I do not know if the girl comes here because of that history. It is long past, and the boy's presence only a memory, I could tell her. The only life I scent as we descend to the shadowed chamber is of my own kind and of those we hunt. Even that rind is long gone, its waxen edges gnawed by dozens of ceaseless teeth.

She checks the makeshift cupboard anyway, though surely she must know it will be empty. It is, and I see her body sag. She leans against the wall, her head hangs down. I do not think she grabbed the envelope of bank notes in her rush.

'Tick,' she says, and I realize it is not food she hungers for. She repeats the boy's name, and I cannot help myself from bristling, my back arching slightly even as hers slumps. I do not trust the child. He is a slave to hungers, to pressures that she has proved herself immune to – he has shown a taste for the illicit drugs that tore his mother from him. Still, her longing – for such a weak and wayward boy – makes her vulnerable as well. Compels actions that are not sensible for a small creature in this wasteland.

And yet her sorrow acts on me, and I would soften it. With an exhalation that would, I believe, almost approximate a sigh, I stretch to straighten out my back and lean into her, rubbing my cheeks and then my long body against her legs, smoothing down my own fur as I comfort her. Even over my own purr, I hear how ragged her breath has grown. She is on the edge of tears, and so I twine myself about her, to warm and distract, and to remind her that, although the boy is gone, she is not alone.

My maneuver works, and she reaches for me, holding me close as she buries her face in my fur. I am not comfortable being held. I do not like having my freedom restricted, as too often my own survival has depended on the ability to jump and twist and run. But I cannot resist the warmth of the girl, of her breath against my scarred and weary hide. My eyes close, and my front paws begin to work, despite myself, in the gentle kneading motion of a kittenhood I no longer can recall. As she strokes my back, her hand gently smoothing my hackles, her breath calms and my purr deepens. For a little while, we are at peace.

I did not sleep then, not exactly. Although the girl slides at last to the ground, exhausted from our flight and from the long night before, she holds me close, leaning back against the worn brick. I remain in her arms as long as it is possible to do so. She left the coat behind her when she fled. The basement is hidden from sight, but this close to the harbor the ground is permeated with moisture. This adds to the penetrating chill, and I would keep her warm, despite my growing discomfort with this posture. With the restriction of my movement.

I use the time to contemplate the room, the boy's retreat and onetime hideaway. As spring progresses into summer, this will be a good place to remember – a refuge from the heat where other, smaller creatures will come, too, seeking relief. Many of them will find death here, at my behest or others', but that thought does not trouble me. That this girl not be one of them matters, however. And as she surrenders more deeply to sleep, into dreams that I surmise are full of questions and concerns, I watch, through lidded eyes and listen. I cannot intervene, but I can observe, holding myself in readiness for her time of need.

'Tick,' she says, the name coming to her even in sleep. This time, however, the boy's name is not a cry, not an invocation of sorrow or longing. It is a statement – the answer to the questions she has been asking. But not, I fear, a safe one. I rise at that and stretch and begin to bathe. I do not like where the girl's thoughts are proceeding, but I will not let her follow them alone.

# FOURTEEN

The heat of day has passed before she rises, as meager as it was even at its peak. The timing served to hinder my hunt, a twilight activity at best, nor did my reluctance to leave the girl give me much scope. Still I have found sufficient prey among the basement's crawling things to sustain my strength by the time she rouses fully, and I greet her with my senses sharp and at her service.

'Tick's the key, Blackie.' She looks over, and I blink back to indicate my benign awareness of her words. I am bathing, but I am alert. 'He knew about Dingo – and he knew I'd be there, too,' she says. 'He tried to warn me.'

I pause in my ablutions, waiting, but she does not hear the error in her thoughts. The missed note, so gulled is she by her affection for the boy. 'He acted like a decoy, running the other way like that.'

She is pacing now, inscribing a circle on the damp dirt floor. I recognize the motion, the excitement that cannot be contained. It's a precursor to action, akin to the lashing of my tail. Only when I hunt, I begin with observation. With scent and sound and even, at times, sight. The girl, on the other hand, is acting on incomplete information. She perceives that the boy is involved – and that the boy was aware of her involvement. That he made an effort to shield her, I will accept, though unlike Care, I do not confer motive. What I distinguish, which she does not, is that his appearance suggests a deeper collusion than she would credit. That he may have a larger role, may have been complicit in the arrival of Gravitch – or of the lugs at our door this morning who arrived with some semblance of authority. Of office.

She does not see this, or does not wish to. If I could grant her a more pragmatic outlook, I would. But although she lacks my age and perspective, she has my allegiance, and so I ready myself for whatever she plans next.

That does not mean I am without apprehension when she exits the basement and takes a familiar path deeper into danger. Closer to the waterfront. Some of that is my own history. Although I have some memory now of what happened there – of how I was trapped and hurt and thrown in the water to perish – I do not know everything, and these gaps may prove dangerous, leaving me susceptible to ambush or other attack. Being in the company of the girl is no comfort. Yes, she pulled me from the flood, saving my life in the process. But she too is susceptible, the more so as she is driven by emotion rather than the calm of reason or the cool calculation of the hunt. There is a reason that beasts such as I forget their offspring once they have been weaned. We none of us benefit from such mindless alliances.

My bond to this girl is of a different nature, one of choice and obligation. And although my nature limits our communication, I would wish her to emulate my stealth as we draw near the piers. Perhaps she senses this. The girl is careful to vary her route. We skirt the lot where the hovel once stood, passing behind the building through which we so narrowly escaped. The streets are quiet now, the hum of life as it occurs here subdued in daylight, but I can still scent the dust and other debris on the air. The oil of the machines that went through here, leveling the shack – and most likely the body inside – in their wild passage.

My apprehension rises as we pass further on, into an area where the low brick buildings still stand and serve some use beyond mere shelter. The commercial district, such as it is, and I cannot help the low growl that escapes me as I realize her destination. That brick building – Gravitch's place of business, if not his lair, but marked by him as much as if it were a nest – its street front blind and dull. But not abandoned. A dim light makes the one unpainted window glow, and there is no mistaking the snarl of activity within.

The girl must hear it, too, the rumble that makes the structure itself sound alive. When she stops short of the flagstone paving at its front, I congratulate myself. The girl has learned. She will steer clear. But when she retreats to the building adjacent, I comprehend her more subtle plan. With an energy I envy, if without the grace that is second nature to me, she jumps and, grabbing the lowest rung of that rusted fire ladder, she pulls herself up. There is no platform, no access to the building it would serve. But from her perch, I see her squinting. Leaning forward as if to leap—

No, it is too far, and when she lands back down beside me, I understand. Although I could not emulate her feat, I too would spy out what may lie within. And from that rusted perch, she may have been able to see into Gravitch's sole unblocked window. If, that is, there were anything to see.

'Damn,' she curses softly to herself. 'I was hoping.' And as I butt my head against her in both inquiry and comfort, she explains, 'I saw a couch, but it must just be his office. Not his home.'

I find myself relieved, for reasons I cannot entirely explain. But as she makes her way around the building, skirting the stone to enter the alley on the other side, I reflect on the woman we saw leaving here. Of the appetites she serves, as well as the ones she has fostered within herself in her search for oblivion. A couch may be used for more than sleeping. But she is not here now, and I find no fresh indications of her passing.

Indeed, the scents in this passage are male and rank, calling to mind the young tom, of the traces on those papers. I consider the boy Care seeks and wonder again at his involvement. I would that she could forget him. I fear what he may do, wittingly or not, to ease his own burden.

I know she is thinking of him, too. She has retreated one structure beyond the alley, where a once grand stoop offers a modicum of cover. From here she watches the stone piazza, the entrance to the alley. I am reminded of the vehicle that pulled up at the alley's other end, of its unseen driver, and his connection to this low place, but if the girl does not make that connection – does not choose to explore it, then I am content. The woman, Gina, met unkind handling from the occupant of that vehicle, and I would keep the girl from them both if I could.

The light fades as we wait, both hidden in the shelter of that stoop. After the fashion of my kind, I curl up, making of my own tail a cushion for my chin. I have slept in low places for long enough that this hard berth does not discomfit me. I begin to slip back into my usual dream, while remaining aware of the gathering dusk. In other parts of the city, this would be the hour of exodus, when workers leave for their homes or gather in places like the one we visited last night. There is no siren here, no bell to stop the machines that grind and whir, but time is passing. The girl huddles down as the evening chill descends and the damp of the day coalesces into a mist. She wraps her too thin arms around her torso, and I rouse enough to lean against her. As I do, I hear footsteps. The girl unfolds herself to peer over the stoop, but before she can make a move I gauge the shadow and I leap. She gasps as I pass by her, but then she holds her peace, noting no doubt how I hang by the building's side, another darker shade to all but the most perceptive eyes.

Two men, full grown, are walking toward us. They are not the youths I have sensed, but there is something familiar in their voices and their stride. They are laughing, mouths wide open, as they walk, but as they pass in front of Gravitch's building, I catch their scent. They were part of the assault last night, two among many but their unwashed bodies are as distinctive as any other beast's. I believe the girl is waiting for Gravitch, looking to question the man who hired her, but I trust she has the sense not to approach these in search of information or access of any sort.

'Oi! There you are!' A third male, emerging from the alley. He turns toward the newcomers, but Care shrinks down anyway. It is a healthy instinct with brutes such as these about, and I myself push further into the old doorway. 'What took you?'

'Had to clean up a bit,' the smaller of the two responds, as his companion laughs. He raises an implement – a tool of some kind, for machinery. It has been wiped clean to their eyes, although its appearance evokes more of the same humorless mirth. To me, the odor of blood is as clear as if it dripped still. Wherever these two came from, they left violence behind them.

'Boss gonna complain?' The man from the alley ushers the two before him, and I feel Care breathe more easily as they turn away.

'Nah, this wasn't like the other night. This was on the shop floor. Come on, let's get going. I'm getting wet.' More laughter as the three disappear from sight. I smell as much as see that alley door open. Dust and a gust of heat, a young, male scent. The growling rumble grows into a roar, drowning out that laughter, and then the door closes again, cutting both off with a bang.

As I've said, time means little to me in this form, and my guard hairs are good about shedding the thickening mist. But I am hungry when I wake next, and as I stretch I feel the chill of full night on the bare leather of my paws. The girl beside me has dozed as well, despite the damp, and starts as I rise before peering once more over the stoop. I would tell her not to worry. I would have woken had another come down this way, would have registered even the lightest of human steps.

She does not appear as confident. Instead, she licks her lips and turns both before and behind. I lean against her to give her comfort, but although she smiles down at me, it is an anxious smile and quickly disappears even before she speaks.

'I can't believe I fell asleep, Blackie.' She is shrewd. She keeps her voice low but does not whisper. To any whose ears are sensitive, the sibilance of a whisper would give her away. 'I meant to keep watch. Gravitch has got to come out at some point. I mean, this is his place of business.'

I lack the means to share what I have already discerned. There is no scent of the dusty little man about this building. There has not been in days. But as I pull back, considering how best to move her on, her own body betrays her. She is shivering, and I can hear her teeth chattering in the cold spring night. The mist has changed to rain while we rested, and her thin clothes are soaked through.

'I've got to get out of here.' She rubs her hands up and down her arms. 'I wonder if it's safe . . .' She stands and looks around. Her thoughts would be clear, even if I did not know her this well. She is weighing her options. The makeshift nightspot where she met with Gina. The bare cellar where we last sheltered, and the office that had become our home. She is a practical girl and has been trained in skills beyond mere subterfuge. She was schooled in the hunt, as well, though I did not then call it such. Taught to attend the traces all creatures leave, to weigh and understand.

She must know that those who pursue her can marshal superior numbers as well as brute force. But perhaps she can judge as well how they rely on inciting fear. When she heads back the way we came, I am heartened. The rain is drumming down. Exposure to the night will do this child no good, and I know I can at least do my best to guard her. To warn her if danger comes again.

The office has been ransacked. Whatever could be broken has been, her small store of food tossed to the ground and soiled. The envelope of bills gone. But once we have ascertained that the space is empty – I by quick evaluation, my nose and ears in confirmation, the girl only after a more laborious examination – we find shelter of a sort. The gutted sofa cushions piled are softer than the floor. The retrieved overcoat still serves well as a blanket, despite the tear that splits its back. Even the office placement serves us on this cold night: two floors above the street, the radiant heat of bodies and of more affluent tenants, those whose radiators hiss and bang, seeps in. Although she has the prudence to leave the window ajar, a gap large enough to serve as my egress, we are warm here. We are dry, and I would we sleep. Exhaustion and fright take the girl first, and soon she is breathing evenly, the worries of the day dispelled. For me, rest is more elusive. Even when I do succumb, I dream of three men, of hunters, and I know that I have become the prey.

# FIFTEEN

By first light, I have roused. The rain, which continued through the night, provided a thrumming lullaby that lulled me into a deeper sleep than I expected, into dreams of the hunt among the rumbling of machines. I wake suddenly, as is my wont, and to a sense of urgency that sends me out to scour the grounds around our violated sanctuary as the weak sun rises over oily puddles.

On my return, the scuffle of movement behind the ruined door makes my heart race. Makes me curse those memories I cannot quite recall. I still myself. I wait outside, listening and poised. And then I recognize her light step, her gentle breath, and know I can relax. Uncoiling my readied limbs, I slip back through the shattered frame.

'Blackie,' she calls softly. The rest has done her good. Despite the pallor of her cheeks, her eyes are bright and the hint of a smile plays on her face. 'I've got something. I can't believe I didn't see it.' She holds up a paper and so I leap up to the desktop. It's the eviction notice: I recognize the shape of the imprint. The smell of its ink. I lean in, to examine it further. But she misreads my action as affection and moves the page away to rub my ears. This frustrates me, but she continues. It is an enjoyable sensation, I must admit.

'It's a corporation, see?' She pauses in her ministrations to indicate a symbol. The peaks of a mountain, or of shadows looming. I reach to sniff it, and her smile broadens. 'I'm underage. But maybe if it's just some corporate board, they won't care. I mean, if I can come up with the scratch. If I can just figure out how to reach out the right way. More Corp? Moon? At any rate, M— something . . .'

I pull back and regard her, meeting her gaze with my own. Her eyebrows arch and that smile broadens, as if for a moment . . . 'I swear, sometimes I'm sure you can understand me, Blackie,' she says, her voice soft.

My heart stills, and I open my mouth to speak. That logo, her words . . .

'Mew.'

I am humiliated. Frustrated to the extreme, and as she chuckles, I jump to the floor. If I cannot express my more subtle emotions, I can at least signal my readiness to leave this space. Whether she understands or simply agrees, I cannot tell, but she begins to pack up her bag, adding some of the other papers that she had left in our hasty retreat. I wait by the door, alert for the sounds of others. Returning to this place was a necessary evil. Remaining here, while the girl is hunted, would be foolish.

'You're ready to go out?' The girl smiles down at me, the dangers we have faced seemingly forgotten. I lash my tail, but she pays it no heed. Despite our flight from this very place only a day before, she appears to be of a cheerful demeanor, and I find myself disturbed. I would this girl be more cautious. Be more wary of the dangers of this city. And yet, as she reaches down to ruffle my fur, I cannot resist pushing my head into her hand as a purr rises deep within me. There is joy to be found in a bright morning, in the company of one whom may be trusted.

In the richness of the world as well. And as we turn toward a ripening I know well, I race ahead. We are headed toward the workhouse, the girl and I. And much like the rat, whose stink beckons even as its corporeal self disintegrates, if the man whom she approached yesterday is no longer accessible, there will be another. These prisoners have their own means of passing information along, and the meager reward that the girl can offer has concrete value.

As expected, the rat is nearly gone. There are other, less fastidious, creatures about for whom its peculiar perfume is a particular enticement. They scatter as I draw close and, to my dismay, do not return. The man with whom Care spoke yesterday does not approach either. No one does, although the girl presses close to the fence to scan the crowd. With frustration or perhaps concern, I note that she consults the tower clock more than once.

I make use of the delay to scope out the alley. In response to the rain, life has re-emerged here. Slugs and worms have been brought to the surface, the city-hard earth having become quickly saturated in the night's downpour. Rodents and other scavengers have enjoyed the bounty, while larger hunters have feasted in turn. Some of my own kind have been through here, but theirs is not the scent that causes me to pause, making my wet nose pad twinge. No, it is a human scent, a combination of unwashed flesh and waste that urges me to stick closely to the girl.

Someone has spent the night out here, despite the weather. A woman, not young. And while there are many in this city who lack shelter, this alley is not one of their usual gathering sites. Not a place to drink or to consort, but for a female – an older one – its isolation may mean safety, if not comfort. I begin to work my way through the refuse that is piled here, taking my time to process what may be hidden beneath the rich aroma of new mold, when Care gives a small cry.

I turn to see her staring into the yard. At the men caged there within. But something has changed in their routine. The men emerge from the stone building, but they remain in lines today. The lines form a circle and as we watch they begin to walk, feet dragging and shoulders hunched forward.

'Come on, you slugs!' The yell carries over the paved yard, although it does little to speed up the circle. The sound of a blow, muffled by cloth or flesh, and a brief cry. But the speed of those walking barely changes.

'Someone's in for it.' The familiar voice makes Care turn. I could have told her that the woman has been waiting. I have been eyeing her, watching that she kept her distance, as Care pressed against the fence. Blowsy and unclean, her scent is one of the many in this alley. She did not spend the night here, unlike that other, older female I have sensed. But she has been here since the rain, since leaving that low bar last night. Her appearance perhaps no more than a return to a usual post.

'They're on lockdown,' she continues, her voice is low, her syllables elided. The drink – or the men – of the night before have left her drained. Arms crossed for warmth, she raises her chin to indicate the yard, the men within. 'Nobody's going to be coming to the fence today.'

They watch the men in silence, but I can see Care's eyes glancing over at the woman.

'This about Dingo?' she says at last. She's reaching, the girl. Throwing out a line in the hope of drawing the woman in. A tease, in lieu of liquor or of coin.

'What about him?' She aims for impassive. Wooden. Still, there's an edge to her words that hint at some urgency, some emotion.

'You heard. You must have.' Care keeps her voice level, watching. 'The stiff at his place? That was him.'

The woman flinches as if slapped. As if her denial of the night before has made her weaker, somehow. More vulnerable.

The girl sees it. She speaks again, her voice low but clear. 'Dingo's dead, Gina.'

Gina turns away, as if aware of the scrutiny. As if aware that her heavy makeup will not hide everything. She is facing the yard but her jaw is slack, her gaze unfocused. Whatever she sees, it is not the men circling. 'Yeah,' she says at last, when it becomes apparent that some response is necessary. That Care requires one. 'Yeah,' she repeats herself and looks down. 'I heard.'

Care's face softens, although the woman does not see it, and I sense a wave of sadness coming over her. She did not know this man, the one she was paid to find. But the woman beside her did, and everything about her posture – the way she hugs herself, the way she kicks at the base of the gate – suggests she mourns him, in her fashion.

'Maybe one of the inmates knows something.' Care pauses, considering her next gambit. She would entice this woman, draw her out through her self-interest and her loss. 'Maybe that's why the lockdown. Maybe he was in league with them.'

A laugh, or something like. 'Hardly,' Gina says, and shifts, wrapping her arms more tightly around her bust, her low-cut top too thin for warmth on this chilly morning. 'Dingo was one of Gravy's top guys. One of his trusted ones.'

'Really?' Care appears to consider this. I see how she is watching the woman, though. Wondering what else she knows, and what she will volunteer.

'Always in and out of his office,' she says. 'His inner sanctum.'

She is reciting words she's heard. 'I should know.' Another
laugh, although there is no humor in it, and then falls silent.

'You should know?' Care's voice is an echo. A prompt, no
more. In the yard, the guard shouts an order. The men shuffle
to a stop and he shouts again. The line begins to move.

'Gina?' Care should wait. She should give this woman time,
but she has seen the woman straighten and begin to turn. A car
has appeared at the end of the alley. In the shadow it resembles
the car that picked her up the day before, but newer, maybe,
with chrome that reflects the morning light as do its tinted
windows. Gina looks at it as if sizing up the money spent on
those fancy rims, on keeping its paint so clean and white, and
then turns back to Care.

'Look, kid,' she says. From the way she licks her lips, I
gather she thirsts and would be off. That car waits, its engine
a low purr, rich with promise. She glances back at it, anxious.
I do not believe it will wait for long. 'I owe you. I shouldn't
be telling you this, but Dingo was one of the good ones. He
didn't—' She breaks off. Shakes her head, as if responding to
some internal reprimand. 'Not that,' she says. Pulling her top
into place, she walks off, wobbling on the broken pavement.

Care stares off after her, as she gets into the car. Creatures
such as she do not offer their gifts freely, and I consider what
this means. Care has helped her, that is sure. She has also bought
her drink. But where Care has provided, others may pay more.

Care sighs and sucks her own lips, though I gather doubt,
rather than any hunger, is behind this simple act. I am glad.
The girl is smart and she has been trained well. But she is too
quick to take in those in need. Though I do not trust the boy
and I am glad that, for now at least, he is gone, I have less
confidence in this woman, and in the debt she would have Care
believe she owes.

# SIXTEEN

The girl has the wit to drop back as the car drives away, sheltering in the wall's shadow. The occupant had been waiting for Gina. The door opened before the woman reached the end of the alley and closed behind her as she slid in. But what may have been a simple transaction has taken on suspicious ramifications. Although the woman may have been following the same leads that brought the girl here, her appearance is curious. We have been in this alley, many times. Yet I do not recall her presence here before Care was hired by this Gravitch, with whom the woman has dealings. Not before she sought the information that the woman drops so casually, like a trail in the dirty alley.

The idea that this Dingo was a valued member of Gravitch's team has merit. The oily man paid quickly what Care requested to seek him out, to observe him and report. And she has heard others, members of his crew, remark on his absence, reinforcing the woman's words – that Dingo was one of the 'good ones,' valued and deserving of a better end.

As I stare up at the girl's face, I find myself trying to read her. To understand what she does, and to follow how she thinks. Surely, she must wonder at her hiring – and at the timing of the missing man's death. Surely, she will not forget the bright lights of the authorities or the hammering that broke down her door.

She is owed payment for the job, a commission that she fairly earned, for she did in fact track the quarry as agreed. But I do not believe this is why she will not let the matter rest. Nor is it because she has been looped into the killing of a man she did not know. Nor because her trade – the training she received and the memory of he who introduced her to it – has been leveraged to trap her, to take advantage of her youth and inexperience. No, I see the conflict of emotion on her face, the way she chews her lower lip as she stares down the alley. She would finish this job because she has accepted it. Has bound herself to the responsibility, employment of a sort as her options narrow daily. And because she saw the pain on Gina's face, the loss and sorrow of a woman similarly bereaved. Who searches, also, for a boy.

I do not realize that I lash my tail until it strikes a chunk of asphalt, a black and broken slab kicked up by Gina's toe. It is this last factor that infuriates and sets my tail to moving – Care's disregard for risk as she seeks the boy. He is alive, but that does not suffice. And I, who would protect her, cannot point out this simple fact.

Now I must watch and wait, unable to guide this girl, my charge. She is thinking of the woman, it is clear. She stares toward the street where the blowsy blonde got into the car, her face drawn as she considers what the older woman has said. What she, both here and in her cups, has been willing to share.

I would advise her, if I could. While it is possible that this Gina has gathered this information over time and would share it with another female, also bereft, who seeks information about a boy, it is not likely. Not for free, nor for a tumbler of cheap whiskey already drunk. I understand that Care seeks the comfort of kinship. That she would make allowances for this woman, worn down by her trade. But I would have her notice the repercussions of this trade, of the woman's diminishing market value. She has learned to see the world in terms of her low occupation, and that information may be a more durable asset than her body.

As Care makes her way down the alley, I believe she has marked another sign that all is not as it would seem. To start with, the car that had pulled up was large and clean, indicating not only a newer model but one on which more has been spent than is usual for this part of town – or for that kind of companion. In addition, despite the obvious effort expended on the vehicle's upkeep, it would appear to have been flawed. When that door opened for the woman, no light went on inside.

There is something more. As we reach the road, I scent it, nearly hidden in the rich atmosphere of the wet earth, the mix of refuse and waste that serves as the alley's loam. If I were a younger cat, perhaps I would have caught it earlier, even from where we stood. Perhaps I was distracted by the interaction between the two – by the girl's concern and interest with the caged men. Perhaps it wasn't here.

In the hours since the rain has stopped, the city has sprung to life. The rats and insects, I have noted. The woman and her trade as well – men since the two last night. Others who did not usher her into a vehicle or take her away. The ground around us spews forth scents in a maddening mélange – mud and paper, rot and debris. But among them, half buried beneath a high-heeled footprint, I have found the remains of a matchstick, the chewed remnant of sulfur sharp to my wet nose.

'Gravitch,' says the girl, and I look up, startled. For a moment, I wonder if she too has picked up the match's sharp smell. But, no, she does not share the acuity that has come to me with this form. She is merely thinking of the woman and where she may be found. Of how she knew the dead man and his cohort.

I am relieved to see, when she looks down at me, that she is troubled by her thoughts. She does not rush off without consideration, and I sit and stare back up at her, willing her to take her time.

'I wish I . . .' She pauses and shakes her head. Glances back at the yard. It is empty now, the men have filed back inside. She knows their schedule, that they will not reappear, but something in her continues to hope.

'Those pages  those were lists of case numbers. I knew the sequence was familiar. Nine digits. I had one myself. And Tick is tied up with him somehow.' She is talking to herself as much as to me, and as she strolls back to the railing, I remain silent, bidding her to process as she has been taught. Besides, better here than by the road, exposed. 'The case was a fake,' she says. 'But why?'

Again and with a renewed pain, I regret my muteness. I cannot tell her about the third man – the shadow who haunts my dreams. The maze of deception and machine. I would not have much to share, not knowing myself who this creature is or why he haunts me so, but I would warn her, if I could. Tell her that there is such a one, a creature who wields a power over this city, and that Care has hurt him, by her dealings. By her efforts to free herself from the lower trades of this city. And that I have put her in his way by helping her. It is this that binds me to the girl, a knowledge and a past that I cannot communicate and do not fully comprehend.

Thoughts of this man are why I start at the sound of footsteps. Cheaply made shoes, they slip on the stone of the courtyard, moving quickly and with stealth. But I am prepared. I arch my back and hiss, ready for the grab – the fight – and this is what rouses the girl, who starts, stepping away from the fence. In truth, the man who approaches, crouching as if he would evade some watchful eye, is not the fearsome apparition I had expected. This man is scrawny, his body bent and his face bruised. He reaches through the bars and gestures, and the girl steps hesitantly forward.

'You, girl!' His voice is more breath than sound, but still he looks around, haunted. The bruise on his face is fresh, and there's a strange pitch to his voice – a high whine of panic – that calls rodents to mind. 'This is for you.'

He reaches inside his filthy shirt and pulls out a bundle. Folded cloth, it appears, though of a sickly yellow green rather than the grey denim that the prisoners wear.

'I don't . . .' Care keeps her distance, watching the little man as he holds the cloth toward her. As he shakes it, urging her to reach forward. Still she holds back. I do not believe she can hear the fear, that strange high whine, but she can see the bruise, and she understands what pain and fear may make men do.

'From Big Al,' he says, as if that name should mean something. 'Him you gave the apple to. Wanted you to have this, didn't he?'

'Why?' The girl steps forward. 'Did he find out anything about Tick? About my friend?'

A puzzled look, the bruised lips drawing down into a frown. 'I don't know nothing about that. Only Big Al was my friend and now he's gone, more's the pity.'

'Gone?' Care's voice catches, but the little man shakes his head. 'You mean . . .'

'Nah,' he cuts her off. 'Big guy like him? He's worth something. They jobbed him out, the bulls did. On a work detail. That's when—'

'I know what it is,' Care cuts him off, her voice sharp. 'There's a tone I do not recognize – harsh with pain, I believe, or with regret. I see her jaw tense up as she bites down on the words. The man addressing her does not. 'He's lucky,' he says, his voice growing soft with longing. 'They put him out on the river. Real work. It's rough out there, they say, and ten years will be hard. But who knows? I hear they're getting sloppy. Losing their edge. Maybe he'll get away. Maybe he'll end up on some island somewhere, far away from here. That's what I want to do.'

The girl leans in, the sadness in the man's voice draws her. I would alert her to the panic, to the pain, if I could. Instead, I must watch and listen as she draws him out.

'Do you think you'll follow him?' Her voice is soft again, and he relaxes into its comfort. Into his dreams.

'Me? Nah.' He huffs in what I assume to be humor, and I can smell his breath. He is half-starved, and his teeth are rotting. 'Little guy like me? I'll be lucky if I get the factory. That's tough, too, they say, but it beats being here.' He holds the bundle out again. 'Besides, you get to make some pretty things,' he says. 'Take it, Miss. Big Al said I should give it for you. Told me, "Eddie, give this to the girl." In memory of your old man, he said.'

'What?' Care leans in. 'The old man?' My ears prick up at the words, but not the tone. This man is weak and dying.

'Your father!' The skinny brute leans against the bars, his arm extended, the bruise over his temple growing more florid with the effort. Care looks at the bunched fabric, but I take in his bony wrist, the blue-black marks that hands or shackles have left. 'Big Al says he knew your father.'

'Oh, that's right.' The girl sounds deflated, and I experience a strange rush of pride. The old man – the one who mentored her – did more to prepare her for this life than did her father, I suspect. I know the girl still mourns her parents. Vague memories pass through my mind – her face was rounder then. Her lips trembled as she wiped tears away. But it is the old man she seeks to emulate. Whose career, as well as whose office, she has taken over.

There is no time for reminiscence now. The scrawny man has spooked at something. He tosses the bundle, which falls open as it hits the pavement. I approach, gingerly, waiting for whatever may crawl out, but my ears register his footsteps as he runs, darting, back toward the building, toward the relative safety of his own kind.

'For my father?' Care has crouched beside me and eyes what appears to be a sweater, knit of some soft, cheap yarn. It has a familiar funk to it – a mix of dust and something else – but as I step closer, she lifts it out of reach. In the yard, a cry, quickly broken, and then the sound of feet. A guard, his leather boots making more of an impact on the courtyard stones, gives us ample warning, and Care tucks the item under one arm and dashes away, back toward the street – toward where the car picked up Gina. By the match.

There is no traffic now, although the day has blossomed bright and clear. The sun warms my black fur, but I can see how the girl's flesh dimples in the breeze. She is ill equipped for this city, even in this more moderate of seasons, and I lean in to share my warmth with her. As she contorts, I look up. She is pulling on the garment, its unnatural green playing up the strange pink of her hair. It is tight, and the arm begins to pull from the body even as she works her hand through the sleeve. Clearly, this garment did not belong to Big Al. Even in his emaciated state, it would not suffice to cover him. Not even his bruised friend could have fit into the sweater Care has donned. Her arms are covered, but as she pulls the fastening close in front a tearing sound announces a new rent in its back.

'Well, the idea was nice.' Care peels the cheap cloth from her back and looks it over. She has learned, this child, not to discard anything that may be of use, and I see the play of thoughts across her face. I could by this time almost narrate them. Perhaps the piece will serve for barter, she is thinking, or for some other purpose in the constant market that keeps this city on its feet. I do not indulge in such exchanges. My life is more basic – I hunt, I feed, I sleep – but like her, I gather knowledge in the pursuit of these activities. I do so now, taking in the fruitful air with all its prompts. That one scent bothered me, although I cannot place it, but already it has passed, superseded by fresh traces of prey and of freestanding water. The rain has provided both, and I approach a puddle with a sniff.

Oil has risen from the stones beneath, and filth of other sorts. But the source is new enough and clean, and so I lap, the brimstone tang a bitter reminder of my station here, my place. And something else – a memory. I pause, head up, to take it in. My senses now more acute than once they were, but it is gone. I am old, and I no longer command the faculties that once were at my disposal. This scent . . .

A gasp. I freeze, but the street remains empty. It is the sweater that has caused the girl to catch her breath, to blink. She stares down at it now, its thin collar in her hands. One arm hangs down, its cuff already fraying, and so I turn to sniff – the friable yarn has more in common with the oily street than even the wear-softened denim of the girl's jeans.

The sleeve is jerked away as the girl grabs it up, turns and digs in her own pocket. I sit back and watch as she searches in a frenzy. I did not expect a flea, though both those men were verminous enough. But, no, her pawing ceases as she pulls a small thing from a pocket. The scrap – the label, she called it – that she had found. That she had shown the woman. She holds it now up to the collar and nods, her mouth set in a firm line.

'This is why he gave it me,' she says, her eyes meeting mine. 'This is what he wanted me to see.'

She squats beside me, as if to show me the similarity. I see the label, of course, but the writing on it is just so much scrawl. Still, the girl has made the effort and so I approach. The warmth of the girl is on the garment, although it is dissipating quickly from the slick and tawdry yarn. Her fingers frame the tag and I move toward those, the wet leather of my nose brushing the back of her hand. And then it is my turn to freeze – my whiskers and all my fur going on the alert.

'You know, don't you?' The girl looks down at me, her young face serious and sad. 'I don't know how, but you do – you know this is the same label we found in the garbage. It's one of Gravitch's products, isn't it?'

I look up at her, mute as any animal and nearly mad with it. My mouth hangs open, and I know she can see my fangs, see the heaving of my furry body as I begin to pant. No, I did not know this cheap thing was of Gravitch's making, nor how it came to be within those prison walls.

What I do know is that this garment has another marker on it beyond the script she reads. There is blood on this cloth, fresher blood than that which stained the scrap we found in the bin. And some sweet remnant of it does recall the boy. She cannot know this, I am sure. She is clever, quick and purposeful at reading that which the world places before her. But although they are sharp, her senses are but of her kind, incapable of catching that sharp tang, the iron bite of blood still new and raw.

No, something other than the scent I have discerned now drives her. Makes her bite her lip and mumble, turning the torn garment in her hand. Some knowledge of the world, perhaps, some intelligence I have forgotten in my current state, must drive her.

'T.G. Fashions,' she says, and nods her head. Her face is grim, the bead of blood upon her lip no more regarded than the beetles underfoot. 'Tick,' she says, and that is all.

At moments such as this, I know despair. Not for myself, but for my purpose. For the girl. I would turn her from this path. The boy is gone, beyond her reach. Mayhap beyond this life by now. And although I now well know that what remains may continue on, I do not believe her duty is to follow, nor must she take it on herself to resolve or to avenge. The boy was trouble, always, perhaps condemned from birth. No, I would shield her. Lead her away from the source of this blood, of the unclean tang of the cloth. I would have her leave the boy and client both and seek a safer berth.

But I cannot. This city is all I know, and perhaps the girl as well. And so as she starts out, a resolve fueled by anger driving her steps, I am forced again to face my limits. I call and call once more, suffering the futility. When my best, most piteous mewl does nothing more than cause her to grab me up into her arms, I still myself at last. Content myself with silence. She thinks me tired, I perceive, and believes my protest born of fatigue or pain. It is kind of her to think so, if misguided, and so I let that concern comfort me. She stows me in her bag with gentle hands, despite her mood, and once again begins to stride, albeit at a slower and more thoughtful pace. Inside the swinging carryall, I wait and think and ready myself for whatever yet may come.

While Care walks, she talks to herself – I hear her invoking the father who is long gone, the mother she still misses – and worries, fretting over events of the past. I would comfort her, if I could, but tucked away as I am, I must assume that my warm bulk will do as well. Instead, I conserve my energy, trusting that instinct and habits of long use will serve whatever purpose we may meet. I have gathered what clues I may. The hunt will be joined when it is time.

Besides, the bag is dark and warm, the worn cloth a soft hammock beneath me. There is something to being enveloped so, the sides pressing against my fur as we sway and move. It stands to reason that I too was a kitten once, as young as Care – as Tick – although I have no memory of such. Perhaps my dam once carried me, helpless, from place to place. To safety or to shelter. It is a pleasant thought, although an odd one. It is not in my nature to dwell on the past. Only where threat exists – that man, that shadow – do I return in thought, much as I would seek out a trail when hunting, searching for a trace where once I had a lead.

So, I realize, is the girl doing now. I sit up and shift, my weight throwing me momentarily on my back. I have till now dismissed the purport of her murmurings, believing them the last weak cries of a youngster newly weaned. In truth, they unsettle me. The girl is nearly an adult, I have thought. Plus, I must confess, my inability to comfort her – to supply the loss – has mortified me in ways I find difficult to comprehend. Combined, these factors have led me to dismiss her soft vocalizations as so much self-comfort, a private matter and one in which I have no role. Only now I have begun to catch a repeated refrain. The girl is not simply salving sore wounds, she is seeking to remedy – or, if not remedy then understand – that which has taken her too young from her own.

# SEVENTEEN

As a cat, I am a predator, albeit a small one, I know certain things. To start with, I must hunt to live, and that this hunt is neither fair nor foul. It is necessity, the law of life. I know as well that others may hunt me. Larger predators. The feral dogs, for example, that prowl some precincts. Other cats, especially as I weaken with infirmity and age. And humans too, of the more desperate variety – those driven beyond their kind by starvation and despair.

I know as well that there are other dangers in this world. Violence born of anger and of madness, the quest for dominance even of a lesser kind or for satisfaction of cruel appetites. I take nothing for granted, in this life, and still I have survived only due to kindness. Due to the actions of this girl, who pulled me, drowning, from the flood.

For this reason, as well as others, I would teach her what I know. I would have her be alert to the signs of fear or aggression that I have noticed, and I would share what my superior senses have ascertained. It is not easy. Although I know that my bond with this girl transcends that of many between our species, transcends our very nature, I am limited by my current form. I cannot communicate all I would, nor share that which I have found. It is a pain akin to hunger, a longing that will never be satisfied.

I work with a limited palette – sounds and gestures that fail to convey the complexity of my thoughts. And although the girl has an adult's command of language, indeed she reads and speaks better than many full-grown of her kind, she does not speak to me, beyond the offhand thoughts and endearments one shares with a pet. It is frustrating, to be considered such. But it is secondary to my loyalty, and my fear for her, and that is why when she stops, I make my move. I leap from the sack the moment she lifts the flap, with such alacrity that she steps back.

'Blackie!' she calls. But I have already caught myself. I have not been paying attention as I ought. Have not monitored the scents and sounds along the way. And I am taken by surprise, as much as she was by my jump. We are not, as I had surmised, heading toward Gravitch's office. Instead, we have ventured into the center of this blighted city. To a place I thought she would never dare again.

'Watch out!'

I freeze, as alarmed by her voice as by the truck that rumbles past, and then retreat, to stand beside her legs. Our eyes meet as she glances down, and once again I am struck by the strangest thought. A suspicion, almost, of recognition. But then she is off, striding with a swagger I do not associate with the girl I know, as she heads down the concrete walk.

I stick close in this area of commerce and of traffic, recognizing belatedly her strategy – her gait makes her seem purposeful, one of the throngs who crowd this busy thoroughfare – and trot on the hard pavement to keep up. I am winded by the time she slows, having turned into a rundown and shadowed passage, its gutters still full of last night's rain. It is a place we have been before, an alley where once we hunted and shared our spoils. She pauses by the alley's mouth, regarding the traffic beyond. I progress to sniff one puddle and catch the stink of the city: oil and human waste, soot rinsed from the air.

'This is no place for a cat,' she says, as I look up from the befouled water to find myself in her regard.

I stare back, wishing once again that she could comprehend my choice. My duty. Instead, she smiles, seeing, if anything, only the injured dignity of a creature too small to be a threat. Another truck passes, but she hesitates. 'I wish you really could understand me,' she says.

I would go to her then. Would comfort her with the softness of my fur. Only as I step toward the mouth of the alley, I sense oncoming footfall. By instinct, I draw back, and I am pleased to see the girl does, too. The passersby are men, their clothes are worn but clean. We have left behind the immediate threat of the prison district and the harbor as well, but still they reek of the cage, their skin permeated with the smoke of cheap tobacco. Their pace a jittery tightrope between exhaustion and caffeine. They are too distracted to notice the girl they pass, steps away, and I join her as she leans into the street. As she watches and they turn.

It is a building that she surveils, I realize as I scan her face. A familiar place fronted by worn steps. We have been here before, together, and she before me, drawn through concern for the boy. He is not housed here; I get no scent of him on the damp spring air. I do, however, remember a calming voice and the taste of cream. Indeed, I begin to salivate as I see a large, familiar figure step from the door and descend down to the street.

'Miss Adele,' Care calls, her voice soft but urgent. The woman cranes her head and holds her bulky beige purse close. 'It's me,' the girl calls again, 'Care.'

'Carrie Wright!' The woman hurries over, her steps delicate despite her worn heels. 'How are you?' She pauses, but gets no answer. 'Would you like to – come to lunch?'

Her voice had caught, had changed course, and I look from her to Care, gauging the reaction. A quick nod. Care trusts this woman. 'Thanks, yeah,' she says. But even as she does so, she holds one hand out flat. A signal, too low for the woman to see. A sign that I should wait and not attempt to follow. I am warmed by it. The gesture means connection, that she believes me capable of rational thought or at least direction. I wait as they walk off. Then, of course, I follow.

They don't go far. Either through economy or an astute appraisal of what the girl will tolerate, the woman leads her to a cart. A fragrant steam rises from it, full of meat and so intoxicating that I miss the interaction, and almost as well their exit, as they carry their food to a protected corner.

'I wish I could have you visit him, dear,' says the woman. She holds her food but does not eat. 'I know you care for him.'

Care looks up, chewing. She has learned not to linger, and her stare is as eloquent as any comment.

'He's in a better place,' the woman says.

Care chokes and coughs, before swallowing. The woman, meanwhile, has heard her own words.

'I'm sorry,' she says. 'I didn't mean— He's in the country, that's all.'

I look to the girl, unsure of what will follow.

'He's on a work detail, isn't he?' Care's voice has an edge I do not understand. 'You've hired him out to work. Just like a convict.'

A sigh makes the woman deflate as she faces Care's stare. 'It's the system, the way it functions. He's run away too often for a family placement, even if . . . But it's a good place. Right for children. It's a farm. He'll work hard but he's getting fresh air and milk and butter.' She retreats into herself a little and rallies. 'It's better for him than life was here. You know that.'

Care opens her mouth. She is about to argue, I can tell. About to reveal something of the papers, of what she has deduced, but she catches herself. 'You sure?' she says, and I feel a flush of pride. She has learned, this girl, that information is a currency not to be squandered without surety of compensation. 'You sure he's not in town?' Her voice is low and questing.

The woman nods, and when she speaks, I perceive no hesitation. No sign of doubt or subterfuge. 'There are safeguards now. Check-ups. It's a good system, Carrie,' she says. 'Why, your own father—'

'What about my father?' The girl cuts the woman off, a sudden urgency to her query.

'He would have been clear of debt in only a few more years.' The woman's voice grows careful. Lowers as she picks and chooses words. 'It was a good job for him, Carrie. A clean job, in an office. Considering what he'd been through.'

'If you people had left him . . .' The girl shakes her head, foregoing both caution and training.

'He wasn't supposed to be out that night.' The careful voice – the soothing of an animal – becomes a gentle chiding. 'We've been over this. He didn't have a pass yet. He hadn't earned one. If he had stayed in the dorm, instead of running off to visit your mother.'

She stops. Sees at last that the girl is trembling. That she is blinking back the tears.

'I'm sorry, Carrie,' she says at last. 'And I understand why you don't want to – why you don't trust the system. But it is the best we can do, and Thomas is safe now.'

'Yeah.' Anger has replaced the sorrow. She looks down at her sandwich. Folds the foil over the portion that remains and tucks it in her bag. 'Thanks for lunch,' she says, and turns and walks away.

# EIGHTEEN

I dash back to the alley and assume a pose of sleep. She does not notice that my sides are heaving from the run, too distracted is she by her sorrow, but she seems grateful for my company, slumping down against the wall and putting one warm hand on my side. We are at peace for several minutes, until the intoxicating aroma of the meat in her bag proves irresistible. I nuzzle the flap, rousing the girl from her thoughts. 'I almost forgot.' She retrieves the package and peels back its covering, releasing the meaty steam. My eyes close and my purr deepens as she places several slices on the foil and sets them before me. A vague sense of shame – I am the hunter and I should have provided for this child, not vice versa – gives way to satisfaction. We make quick work of it, and after, as the girl sucks the last of the juices from her fingers, I regard her anew. She does not, cannot, comprehend what I know. She cannot benefit from even the most basic of my skills, and yet she shares her takings with me. It is odd to be treated thus, as if I were a creature of a pack or den. But it has its benefits. The drowsiness that follows a good meal soon sets upon us both, and the steady rise and fall of her breathing lulls the same from me.

*The darkness lifts, enough to make out the silhouettes above me. Three men, dark against the light, peer down at me. I cannot see their faces, but I know them. Know their eyes to be cold, their expressions cruel.*

*They have taken me here, a bloody bundle, and now they stare at me. I am still alive, which perplexes two of them. The man in the middle, though? He is merely amused.*

*'Did you really think you could defeat me, old man? Did you honestly believe you could stand in my way? Don't you know that others have tried before, and failed?'*

*In response, I struggle, my limbs constrained by bonds, and at his signal, his two henchman step toward me, arms outstretched—*

'Ow, Blackie!' The voice – a cry of pain – wakes me. But the pain is not my own. Indeed, I am unharmed, although the twinge in my left hindquarter reminds me of injuries past. No, it is the girl who draws back, her eyes wide with shock and sorrow. Her hand is in her mouth, and when she withdraws it, I see the red as blood wells up. I have lashed out at her, my benefactor and my friend. In the panic of the dream, I have hurt her, she who once saved me from those too well remembered foes.

I hang my head, ashamed, my tail lies flat. The ground has grown cold, but I wait as she nurses her hand, still and sorrowful in my regret. When I dare look up again, I am confused. The girl no longer has the unblinking stare of one taken unawares. Instead, there is great sadness in her face. She holds her injured hand out to me but turns the palm up. It is an invitation, albeit a silent one, and I take it, leaning in to rub my face against her soft, warm flesh.

'Poor Blackie.' Her voice is quiet, as gentle as that hand. 'You've had some bad times too. Haven't you? I wonder what you'd tell me, if you could?'

I feel once more my muteness. The limitations of this form, this time. I would share my knowledge and experience. The skills I have honed over one lifetime and the next. The dream is a memory, I know that now. A remembrance of those who hunted me then, and those who hunt her now, and I would share that knowledge. Warn this girl away from such cold-eyed men.

But I cannot. The day is growing dim. The damp is chilling. But we have eaten and have shelter of a sort, and in each other's company both comfort and warmth. She does not flinch as I press against her hand, and so once more I come close and lean on her. This time, I stay alert. My eyes wide open for any movement in the growing dusk. What I fear are not simply the phantoms of my dreams, and I would defend this girl, if I could do naught else.

She sleeps, at last, curled in this alley, back against a wall. Her injured hand lies warm against my fur, her breath soft on my back. I would give much to be able to warn her. Give all I have to save her from those who seek her harm, but I cannot. Instead, I sit and wait, my green eyes guard against the world – one small watcher in the night.

\*     \*     \*

Perhaps it is the food, the stress of running. Perhaps my own small warmth served to give her ease. She sleeps till dawn and wakes slowly, stretching out her youthful limbs.

'Blackie,' she says at last, having brushed back that shock of hair with a hand now scabbed over. 'I think I know what I've got to do. I'm going to report back to Gravitch. I don't know for sure what he was playing at – I don't know why he hired me, or if he was trying to set me up. But it's been three days – and he owes me. Besides, it's too much of a coincidence. That label and the sweater Big Al had for me. I need to check out his place again, maybe get inside. See if I can see more than a grimy couch. Maybe that little guy, Eddie, got a job there. Maybe someone there can clue me in.'

I look up at her, the warmth of the night draining from my bones. I cannot tell her of the scent on that sweater. Of the blood and corruption that I smelled there. But surely she remembers the stench of the bin where we found the label – the perfume of old blood and decay?

I stare, aware again that my face appears impassive to her. Aware that my cool eyes cannot convey the urgency I feel. I share with her the need to hunt. The need to track and understand. But she will put herself at risk, I fear, and I would have her shelter or retreat. I blink, willing her to question, at least, her process.

She is no fool, this girl. For while I fear the danger she may find herself in, she too appears to weigh the risks. I hear her murmuring to herself as she makes her rough toilette, availing herself of a dripping drain pipe to not only wash her face but to slick back and darken that distinctive mop of hair. She pulls the fraying sweater from her bag, regarding it for utility as a scarf. And when she rejects it, shoving it deep in her bag again, I realize that she does understand the value of concealment. She would disguise herself, I see, but that garment may reveal more than she intends.

I am heartened, as well, by the path she takes. She is not a cat, and the stealth and byways open to me are not options for a girl even as lithe as she. However, she does her best, avoiding both the open roads and those alleys that, closed off, may serve as traps to travelers unaware. She cannot take to the rooftops, as I would. But she can climb and does so, working her way through the rubble as we approach the harbor and such ruined buildings become more common. She does not emulate me consciously, I do not believe. But she has learned from those around her, me and others, and chooses her path well. Care she calls herself, and it is a name well chosen. She is mindful, this girl, and I begin to hope.

That hope fades as we near our destination. The sun has risen above the buildings by the time she slows, and at first I believe she has picked up the same traces I have. Dust and oil, and that odd chemical reek – like the hot breath of a mechanical monster – and under it all that strange rumble that shakes the street beneath us.

I glance up at her, uneasy, willing her to notice the vibration, so like a growl. The essence in the air. Something must reach her, for I note how she waits before approaching. And when she does, she skirts the grey stone before this squat structure to peer, once more, down the alley that runs along its far side.

The flagstone doesn't reach here, and what paving remains is pitted, holding traces of those who have passed. The walls as well are porous, their brick softened by the damp and the winter past, and from them I get traces of those who have passed. That woman, Gina: her perspiration and cheap perfume, although I do not believe she has plied her trade out here. The refuse left by passersby. The fresh kill of one of my own, and the less fresh stink of the corpse that we ourselves had found, only a few streets away. To these are added other, more familiar scents: the chemical bite of fuel and oil, which slick the roads and no rain can wash away. The sting, as well, of cheap food, badly cooked, a reminder of the desperate souls abiding here, even if they do not now appear. And that curious mixture of dust and oil. Of steam and something I do not know what to name.

That residue – as well as the low thrum of these walls – serves to warn me; the girl is in danger here. I do not believe that the discovery of that body was an accident, not when the authorities followed so closely on our heels. I know the girl teeters in her belief. Know as well that she would that it were otherwise. She needs the custom that this Gravitch promised and wants him to be true, despite his unsavory manner. I do not believe she will let emotion sway her, but of this I am not sure. She is young, for all her untimely experience, and she had placed great importance on this commission, particularly now that she has lost those bills.

At times like this, my limitations gall. If I were other than I am now, I would be able to advise her. To explain the importance of patience. The value of the careful wait. I lash my tail in frustration, wishing even that she were other than she is. That she would observe how I hunt, with stealth, yes, but with perseverance and restraint as well. Then again, were she other than she is, then I could provide for her, in my manner, as I may have provided for others in the past.

The alley appears empty, quiet now but for the sounds of the low creatures that call it home. The streetlight at its far end is blank, its sickly yellow light extinguished by the dawn. But as she creeps along the alley's length and peers around the corner, we see the reason for its presence – perhaps for the traffic that drew Gina, as well. An open area, its paving better and less marked than other streets nearby. And backing up – a truck, its rough engine growling like some unwieldy beast, as it slowly makes its way across the street. Toward the building. Toward, I realize as my fur bristles, the alley where we stand.

The girl pushes back against the wall, the morning sun still low enough so that the low brick building casts dark shadows.

'Hey there!' A man yells and jumps from the cab, its open door blocking, for a moment, the driver's line of sight. A grating noise, the movement of metal, and the air changes again. Dust and something musty, an overlay of sweat. Unlike the girl, I can explore unseen. I inch out toward the street, my belly low to the wet ground.

Behind me, I hear her intake of breath. 'No,' she calls in alarm. 'Blackie!' I pause and glance back, willing her to understand. She cannot do as I do, but I may discover what there is to be seen in this turmoil of scent and noise.

'Blackie!' Her voice is louder now, and only the rumble and thud around the truck keep the men from hearing her. 'You can't— No—'

I hesitate, fearful that in her concern, she may follow and

that the driver will step out from behind the cab door. But I am beyond the alley now, near enough to the curb so that I may press myself low. Unless one seeks me, I will appear no more than a shadow or – I force myself to admit – one of the lower vermin, fur slicked dark with oil. From here, I spy the source of all the tumult: where the truck has backed, a bay of sorts has opened. The metal barrier is rolling up, its mechanism creaks and groans. And as it does, the ever-present rumbling grows to a roar. A fiend is being unleashed. A monster. I flatten myself to the ground, heedless of the filth – waiting for the inevitable attack.

Which does not come. Although as I dare a look, I see that the driver is waiting too. He leans on the truck, apparently unconcerned with whatever lies within the building's gaping maw.

'You, boy!' The driver, standing, shouts. His voice is barely audible above the clangor. But even with the tumult that issues forth without a break, I hear a gasp nearby. It's Care. She has followed me, but mimicked as well my lead, staying low to the curb. She is too large, of course, to hide behind it. But with the arrival of the truck and the rolling of the gate, her presence is not noted. Indeed, even I had barely registered her movement, intent as I was on an incipient attack.

'Come here!' The man gestures, and I see what must have elicited the girl's response. Tick, the scrawny boy, jumps from the dock and runs toward the truck. In his haste, I see not eagerness, but fear. The manner in which he stops just out of reach, the way his head draws back, speak of blows and lessons learned.

'You got a delivery for me?' It is not a question, but Tick nods, his slender body shakes with the fervor of his assent.

'Yes, sir,' he yells, and then turns and pulls himself back onto the dock and disappears into the hellish noise.

'What's that about?' The girl crouches behind me, her breath warm on my back. She does not speak expecting an answer. I know her process by now. She talks to give her thoughts free rein, to visualize the possibilities. It is a useful exercise, as long as she keeps her voice low, and, whether she is aware or not, I appreciate the insights that it gives. 'That truck . . .'

Besides, it is a question I too ponder, as the boy disappears inside. Other boys, older but not yet men, have appeared. Together they push a palette from the dark interior out toward the truck. I raise my nose, questing for traces of drugs or other contraband. But all I get is that dusty, oily scent. Cheap fabric, packed for shipping.

'Care!' The girl whips around at the sound of her name. It is Tick, standing by the alley, his eyes wide with surprise. No, with fear. He is gesturing, his hands low to the ground.

'You can't be here.' He mouths the words, his voice scarcely above a whisper and nearly inaudible against the din. 'The shop— You can't.'

The girl begins to rise. 'It's okay,' she says. 'I've got business—'

He motions for her silence, the desperation on his face stilling her words. Back behind us, in the alley, the blind metal door has opened. Men, burdened, are emerging slowly. I look up at the girl and at the boy. If I growl, I will distract her. If I do nothing, she will be caught.

'Go!' He mouths the word, and then he turns. 'Can I help?' He speaks loudly, addressing the alley behind him, and by some instinct Care reacts. Not crouching down, as I do, but with a fast survey of the landscape, she races into the street. All eyes are on the building on the bay and she makes her way around the front of the truck and crouches by a tire. It's a smart move – between the shadows and the commotion, she's beyond their range of sight – and I settle in my gutter to keep watch. There is a marking on the truck, on its cab. Writing, of the sort I once could read. It is familiar . . .

'You, boy!' A male voice, breathless. 'Get over here.' Tick sprints to obey, his cheap shoes slipping on the wet pavement. Grunts and a muttered curse. Two men, I believe, as well as the boy, who now sounds like he is burdened with something past his weight. Care must hear this, too, and I hear her adjust her position. Surely, she has the sense not to come to his aid, but no, she is sidling back as the truck's driver saunters over.

'What?' she asks. I raise my head above the curbstone. The men have emerged from the alley. They carry a roll of that same, cheap cloth, only this bundle is different – it is poorly

packaged and sags in the middle, where Tick now shoulders
the thickest part. I smell the dust of the workplace, the sharp
chemical smell of the fiber and something else – something
sharp as iron. I recall the sleeve of the sweater Care was given.
How it carried the taint of blood.

'No, no way.' The driver has his hands up, as if he would
block the progress of the porters and their bundle. Between
them, Tick staggers and the man behind him curses under his
breath.

'I've got a delivery to make,' says the driver, shaking his
head. He points to the cab, where a picture – no, a *letter*, the
word comes back to me – is inscribed. Two peaks threatening,
like tall men leaning forward. I stare, looking for the third. The
one who looms over all. The one in command. Tick, meanwhile,
has recovered, has gotten his shoulder under the drooping
midsection of the bundle.

'I can't have that on my truck,' says the driver. His arms are
crossed. 'Not when I cross the border.'

'You won't.' The man in front motions to Tick, who slides
up to take the front of the bundle, while he steps toward the
driver. He keeps his voice low, but I have grown almost
accustomed to the roar beyond and my ears pick up everything
– from the words, to the strange inflection, part promise and
part threat. 'Just drop it by the piers. In the water, if you can.
Roll it out. It's worth an extra hundred, Hugo, and I know
how much you like your toys. Besides, the boss will hear
about it.'

His voice sinks lower. Serpentine. 'Hear it if you don't, too.'

The driver glances up at that last bit, his mouth goes slack.
'Oh,' he says, and blinks. 'Yeah, sure. Sure I will,' he says
again, as if he can erase his earlier reluctance. I do not need to
see how he shifts to understand the balance has changed. How
he now holds himself tight in readiness of violence.

'Here.' The man before him reaches into his pocket, and the
driver cannot help himself. He stumbles back, his hands rising
in a plea. But when a roll of bills emerges, those same hands
wave in dismissal.

'No, that's not – really.' He looks at the money as if it were
indeed a weapon.

'Come on, Hugo.' The man peels off two bills and holds them out. He's smiling now, relishing the power of his role. 'The boss would want you to have it. We reward our own, don't we?'

'Oh.' Hugo blinks again, reduced to a scared rodent despite his bulk. The man holds the bills out, pushing them into the driver's chest until he reaches up to take them. Until he shoves them in the pocket of his begrimed pants, uncounted.

'Boy.' Transaction made, the first man turns toward Tick. 'Make yourself useful. Help Hugo here get that rubbish loaded.'

'Yes, sir.' Tick steps forward, but the bundle is too heavy and he's been standing under it too long. He stumbles, falling to his knees on the wet pavement.

'Watch it.' The man behind him, silent until now, barks. 'You,' he raises his chin to the driver. 'Get up there. Help the kid.'

The driver does, clambering into the bed of his own truck and reaching down for the bundle. It's an awkward handoff, Tick too short and too weak to properly lift his end. Hugo, the driver, has to reach, grabbing the edge of the fabric. It pulls loose, releasing more of its strange metallic bite. But as I raise my face, eager to find out more, I hear a quick intake of breath. Care, in her hiding place, has seen the handoff. The accident. But it's not Tick's stumble or his struggles now with the oversize load that has shaken this sound from her. Not the boy, whose torn pants leg reveals a skinned and bloody shin, to whom she reacts. No, as the driver pulls on the end of the roll, with a final heave levering the bundle at last into the truck bed, she has seen what the cloth conceals. It is the face of the man she had given the apple to, cold and bloodless and bereft of life.

# NINETEEN

She may be startled, but she does not lose her wits. As the package is bestowed with more curses and grunts, Care makes her way around the far side of the truck. And so when the man in charge – the man who has dispensed the bills – pulls the door down and slaps its side, Hugo mounts the cab without further incident. Still glassy-eyed, still shaking, he may not have noticed one slight figure darting into the shadow, but one of his colleagues might have, and I am grateful that Care has the sense to make herself scarce.

I lay low, watching as Tick is herded back inside, the bay door closing with a clang, lowering the volume of the roar as it cages the beast within. Care must have witnessed this exchange as well, but when I find her behind a pile of rubble – her scent accentuated by distress – she is poised, crouching, as if waiting. Staring, still, at the building across the street into which Tick has disappeared.

'That poor man,' she says when I make myself known, rubbing the length of my body against her knees. 'I wonder if it was the sweater, the one he asked his friend to give me? I wonder if that's what . . .'

I have no response to this, nor would she understand if I did, and so I brush against her once more, butting my head against her leg. She places a hand on my back, and I feel her pulse slow and steady.

'We – I – have got to get Tick out of there,' she says, after a few moments of silence. 'It's not safe.' I lean against her, willing her to relax. It is difficult to relinquish control but it is the only sensible response. She needs to be thinking of shelter and of food. I trust she has given up the foolish notion of confronting Gravitch, of seeking the remainder of her fee; the man is a predator, with the scruples of a rat. She continues speaking, softly, to herself, and I pitch my ears for any mention of his name. Today was to be the day she reported back to him.

Surely, she must realize that the contract is void. Bodies are accumulating. If any reason could excuse him of culpability for this most recent corpse or that of the one we found, it must surely implicate him in the ill-timed raid that nearly caught us in its net.

'Tick.' She says the name again, only this time with an intake of breath that makes me look up. Yes, across the street, a movement in the alley. A small form, his face pale despite the dirt smudged across his cheeks. He is looking around, furtive and lost. 'Tick!' the girl calls, rising slightly. Her voice is quiet, but clearly audible on the deserted street.

He looks up and nods, and she sinks back down. We don't wait long. The boy runs fast and low, like a sprinter.

'You've made it.' The girl embraces him, despite his filth. 'You got away.'

'I'm going back,' says the boy, pulling himself free. He steps back slightly, although she still holds him, and stares into her face. 'I've got to, but I had to warn you, Care. Warn you off.' His eyes are wide and shadowed, his expression too serious for one so young. He stares into her eyes, and she stares back, dumbfounded.

'What are you talking about?' she manages to ask. 'What do you mean, you're going back?'

'I have to,' he rushes to explain. 'I only – there's a space. The door's bent from when one of the trucks backed into it. I'm small enough so I can squeeze through. That's how I get out sometimes. How I got out to warn you before. But, I can't – they'll notice I'm missing soon enough. And, Care, you've got to get out of here. Fast.'

'No.' The girl keeps her hands on his arms, ignoring his words. 'You're not— We've got to run. Together. That man – the one you put on the truck? Tick, I knew him.' She bites her lip, her struggle to find the right words evident on her face. 'He gave me something, and I think that's why he was . . . you know.'

'No, nuh-uh.' In a strange turnabout, the boy is reassuring her now. 'No, you didn't do anything. He wasn't – that was no punishment. It was the bobbins, Care. He was too big to work the machinery. You've got to be small, like me. Small and fast.'

'Bobbins?' She pauses. There is something about the monster within the building, about the cheap cloth that issued forth that interests her. 'That's – you can't be working here, Tick. This company – this business . . . It's not safe.'

'Care . . .' His voice rises into a whine. 'Please.'

'I'll go,' she says. 'But you're coming with me. We can get lost. You know we can. We've done it before.'

The boy wants to follow her plan. The longing is apparent in his eyes, by the way he must clamp down on his lower lip to keep it from quivering.

'He'd find me.' His voice has sunk as hers has risen. Even I must pitch my ears forward to make out his words. 'The boss . . . you don't know, Care.'

'We'll go to Miss Adele then.' He jerks back, but she holds his arms firm. 'Look, Tick, you're not supposed to be here. I went to her, when I was trying to find you. She's not – she doesn't know that you're working here. She thinks you're on a farm somewhere.'

'No.' He hangs his head, addressing the pavement. Only the movement of his head shows he still hears her. 'No,' he says again.

'Tick.' She shakes him. She is desperate to convince him. To make him face her again. 'I'm sorry. I know about Miss Adele. About the services. They're not going to put you with a family again. Not like before. And even if they do send you away, send you to a farm, it'll be better than this.'

'You don't get it. Do you, Care?' He looks up at her once more. The trembling has stopped, and he appears suddenly to be the older one of the two. 'The rozzers, the services – the boss owns 'em all. You report me, and I won't go to a farm. No way. I'll go – Care, the boss, he's got other places for boys like me. And I'll – I'd kill myself, Care. I like it here. It's a good job. We, you know, we make things.'

'Tick.' Her voice is sad, but not surprised. She raises one hand to his pale cheek. 'These people. This company. You don't know—'

'Care, you've got to go.' He doesn't hear her. Doesn't want to. 'You've got to run. He knows who you are. What you did.'

Now it is her turn to simply shake her head. 'Of course, he knows who I am. He hired me, though why he did—'

'No.' His whisper grows adamant. 'Not really. He couldn't really. Things are too – they're messed up now. I meant the big boss – he knows who you are. I heard. You're costing him, they say. Costing him coin.'

He stresses the last word. It doesn't help. Her face remains blank. Behind them, a grinding noise and that roar. The gate over the bay rumbles and begins to rise, stopping halfway as a man ducks under it and stands surveying the street. The girl freezes, and Tick peers over his shoulder. I can hear him gasp, but when the man places a cigarette in his mouth and pulls out a lighter, he turns once more toward the girl, his large eyes intent.

'Please, Care,' he says. He turns once more toward the smoking man. Toward the open bay. And then he is gone.

# TWENTY

Care sits down hard on the curb, oblivious to the damp as she watches the boy skitter, rat-like across the open space. The man tosses his cigarette to the pavement and turns back inside. The gate rasps its way down, as a shadow darts toward it. It is the boy. He ducks under the closing barrier and disappears inside.

'I don't understand.' The girl isn't talking to me, but I go to her. Her hand reaches for me without thought, and I am glad to give her the comfort of my fur, of my wet nose against her palm. 'How can he . . .' She pauses, her shifting expression revealing the turn of her thoughts. 'What did he mean, Gravitch didn't hire me? He did.'

As if mere paper could deny the evidence of her eyes, she opens her bag, seeking, I can tell, the contract that greasy man signed. The first page at hand is not that, though. From its scent, from that strange imprint at its top, I know it as the letter that came under the door. I do not reckon time as she does, but I recall her words. She has only days now. Two, I believe, remaining to gather up her few possessions. To vacate the office that she had come to consider home. I study her as she reads it and see the pain and recognition begin to sink in.

When she shoves it back into her bag, her body slumps. She no longer searches for the contract. She has given up on it, I can see. Given up on the promise of pay and of more custom to come. Instead, she stares at the closed bay, her eyes dead and cold. If I could communicate more directly, I would remind her that these men deal in betrayal, as well as death. I would remind her that she has already interfered in one criminal enterprise. Caused the arrest of several people and the confiscation of their illicit goods. Surely, she cannot be so naïve as to imagine that such acts do not have repercussions, that the underworld that controls this city is not alert to such moves. She cannot be so unaware. But I see no such cognizance in her, and

I am reminded once again not only of her age but of her inexperience. The affection she has – still has – for others. The lingering belief in a system of justice. For all the skills she has worked so hard to attain, Care is not a child of the streets. Not originally, and she is vulnerable. If she is to survive, she must learn to make these connections. To read these signs. To listen to what she is told.

The boy, for example, has done her a favor, advising her to flee. Now that he has confirmed my worst fears about this place – about this job, I would she heed him. More vital still, I would have her question his sources. His very appearance is suspect, to an unbiased viewer. How could the boy elude his erstwhile employers, not once but twice? Even if he believes he did so independently, outwitting their watchful eyes, can such an escape be trusted? Is it not as likely that he has been permitted to leave the premises, as a lure to the girl? In which case, of what worth is the warning he has brought?

I am troubled that she does not ask any of these questions. Instead, she seems consumed by another thought – that notice, no doubt, or the body of the man who tried to be kind. She shakes her head. Her lips move, and I make out words. The letter, she says. The truck. And then the name of the boy, as she folds herself down, her head in her arms, and begins to sob. It is now that I most regret my current form. For while I would take her in my arms and hold her, it is all I can do to lean against her heaving side, offering the poor consolation of my soft, dark fur.

I will give her this. She does not cry for long, this girl. She vents her sorrow, her frustrated love, and then she rises, wiping her face on her dirty sleeve.

'Thanks, Blackie,' she says, looking down at me. I stare back, my visage will appear impassive, I am aware, but I am warmed by her words. Warmed, as well, to see her readying for action. My tail and whiskers perk up; my ears, despite their ragged state, stand upright and alert.

'I guess we should be going.' She forces a smile, more to hearten her own resolve than for my benefit, I must believe, and then she looks around. I know these streets, and I would guide her. Away from the harbor would be best. Away, even, from the city, although it is all that I have ever known. When she spoke of her father, a memory awoke – not of my own lives, but of hers. She had told me, once, of her family. Of its ruin and its flight to this ugly, desperate place. Her mother shrank within herself, she said, when the small family lost its home. And once her father was imprisoned, her mother lost the spark of joy, the will to live, almost, despite the girl's best attempts to cheer her.

She blamed herself, of course, for failing them. Her mother, for her despair. And her father, because she told him, sobbing out the truth during the monthly allotted visit. She'd had no choice, of course. Her mother's absence had had to be explained, and better sickness and despondency than death. Besides, he would have seen for himself how his young daughter was dressed, her apparel ragged and outgrown despite the weight she had lost.

He was trying to right their little ship. She has told me of his struggles. That he was fighting the charges that had impoverished them. The system itself, he had claimed. But the law is slow for those without the wherewithal to grease its wheels, and Care's dismay was real. No wonder, then, that he had taken advantage, abused the relative privilege of a prison clerkship and snuck away. He should have been back by morning, unnoticed and unregarded. He would have been eligible for parole in a few more years.

'This can't be a coincidence.' The girl is staring at the brick building. At the shuttered bay, the rumbling within contained but constant. 'I think that's what my father was working on. The information he was trying to get out to the authorities, Blackie. I think, maybe, if he and my mom hadn't arranged that meeting. If they hadn't borrowed that car that night . . .'

I do not trust machines. They do not respond as we do, we living things, to each other and to the world. Perhaps that is why my fur starts to rise along my back. Or perhaps it is the resolve in the girl's tone, as she steps out from the shadow.

'It's time to finish what he started,' she says. 'I'll do what needs to be done.'

# TWENTY-ONE

' I need your eyes.'

Her voice is low, but insistent, and the little man before her winces. Quirty – the keeper – had been surprised to see her. Those eyes she references opened wide when he answered the knock upon his door. At her request, he recoils, and she stumbles over her apology.

'No, no, I'm sorry.' Hands up in submission, she begins to back away, up the steps to the alley. 'I mean, I need you to look at something. Please.'

'Of course.' He ushers her in, then, and pauses, skinny neck craning this way and that. He need not worry. The girl is careful. We have arrived at his office by a convoluted path through the narrow streets of his district – Kern and Leading and Type. Waited for the shadows to stretch even across Ink Square and further obscure our passage.

His caution speaks of more than custom, however. More, perhaps, than the shock of seeing the girl again, and as he peers up toward the street, I slip by his ankles and find sanctuary beneath his desk. I had not intended to follow her inside. The day has been long, and I would sate my own needs while she fusses over paper and ink. But there are factors in play that I do not fully understand. As well, Care did this man a service, and I would ensure that her trust is justified.

She is seated before me when he returns. It is warm here, and secure, and I do not realize I have drifted off until the rustle of paper rouses me. She has shifted, taken something from her bag, and lays it before him. A single sheet of paper. The notice?

'I got this almost a week ago now,' she says. Yes, I am right. But . . . a week? The parsing of time is strange to me. In my dream, I was more aware, although others senses lagged. I would return to it. Would understand – only as I muse, I miss her next words. Questions about the notice's significance, which surely she has ascertained.

'This . . .' His voice wakes me, its slight tremor of anxiety as alarming as a bark. I am alert once more. A rustle. He has taken the page up to examine. 'You know what a holding company is?'

A soft demurral. 'Not really.'

He sighs. 'This logo – Metric – it's not a real firm. It is – it was how business was done, back when . . .' He does not finish his sentence. Does not need to, apparently, for Care is nodding as if to move him along.

'So how do I find out who to contact?'

He interrupts with an uncharacteristic fervor. 'No,' he says. He is waving her down, as if she were rising. 'No, you don't. If it were a simple lease – a simple landlord – I could try . . . I could negotiate for you. Take the office in my name. That is among the services I offer. And, in truth, I would be happy to do that. In fact, I can begin making inquiries. Looking for a suitable situation for you.'

'That's not what I want.' There is an edge to her voice, though it is unclear whether in frustration or because she is worrying over a notion unspoken. 'The office is home to me. Home to my friend, too, if he ever gets out. No . . .' She pauses, as if considering. 'I need to find out who runs Metric. This M—'

There is another muffled sound, as paper changes hands, but it scarcely registers. I am bothered. Haunted by a word, a name. My recent inability to step into the open. To speak my mind. To read. Only, what would I say?

I too am a hunter, but the prey this time remains elusive. Besides, I am hungry, and my questions are both futile and discouraging. In the silence that follows, I set them aside. Examine my shelter for signs of life. No building is without its unseen tenants these days, and I sense the presence of game. From my covert position, I can see one particular crevice that interests me, over by the exterior wall. Only the constant move- ment of this little man's feet – an anxious jangling beneath the desk – distracts me. I approach gingerly, unwilling to have him notice my presence. The mud of the harbor is common enough. So is the sweat and stink of fear.

If I could read, perhaps – if I could remember. 'Metric might be anything,' he says, his voice distant and restrained. 'Might be one man.' It is difficult to sniff an agitated foot, and I draw back for fear of being kicked. 'For all any of us know, it might be a ghost.'

# TWENTY-TWO

When she heads back to the office, I am, at first, relieved. The girl is tired, stressed from the long day and from the shock of what she has uncovered. Sleep is restorative, and I expect her to hole up as she did the night before, creating a nest of the old sofa cushions and whatever clothes were left unsoiled.

She starts off in this vein, securing her ruined base. Righting the chair and using the heel of her palm to drive a shattered board back into the rear of the desk. Some creatures nest, and while I am not one of them, I can understand the impulse, after a fashion, and I begin to relax.

But once the office again more resembles its staid self, the girl does not recline on the sofa. Nor does she lean back in the chair, her feet up on the desk while she reads. Some of this may be the absence of books. All but one has gone, sold or exchanged for food. Instead, she sits, her back stiff, facing the door. From my perch on the windowsill, I can see the tension building. Although she is too well disciplined to fidget, her hands clench and unclench on the desktop. Her lip, too, is bitten to the quick, and her tongue, darting out, must taste the blood that wells up on it. It is not likely that she can smell her own sweat, the acidic tang that comes with anxiety, but I can, and it keeps me from my own rest. She is still, but she is not at peace.

I would sit with her, keeping watch, if my own wakefulness would serve a purpose. It will not, I realize, as I jump down and approach, rubbing against her shins. She starts when I do this, so consumed is she in her thoughts, and then looks at me with concern.

'Shoo,' she says, a word I do not associate with her. 'Go, Blackie.' She waves one hand toward the window. 'It's not safe.'

I retreat then, back to the sill, but not beyond. I do not wish to increase her burden, but neither will I desert her. And so, at last, when I do sleep, it is with a kind of half-wakefulness, mindful of the window, of the room and of the world around us.

At first, I hear little but the scratching of small claws. As the day winds down, the creatures of shadow become active. It would be a good time for hunting, were I not on another duty. Vehicles on the street below, including one rumbling truck that causes Care to tense, although she keeps her seat.

What I do not hear is the approach of other humans. There are passing voices below, as the few workers who remain employed in this dying city leave their offices for the day. The tired sigh of the vagrant who each night makes his own nest beneath our stairs. But that is all. This building must have been respectable once. I know the old man rented it for its utility, a meeting place amenable to a wide range of society, all of those to whom his particular skills might be of value. As the day fades further, and the passage of the daily traffic is replaced by other, more nocturnal sounds, the girl relaxes. A car slows and its driver murmurs to one in the shadows. The transaction completed, it drives off. A man whistles, the jaunty sound both a warning and fortification as he swaggers down the street.

Somewhere close, an iron grate is rolled down over a storefront, its rattle and clank reminiscent of the bay door. I would question the boy, who shelters with monsters inside that locked box. I would better understand the ease with which he appears to leave it, whether on his own or another's bidding. I think of cages and restraint. Of beasts and of three men watching and waiting, as another, held captive, knows that all hope is lost.

And it hits me – understanding, like a bolt of lightning – waking me instantaneously from my musing dream state. From my memories. She is waiting, sitting at her desk like that. She waits, this girl, for the man to reappear. The greasy one who hired her. I am not one for calendars or timepieces. Not anymore, but it has been three days since he appeared here, with his ready cash and the promise of more. She is tense because she has finally accepted, as I longed desired, that he may well be the reason for her near capture in the hovel. Because she has learned that he has her friend in his control, and that – if the boy is to be trusted – he has aims for her that are not those he has announced.

She is tense because she does not know in what form or in what company he will appear, here, as he promised to do three days ago. She is anxious, as well, I see as the sky blackens further and the room grows dim, that he will not come at all. I wait for the dark to overtake her. I listen for the even sigh of breathing that will signal sleep. She is young and healthy, despite her hardships, and it is the natural order of things that she should rest when she can, when the world is in night. She almost succumbs, I believe. And then, blocks away, a car backfires and she jumps awake, nearly leaving her chair as she tenses.

'Enough,' she says, rising. I wait by the door as she gathers up her bag, takes a deep breath, and steps out into the dark world.

She leaves the building almost as quietly as I, scoping out each corner as she descends. The vagrant below the stairs does not wake as she passes by, and I barely slip through the front door, so slightly does she open it for her own passage.

It is only as she begins to retrace her own earlier steps, however, that I begin to grow concerned. The girl is desperate for an income, I understand that. She seeks to become self-reliant. To establish herself in a trade or with some form of barter, as unlike me, she cannot procure both food and shelter directly. Nor, we are both aware, can she survive on the small jobs such as the keeper brought to her. In other circumstances, she might have the luxury of time. She may still occupy the old man's office but she will lose it before her reputation is as solid or as widespread as his once was.

Perhaps this is for the best. As I follow her through the dark streets, I ponder how her mentor met his end. How he – how *I* – became entrapped. Yes, that body was aging, and, yes, perhaps its perception had begun to flag, leaving me unaware of warnings of which a younger, brighter version of such a man might have taken note. However, the more I recall from that past life the more I come to believe that it was indeed his – *my* – earlier success that led to my demise. That my ability to foil some of this grim city's malefactors brought me to the attention of those who consider this town their own personal property, a mill that grinds its less fortunate inhabitants into grist on which to feed. To the attention of one creature in particular, a man I know only as a dark silhouette. A voice that could chill my blood.

My profile now is not what it was, a fact for which I am grateful as I dash across pitted pavement into the deeper shadow beyond. I am beneath the notice of most on the street, or worthy at most of pity. I see how a streetwalker looks at me, her eyes sad above that painted smile. She would reach out to me, I believe, but for a slowing auto that offers the promise of income and a brief respite from the cold.

I circumvent the exchange watchfully, wary of the vehicle, its engine still running. Wary, as well, of the woman's hungry gaze. Hunger and violence breed on each other, out here, when other consolations are denied. And besides, the girl has moved on. I race to catch up with her, aware all the while of the city waking around us. The spring night is chill, but the last freeze has gone, and the damp has freed the full sensory range of the night. A possum, still nursing, has gone to hunt. She is drawn to the ripe garbage down the alley, and with reason. I can hear, as can she, the rustle of rodents, made careless by surfeit.

I have no time to do likewise. Care has crossed the street again. Even before I can sense those strange vibrations, I suspect she is heading back to the growling building – the so-called shop – where her friend toils. And sure enough, as we approach I feel them. Sense as well the monster's fetor. Dust and something more: I work to isolate the elements. Steam and sweat, and the throat-catching bite of burnt plastic and oil.

I do not like it, and not simply for its mechanical sharpness. There is something of dread about the place. A crushing mindlessness that has already claimed one victim, discarded as casually as a rag. Something cold as stone, despite that continuous growl, and as unresponsive. Something, I realize with a chill that sends a shiver through my fur, that I associate with those men – that shadow. My memory – as I now know it to be, fragmented and incomplete as it is – does not present itself with the full panoply of sensory information. It is a vision and a scrap of sound. It dates from before my hearing was as sharp as it now is. From before scent fleshed out my appreciation of the world, and I regret it. If I could smell that man, that evil, I would feel more sure of myself – and of the girl. I am handicapped in this way, more than by my current form. More even than by my present inability to speak.

Which is not to say I do not sorely regret my inability to make myself understood as the girl approaches the building once more. If I could call to her, if I could warn her of what I fear . . . but she has circled the building by means of the next street over and come back, avoiding that strange stone paving entirely to approach the now deserted bay. From where she stands, she must have a clear vision of the door through which that body was removed, but she has stopped. She stands still, and for that I am grateful.

In fact, as she steps back, out of the sick yellow glow of the streetlight, I find myself quite pleased. This girl is not rash, despite her youth, and she has retained at least some of the lessons I once was able to impart.

Indeed, I feel a kinship now, as she leans against the soot-begrimed brick of the neighboring building and settles in, as if for a long wait. So have I calmly kept watch on an outlet, a hole, waiting for prey to emerge. In her case, the hunt is fraught. The one she seeks may turn on her, making her the prey. He may also, I realize, recalling light on chrome and the rush of tires, leave this place in a vehicle.

I cannot give her more than companionship, but I do listen for the approach of an engine or of other men. The deep rumble that emanates from this building hasn't faltered, hasn't dimmed, and its low drone could mask other sounds, particularly for one whose senses are less acute. I will myself to remain alert, despite the apparent calm. If need be, I will warn her, by any means at my disposal.

I am not asleep when the sign comes. I have been mulling over the affairs of the last several days. Trying to place them against what I remember, to separate my vague dreams from remembered events. Still, as is the manner of my kind, I begin to drift – those silhouettes becoming as real to me again as the trash bin behind which we shelter. And when I hear the laughter, the squeal, I start. For a moment, past and present have blurred. Laughter – men – and my fur bristles.

'Shh.' Care, crouching beside me, puts her hand out as if to signal me to quiet. Her palm brushes the end of my upraised fur, and through it I pick up her warmth and also something more dire. I recall her tears, and it is their salt that I scent on her hand. They have dried now, however, and along with their trace, I sense a resolution – a determination signaled as much by her current calm as by the dried sweat that marks a decision wrestled with and made. When I glance up at her face, hidden by darkness to eyes less acute than mine, I see the set of her mouth. She is watching, waiting, still. Readying like the hunter I would have her be.

The men step into the alley, and the door clamps shut behind them, but they do not proceed toward us, toward the streetlight or the avenue beyond. Instead, they set out toward the unused front of the building. Care curses quietly beneath her breath, and I am confirmed in my suspicion. She does not seek to enter the building, upon their departure, nor wait for the emergence of her friend. She is intent on the men – on Gravitch, whose coarse chuckle joins those of his colleagues as they saunter toward the street. If a vehicle awaits them there, she has lost them, and it is a testament to my own concern for her that, for a moment, I wish this to happen.

It does not, and as they turn down the dark road beyond, she makes her own way through the alley, passing quickly by the closed door. They would be easy to follow, even without our combined skills. They walk three abreast, their voices loud. Leather-shod feet hard against the smooth stone at the building's front. The other sounds of the night quiet as they pass, as if aware of their capacity for violence. Three men – two taller and Gravitch, the short and stumpy one between them – the alpha predators in this jungle, or almost. I find myself relaxing as I pace the girl. She has the wit to hang back, to not dare the open stone until they have moved on. And even then, she is wary, making use of such cover as the broken buildings and torn pavement provide. As her quarry walks freely down the empty street, she moves from rubble heap to burnt-out car almost as silently as I. But that alone is not the reason for my ease. It is the men, the three. They are dangerous, of that I have no doubt. But as they have walked – moved from the hard stone to the dirty street – I have been able to appraise them. Judge their gait, their sounds and smell. They are not the three from my nightmare. The monsters of memory, of whom the central character – the leader – still looms large.

When they approach the ramshackle building where Care met with the woman, my concern heightens. Now is the time to double back. As they push that warped wooden door wide, they are greeted by loud voices and by light. Surely, they will remain for some time, enjoying the spirits and the companionship they will find – or purchase – in this low shebeen.

But even once the door has swung shut behind them, dulling if not obscuring the raucous tumult within, the girl does not depart. Instead, I realize, she is readying herself to approach, steadying herself with a series of deep breaths and smoothing her wrinkled top in what I recognize as a version of my own grooming.

And then she walks up to the door.

I do not panic. It is not in my nature, although I can react almost instantaneously when need be, with claw and tooth – or with swift flight when such a retreat is best. I am, however, alarmed. Not merely at the girl's approach, but at my own inability to guard her. To warn her. Or, to be honest, to have foreseen this particular development. With growing apprehension, I lower myself nearly to the ground and creep closer. The door hangs badly, light and raucous laughter alike leaking out into the night. The door opens outward, and so I pass it by, seeking once again the rotted place in the boards where I may make my entrance unannounced.

The room is as I remembered. A rough board serves as a bar, although tonight more patrons cluster around its few low seats. The barkeep is busy, filling their glasses with a brown whiskey that smells more like the effluvia of the streets than of anything potable, and keeps his head down. The boisterous laughter has not yet reached out to include Gina, who slouches in the corner, her back curled against the draft. She is not drinking, I notice, although I suspect her abstinence springs from poverty rather than desire. Her empty flask lies on the bar beside her, its top unscrewed and open.

'Care.' She sits up as the girl pushes through the door. She has remembered her name and appears pleased to see her, despite the grilling she received when last they met. 'Come here.' She pats the stool next to hers, a barrel put to use as seating when its contents emptied, and it occurs to me that she is not fond of the girl so much as she remembers her generosity. The proffer of a drink without the usual payback is recalled as a strange beneficence by this sad, used woman. The disappointment that drags her face down when Care shakes her head and turns away shows the intensity of her thirst, her need.

'Whoa, who have we here?' A gruff voice, tempered with humor. From my vantage point, near the wall, I cannot see the speaker. I do not need to. It is Gravitch, warmed by drink and in the company of his fellows. Any trace of nervousness has been dispelled by the surroundings or the strong drink he has already managed to down. I see his hand, pounding his empty on the board for the barkeep's attention.

'It's Care. Carric Wright,' the girl says, as the murky brown liquid fills the glass. 'I've come to see you, Mr Gravitch. If you have a moment.'

The room does not quiet. It is too loud, its inhabitants too eager for the release of drink, for that. But a kind of hush falls as the men at the bar turn at this unusually formal address.

'If I have . . .' He leans back, tipping his seat as he regards her. 'Learned some manners, have you?' The glass is raised out of my sight, only to return a moment later, empty once more. 'Learned to respect your betters, I see.' The rasp in the voice has softened slightly, but not enough to indicate befuddlement or weakness. I do not know what the girl is playing at, and I make my way closer. I am confused, and I am concerned.

'Yes, sir.' She speaks, but her voice is so soft, he doesn't hear. He doesn't need to, as he recognizes the subservient tone. I have circumnavigated the room, coming up from behind the bar to a position near the drinkers. I can see her face. The effect of the deep breathing has worn off, and her pulse is visible in her neck. Despite the chill, the draft that whistles through its unsound walls, the place is close. Ripe with the odors of unwashed men and their foul refreshment, but through even this I sense her warmth. She is scared and sweating, despite the cold. Still, she holds herself firm.

He sees it too, and turns toward one of his colleagues, making a lewd comment audible throughout the room. She resists the urge to wince, a slight tightening around her mouth the only giveaway that she is afraid. That she would rather run, and I watch her in both fear and awe. Like the drinkers, I wait, knowing that she has not lain down her final card.

'I'm here about my services,' she says. Her words sound rehearsed, and she quickly amends them. 'My services at detection,' she says. 'I know how to find things, to find people. To locate that which has been lost.'

A pause as the words sink in. 'You know I found Dingo for you. I did as you asked.'

'Wasn't too pretty when you did, was he?' He looks across at Gina, who turns away. 'Our Dingo was quite the dog when it came to women. Maybe that's what got him offed. You think?'

Murmurs of assent, but Care only nods, her suspicion confirmed.

'You were well paid, too, girl.' Gravitch leans back, his chair scraping on the floor. 'Or is that it? You want the rest of your money now?'

'No.' Her voice is growing stronger. She is reaching the crux of the matter. I creep forward, toward Gravitch's chair. The man is rank, with more than filth. There is blood on him. Blood that has dried and rotted in the crevices of his skin, despite the harsh cleansing agents he subjected himself to. Despite the perfume. I cannot help the low growl that forms deep in my chest. The lashing of my tail. This man has been involved with pain and violence. With the death of the poor slob who was removed to the truck, and with others, older, as well. I recall the corpse we found, bloated and foul. I look up at Care, her face so calm and pale, willing her to truly see. To discern the brutality beyond Gravitch's rough humor. To perceive the warning I would give. The truth.

I crouch, readying for a leap. If she does not leave, I will launch myself at this man. I will claw and bite. I will not win this battle. He and his colleagues will dispose of my body with less thought than they did Big Al's. But if I can buy her time to escape, I will consider my choice wise. My hindquarters twitch. I prepare myself for the spring, blocking thoughts of the blows and pain to come. I am ready—

'That's not why I came.' Care is speaking again, inciting me to wait. As much as I want to protect her, I understand the importance of letting her speak her piece. Also, I am curious.

'I'm not here for the remainder of my fee,' she is saying. 'In fact,' she pauses, but does not lick her lips, as is her wont. She is waiting, too, I realize. Gathering her audience's attention. 'I am willing to forego any monies owed. I am here to make an offer, one that I believe will be worth your while.'

A low hum goes up at that, and another crude joke falls flat. Gravitch isn't listening to his cohort now. He's staring at the girl, doing his best to read her. When he fails, he sits back up, relieving me, for a moment, of the worst of his stench. I do not need to see his face to know that he is both puzzled and intrigued.

'You got something to offer me?' He tilts his head. He does not cogitate easily, this man. I wait for him to pull out a match, moving slowly closer. 'Something worth more than your scrawny little—'

'I do,' she says, her answer short and sharp. 'I'm here to make my offer. I want you to release one of your workers.' She stumbles a bit on that last word, but I do not believe Gravitch notices. 'I want you to give me Tick,' she says.

I stop short, taken aback by the realization: the girl knows. She is aware that Gravitch is not on the level, that he is, in fact, complicit in the dealings that keep her friend virtually enslaved and, more dangerous still, in the death and successive frame-up attempt at the hovel. But does she sense the shadow behind him? The mastermind who runs Gravitch? The tall, dark man? Surely, she must see that this round, greasy figure is too nervous for one in a dominant role. That with his tics and insecurities, he is incapable of leading. Incapable of anything but brute enforcement. Surely, she can tell that he lacks the intelligence, the pure drive, to have created such an intricate web of corruption.

But she is still speaking. Addressing him in a tone of deference. 'In return, I am offering you my services in detection,' she says, her voice both low and clear. 'I'm offering you my allegiance.'

The loud guffaw sounds like a thunderclap, assaulting my ears and making me jump back. It serves to cover my move-ment, at least, and from here – behind Gravitch – I can see

Care. She is still standing, holding her face impassive as the men hoot and call. Only I, who know her, notice the slight tremble of her lip. Only I, who love her, feel how her heart must sink.

'Your allegiance, you say?' Gravitch looks around at his colleagues, making sure that they have witnessed his triumph. He adjusts on his seat, releasing his odor again, rank but stale. He is not excited by the girl per se. Rather, he is relieved; his fear has dissipated, dispelled by her concession. By her surrender. 'So I can use you?' He is preening.

'My skills.' She seeks to set boundaries, only it is too late. I sink to the floor in despair. That she loves the boy, I understand. That she will barter away her autonomy, her independence, I do not. 'If you let Tick go.'

'Hey,' he says, the match dangling from his lips, 'I got no control over that. The kid's in the system.'

She blinks, saying nothing, but in the split second before her face becomes an impassive mask once more, I see a reaction. He has acknowledged the boy. He knows of whom she speaks. I feel hope flutter in my breast. Perhaps she does understand what this man is, what a small part of the organization he is. Her silence, now, is a force. The onus is on him to respond or not. Only a few seconds pass, but they are enough.

'I'll tell you what,' he says, at last. The men watch him sideways, waiting for him to reassert the dominance he crowed about only moments before. 'You come back to me tomorrow.' He removes the match, points it at her. 'I'll have a job for you.'

'And Tick?' She raises her chin. She is hanging onto her pride.

'Depends on how well you do the job,' he responds. 'Don't it?'

With that, he turns back toward the bar. She has been dismissed. Still, for a moment she stands, the struggle clear on her face. She wants to insist. To obtain promises, a timeline. But she has nothing left to offer, and so she turns too, leaving behind the rude place for the night. Behind her, the door swings shut but does not hang true.

I slip through, pushing it open with little effort, and find her there, bent over with her hands on her knees. She did well, in there. As much as I did not approve of her actions, could never condone the deal she made, she did it with a show of strength that that greasy man could not ignore. Now she is trembling and breathing hard. I glide through the shadows to join her. To comfort her as she gasps in air.

Another shadow passes first, and I freeze, waiting to see what form it will take. Gina has snuck out quietly, or as quietly as her type can, her footsteps masked by the loud laughter at the bar.

'Hey,' she calls softly. Care looks up and then straightens. The woman stands waiting. 'That was something, what you did in there. For your friend.'

Care starts with the recognition. The unexpected empathy. Then she shrugs, as if to downplay her sacrifice. 'It's business,' she says. 'It's a straight-ahead deal.'

'Yeah, sure,' says the woman. She glances back at the building. The light from inside shines on her face, highlighting the lines drawn through its sad bloat. 'Only, you know what it means, right? That he'll own you.'

Care's head jerks back. She catches herself, but I see it. The woman does, too. She pretends she hasn't. Looks away, blinking. 'That's not—' She stops. 'You should get yourself something. Something like this.' She opens her bag and tilts it forward. I too see the small dagger inside. 'They can get rough,' she says.

'I gather.' Care's voice is flat.

'They're not all bad.' The woman is speaking quickly. 'Dingo gave me this. After – well, to keep things from getting out of hand again.'

Care nods, but the woman isn't done. 'If you could get my Billy, I could help, you know. If you would get him too.'

'What do you mean?' Care eyes the woman. 'How could you help?'

'You know it's not him in charge.' The woman's words confuse Care, but I regard her with a new respect. She has knowledge that she has not revealed before. 'Gravitch, I mean,' she clarifies, as she nods back at the door. 'He works for the machine.'

'I know the system's rotten.' The girl's voice is bitter. 'That a lot of people are involved in it. Tick said—' She stops, shakes her head. 'I wanted to call the authorities,' she says now. 'Wanted to turn them in. Turn them all in.'

'Uh-uh.' It's the woman's turn to shake her head, even as she reaches for Care. 'You can't. Really.'

Care steps back and Gina drops her hands, but she continues to lean in, her voice growing soft. 'Someone tried that. Someone dropped a dime. A con in records, some paper pusher.' Her voice drops lower still, and Care waits, her face eager. 'They took him out. Him and his whole family.'

'His whole family?' Care's voice has a quaver, an echo I have not heard before.

'That's what I heard,' says the woman. 'Made it look like an accident. Like with a car or truck. He'd been warned, I heard. They told him: "Your wife, your kid. Everyone," they told him. But . . .' She shrugs and stops. Even she must see how Care is staring. How her green eyes have gone wide and glassy.

'It's okay,' says Gina. She thinks she's scared the girl. Scared her enough, at any rate. She's wringing her hands, but it is her own tragedy that consumes her. 'Just, you know, keep your deal. Do for Gravitch, right? Whatever he wants. Only, if it does work – if he does get your friend for you, you'll think of my Billy, won't you? He's just a little tyke, and I haven't seen him in so long. And I'm sorry. You know, that I didn't tell you about him – about them.'

'Yeah, I know.' The girl reaches out and clasps those wringing hands. For a moment, the two are bonded. Allies in a strange way. Then the woman turns back toward the bar. She pauses a moment at the door. Straightens up and pushes it open. But I am not watching her. I am focused on the girl, who has staggered away from the pool of light. Her steps break into a run, and I dash ahead, only to stop. She has made it only as far as the next alley, where she has collapsed against the wall. The sound of her sobs fills the air.

# TWENTY-THREE

S he stumbles so and moves with such lurching progress that I fear for her as we make our way from the waterfront. The door to the tavern, as flimsy as it is, did not stir as she wiped her face and set out. Still, I listen for the creak of its rotted wood, for the sound of footsteps shod in leather, as we wind our way back toward the heart of the city. Those men inside did not mean her well, despite their apparent acceptance of her offer. Nor can I be sure of the woman's role in all of this. That she misses her boy and hopes for Care's assistance, I do not doubt. Even were my ears not more sensitive than a human's, I would hear the tight, high whine of longing that creeps in when she speaks of him. And yet there is something about her that speaks of deception: the quick, nervous glances back toward the bar, not entirely explained by her fear of the men – or the custom she might lose. A tension that remains, although she would camouflage it, even after the maternal ache has passed. If I could communicate, I would warn the girl, though I know not yet of what. Something in that woman's words has undone the girl, and I am torn between uncovering the truth and watching over Care.

My concern may, in fact, be moot. In this state, she might not heed me. And that, I realize as I dart toward a less exposed corner, as I take in the dark, empty windows above us as well as the rumble of the sewer below, underlies my unease. The night has quieted, as much as it ever does, and I do not perceive any threats beyond the usual. Two men, more feral than any curs, pass nearby. I smell their bitterness, unwashed and angry. But they do not come near, intent as they are on the offerings in the tavern, both of the liquid and, I suspect, companionate variety. A scent about them – funky and sharp – tickles at my memory. Too late, I lose it in the panicked hush that follows. The world – my world – goes silent, as above, obscured in the overcast that dims as well the stars, an owl flies. I hear the almost liquid rush of air beneath his wings. The breathless pause – and then the scurry as those who smaller than I, and more frightened, make for shelter. I put this from my mind. I am not foolish enough to believe myself too fearsome to be prey. But this night, in this company, I favor other concerns. The girl has suffered an upset of sorts, and I would see her home.

That, at least, is where I believe her headed, much as I would expect any injured animal to go to ground. I expect her to barricade herself in the old man's office. To lick her wounds and rest, regrouping for another day's attacks. When she does not head across the avenue, into the relative silence of the rundown business district, I am curious. I become concerned as she proceeds instead toward the west – toward the yard where first she met the woman, I think. But, no, with increasing unease I ascertain that her path leads to a more fraught destination. She is heading toward that place she terms the Dunstan. The brick monolith where we were almost trapped, where a body was left to bleed out in a bin like so much trash.

I do not like this. But short of rushing her, with claw and fang, I have little means of turning her, and even that would do more harm than good, unsettling still further the fragile peace she has seemed to find. Instead, I approach quietly and let her spy me in her path, before I fall back to let my fur brush against her leg. If I cannot turn her, nor question why she has detoured this way I can, at least, comfort her. As little as that is, I will do.

I am in luck, or so it seems. She has smiled down at me, her green eyes meeting mine, and gained strength from my presence. I note the tremble in her lips, but also how I calm her. To the point where I wonder if I've done more harm than good, easing her qualms about her present path. But whether my appearance has heartened her resolve, or merely cheered her, does not matter. She enters the alley where we were trapped and I see at once that the bin has gone. She does as well, a moment later, although in the dark she searches for it, arms out as she explores first one corner and then another.

'Damn,' she mutters, the word soft beneath her breath confirms what I have feared. She once again seeks to enter this building To find some answer within to the turmoil that the woman's words provoked. For my part, I am relieved. The girl is tired, and she is overwrought. Her mental capacity will have been weakened by fatigue, a malaise both physical and of the soul, and I would not have her go in there. I am glad, as well, that the foul bin has been removed. Although it only retained the miasma of death, it had been used for evil. I would not revisit it, if that could be helped. Yet, its absence does seem curious. I would that the girl ponder this also.

The girl is pressed against the alley wall. She eyes the ledge above her. Runs her hands along the pitted brick, seeking some kind of hold. She will be hard pressed to find it. This edifice is better cared for than many, certainly than the ruins by Ink Square. Despite the stains and wear, the constant drip of water down its side, it was built to resist the casual incursion of such a one as Care, and according to the standards of men, it has been maintained.

My examination finds what has been overlooked. As I make my own perusal, my nose catches the musk of small burrowing creatures. The damp earthiness of the clay. And then the jab of something pungent. Fleeting but – yes – familiar. I reverse my steps, lowering my head to the earth to trace that caustic scent. *Sulfur* – the word comes to mind like the blue flare of a flame. A match.

The bin. A body. A building of importance.

My ears flatten with rage. My fury at my impotence at myself – could cause me to scratch and flail would that serve any purpose. No, I have been a fool. Or worse than that – an animal – reactive when prediction was required. I have been a follower in a most dog-like fashion, and I have led the girl I love to this. I need to find the source of that pungent odor. Need to—

'Blackie!' Care turns. She cannot see me in this light, but she can hear me scratching, furiously, at the earth. Catches the low growl that winds its frequency up to catch her ear. 'Is that you?'

I whine – at my own foolishness, but this she cannot know – but this only turns her blindly toward the alley mouth, and so I lash my tail and spit, knowing the motion will catch her dull eyes in this dark place. I wish her to leave me. To let me track and hunt and find.

'What is it?' I see her turn as she attempts to find me, as her own green eyes peer down toward where I stand. I want to howl at her. To yell out – *Cannot you smell the evidence before you? Cannot you place these occurrences in a sequence?* – but I cannot. Even to howl might be too much.

For I have not counted on her heart. The girl does not understand. She cannot smell what I have. Does not see how the removal of the bin may be tied to the corpse in the hovel, how her discovery may have been a trap conceived to lead her to this place. Or, no, to that man Gravitch, to whose foul purpose she has sworn. But she moves quickly, abandoning her quest to scoop me up in her thin arms. And while I am too startled at first to protest, I realize that her great heart may be the saving of us both. For although I have failed to alert her – to locate the evidence I know must be nearby – she acts. She believes that I am the one in danger or in pain, and she would give over her mission to convey me – to convey us both – out of harm's way.

What I could not compel through reason, I have done through sympathy. Despite my discomfort – especially at night, I would much prefer to move under my own volition than to be carried – I cease my growling as the girl deposits me in her bag and begins to run. Perhaps because we are leaving that place, with its aroma and its memories, or perhaps because of the way her bag swings, sling-like, as she moves, I find myself once again relaxing into a doze.

A stray thought surfaces even as I drift. I have been sleeping more, my faculties fatigued more easily with the passing of years. But this is not the sleep of exhaustion. Indeed, my senses remain alert as the city passes by. I hear the rustle of creatures great and small, the nocturnal cycles of life and death playing out even as we pass. I hear the whispers of men, not much louder than the scrabble of small claws, passing over the stone of the city. Murmurings of a score, of a prize beyond counting. I remember another time, another hunt, when I listened to such hushed words, hard on the trail of that bounty. A pretty thing, valuable in its way, had been taken, and I had been engaged to locate it. Or so I had believed at the time.

I hear such whispers now. The mumblings of men like rats that pick over the city's leavings and feed on the weak. The old and very young. The swaying lulls me as I listen. I hear the tidbits, dropped like crumbs. I pick up the scent and follow the trail. I see the prey, within my sights. I do not see the trap.

I wake with a start, kicking against my bonds. I will not be taken. I will not be shot and thrown, once more, into the river to disappear forever. I will not—

'Whoa, boy!' Green eyes staring down. Familiar, once again, as I wake. As I recall myself as I am now. A look of surprise but not malice. I am on the floor. We are in the office, and the girl has set the bag down, and me with it, the flap open to permit me egress. No matter, I have kicked a hole in it, my claws still as sharp as in my youth. It was this hole that had panicked me, as my hind leg had pushed through and become entangled in the cloth. I pull it back now, retracting my claws, all too aware of the censorious – no, the hurt – expression on the girl's human, open face.

I am ashamed. I bathe.

But as my fur falls back into place, so too do the impressions that made up my dream, that sparked my unnecessary panic. My dream of entrapment was based on memory. I know that now. Know, too, that in my former life I was led by my faith in my own methodology – my own brash conceit – into an ambush, and that I did not escape.

I am a predator, and at times I have been prey. This is a truth of life, and I harbor no illusions, no undue sentiment. This dream, then, came not simply as memory. Not from the discomfort of an enclosed space, or the stiffness of an old injury. No, in my waking life, I feel my years, and at times I fear that my perceptions may be becoming muted. My capacity for reason, however, remains sharp. And what I may miss in the full light of the active hours, I piece together in the feline dream state.

It may have been the memory of that horrid stench that set me off, the unclean gases of a body settling into its death. No doubt it was aggravated by the rashness of the girl attempting entry at that deadly place. Whichever served as the trigger, I know now they are connected. I am left with the certainty that the body in the hovel was intended to be found – the first clue in a trail intended to be followed. That it had been moved, I

was already sure, although I do not know if the girl had time
or illumination enough to discern this, nor what exactly that
movement means. She is smart, this child, and remembers her
lessons well. However, her senses are not as acute as mine, and
she has not my experience with the hunt – or beyond.

Nor does she have my ritual of bathing, which serves a
purpose beyond the proper placement of my fur. When my coat
is smooth, it better protects me from the elements – repelling
water and retaining warmth. As well, the act of grooming has
a meditative quality, the repetitive movement of tongue and paw
serving to organize my observations as well as my thick coat.

As I finish, I step away from the discarded bag, the encircling
canvas now a heap upon the floor. I am aware now of what has
been eating at my thoughts, and my challenge now will be to
convey it. First, I realize, I must get the girl's attention.

A quiver as I judge the distance, and then I leap, landing
neatly on the desk. The girl jerks back with a gasp. I have startled
her, and I realize that she has been engaged in her own delibera-
tive haze. For her, it involves these papers, which lay between
her outstretched arms and which I now sniff. These are the documents she carried from the hovel, that place of death. The smell
of the corpse is on them, as well as the faint dust of insects that
have passed and died as well, their carapaces dried and crumbled
by the simple expedience of time.

But there is more than decay here. More than death. Scent
holds memory, the essences given off at times of heightened
emotion or stress: the still sharp sweat of her hands from when
we fled and, before that, from her surprise upon her finding
these papers, hidden beneath the flooring. But these were
recent additions, and fleeting ones at that. No, these pages
were witness to more than the girl's excitement, to more than
death and dirt. I catch something biting. A scent that cries
out. Pain. Violence was committed near – no, on – these pages,
marking them with the struggle. Blood and sweat were left
here, although their traces are older and are fading now. The
exultation of mastery and of a kind of rage. Surrender, also,
though both these opposites stink of fear. And, yes, that male
effusion – the chemical smell of spunk. Those pages relate a
tale in more than words.

There is another, more recent story to be read here as well. The tale of this girl's time with these papers. Her reaction to them, with what that may suggest. She cannot know what I do, the pain these sheets have witnessed. No, she responds instead to what she has heard. My nose moves over the slight concavity, a warping. A tang of salt. The leather fits neatly over it and I know: the girl has sorrowed over these papers. This is the mark of a tear.

I am not sentimental, but neither am I made of stone. Closing my eyes to the room, to the foulness of these papers, I lean against her forearm, pressing my fur against her bare skin. She responds as I had hoped she would, raising her arm to stroke my back. Her gesture is clumsy; she ruffles the coat I have taken some trouble to smooth into place. But I allow her to continue, gratified in the cognizance that if I cannot always impart knowledge I may, at least, give comfort.

'These were my father's, Blackie,' she says, and I turn toward her, fitting my head to her hand.

'You have no way of knowing, I know.' The sound of her voice, its repetition, lulls me into a reverie. She is dreaming, too, in her way. Reading other than what is on the page – oblivious of what I have found there. Although my eyes are closing, I can glimpse her face. The faraway expression as well as the dreamy tone confirm my suspicion. Her words are more for her own ears than for mine. To me, they mean little. I have no recollection of the sire who formed me. Nor have I a sense of any offspring of my own. 'He kept these records. Smuggled them out. He was the one who figured out that . . .'

Her hand stops, and I tense. Not because of the cessation of the stroke, but at the import of her words. It is as I have feared. The woman's hints have worked as a lure, whether by accident or intent. They have intrigued the girl, who now seeks to draw a connection between her parents' demise and the man she has agreed to serve. Even as she remains ignorant of the violence I have read the traces of here, in blood and sweat and semen. It is this shadow that hangs over my sleep, my dreams. This threat. Behind this Gravitch – behind, even, this recent violence – the man I recall only as a silhouette, a dark shape against the light. He would reach out thus. Baiting his trap with misdirection, he would draw in and destroy all who oppose him. I shiver, the memory overcoming me once more of pain and cold, of the irresistible force dragging me down.

I do not know if the woman is part of the plan or if she has merely in her self-interest and misery helped lay the trap. I do not have proof that what I speculate is, in fact, correct. But I have passed beyond the realm of simple evidence and cogitative deduction and now must trust instinct. The girl believes she is uncovering the source of the pain that wounds her still. It may be so, but she is dangerously close to doing more. To revealing the steel teeth of the trap ready to snap closed. To triggering that trap.

I curl up on myself, pondering how to communicate any of this to the girl. How best to keep her safe. I watch as more tears drop, and she wipes her face. As she finally gives in, resting her head on her arms to weep unfettered, her thin shoulders heaving with the effort. And as she ultimately quiets, drifting at last toward sleep.

# TWENTY-FOUR

I am not sleeping when the door squeaks open. I have been absorbed in my memories, trying to link my dreams with the situation at hand, the woman of the streets with the men who use her so rudely. I do not need my eyes to be open to be aware of my surroundings, and as the broken portal is pushed back with a sigh, I am fully alert.

I am also fully aware of who it is who has come sneaking into the office. His steps are as light as any of his kind can be, and he has the sense to move slowly. The moon has set, and the room is dark. Even I would find it difficult to make do with mere sight at this time of night, when only the dim glow of a distant streetlight separates the dull grey shapes within the room.

Still, I have the advantage and I use it, leaping silently to the floor as he approaches. Careful to stay out of the intruder's path, I take his measure through scent and sound. He is filthy: dust and strange fibers overlay the odors of his unwashed body. Oil and the dank reek of steam. He is hungry as well; his scent gives him away, revealing as it does the desperate chemical interactions of an organism feeding on itself. That lack has been accentuated by his journey here, I judge. His breathing has slowed since he has entered, but it retains a ragged edge, a weakness from something more than cold. And it has taken its toll in other ways, as well. Despite his caution, he stumbles, catching himself with a soft cry.

It is enough. Care wakes. She sits up straight, as alert as a cat, and scans the room as best she can, sweeping the darkness with eyes open wide. I too observe, curious as to how the scene before me will unfold.

The intruder takes another step, and the girl's head swivels. I can almost feel her listening, the way she takes in the sound of the light and careful tread, the height from which the labored breathing issues. Perhaps even the smell, although I know her senses are not half so keen as mine. Perhaps there is another affinity, one beyond my understanding, for before he can take another step, she speaks.

'Tick?' Her voice, soft, is freighted with hope.

'Care?' His response has something of a cry about it, a release from fear. Or, I muse, of despair.

'What are you—?' She jumps up from her seat and feels her way around the desk to embrace the boy, whose small, fragrant form seems to draw her through the dark. 'How did you get here?' She holds him close, and then pushes him away, as if the truth will shine from his face. 'Did Gravitch – did he let you go already?'

'Already? What, no.' The boy shakes his head and pulls away slightly. I can see that he looks down at the ground. Something is troubling him, if he would hide his face so from the girl who loves him. 'Gravitch isn't letting anyone go. I found an escape hole. A way out they don't know about.' His voice grows peevish. 'I told you that, Care.'

'But I—' She catches herself and shakes her head, as if in amusement. 'Never mind, Tick. The only thing that matters is that you're here.' She fumbles toward the door. 'Let me get the candle.'

'Wait, no!' He reaches for her and lays hold of her arm. She turns, and I can see the half smile of curiosity playing across her face. 'It's not safe.'

'But you're here now,' she says. 'We can't stay here, but that's okay. We can find someplace, and I've – well, I've arranged to free you. Not just from the sweatshop but from Gravitch entirely. I don't know what their deal with Children's Services is, but I'll let them handle the paperwork.' She's grinning now. 'If there is any.'

He is not, and in the unlit room, I doubt she can see the look of horror growing across his face. 'You made a deal?' His voice has sunk back to a hoarse whisper.

She nods, misreading his shock as humility. 'Of course, Tick. You're like a brother to me. You know that.' The smile broadens. 'Hey, maybe it even says something about my skills that I've got something worth trading, huh?'

'Oh, no.' If she can't see his face, surely she can hear it in his voice: a rising tone, like a cry. 'I can't – you didn't, Care. You shouldn't have. It's not safe.'

'It's okay.' She hears him, I presume, but she mistakes the fear for disbelief. 'Look, if you want, we can leave the city. In fact, maybe that's best. I don't want to work for Gravitch, and, honestly, I don't trust him. But now that you're here—'

'I'm not, Care.' His voice is louder. More frantic. 'I'm not going anywhere with you. I'm going back. I told you. Don't you get it?'

'What? No.' She reaches for him, but he pulls away and, doing so, trips backward over a torn cushion, the remnants of that sofa. He stumbles to the floor with a yelp, and Care kneels beside him. He is crying now, more from shock than pain, but he lets her wrap her arms around him. He buries his face in her shirtfront as he sobs.

'Oh, Tick,' she says, stroking his back. She must smell him now. Smell the hunger and the filth. The desperation. 'What are you doing? What are you thinking, saying something like that?'

'I've got to.' He chokes out the words, as he fights the tears. Fights to regain his control.

'But why?' She examines his face as he pulls away.

He shakes her off, wiping his eyes with his sleeve. 'I have to,' he says. 'Don't ask me more.' His eyes are clear as he stares up at her. They are close enough that she must see this. She must, at any rate, hear the newly adult conviction in his voice. 'I only came to see you,' he says, 'to warn you. You can't trust them, Care. Any of them. Something's gone wrong. All the guys are talking about it, about a count going missing. About how they need to clean things up. And that lady? She's part of it, Care. I don't know how exactly. Only – you can't trust her. She got Dingo killed.'

# TWENTY-FIVE

The boy is as good as his word. It is still dark when he departs, over the girl's objections. She had given up arguing with him, by then, and had instead tried bribery, speaking of sanctuary somewhere to the south of the city. I do not know the place she spoke of, and from elements in her voice – a certain faraway tone, as well as the lack of specifics – I do not believe she does either, or not very well. She spoke as from memory, much as I would of a dream or of another life.

I would have thought he'd capitulate then. He has eaten – the girl had laid out the last of her stores, pushing what fruits she had salvaged on the boy – and sits at her feet as she speaks, a drowsy dreaminess coming over him that makes him, for a moment, look younger, like the child he ought to be. As soon as she stops speaking, however, he stands and makes to go. He refuses further food, although his yearning is apparent, just as he rejects Care's offer of additional clothes, warmer covering to replace the filthy and threadbare rags he has already outgrown.

'They can't know I was here, Care,' is all he will say.

For my part, I am relieved that he leaves. Unlike the girl, I do not trust him. I no longer think that he would betray her voluntarily. I am not such a brute that I do not see the signs of affection between them, the bonds of loyalty and of love. But he is young and weak, and he is easily used. Even if he does not intend the girl harm, he is not a reliable judge of his surroundings. What he has said about 'a count,' for example, is not to be trusted. Such rumblings are common among thieves, who prey on their own as readily as on others, and may amount to little more than the kind of internecine squabble we have already witnessed. Of more interest – and threat – is his agency. His ability to come and go as he pleases seems unlikely, and I consider him as one would a lure. Tempting, perhaps, but likely to lead to a trap.

His departure has left the girl restless. Although it is the time for her to sleep, she roams the office, repeating phrases that the boy has said. Gina got Dingo killed. A count – or was it *the* count – has gone missing. Papers of some kind are involved. She has denied knowledge of any such, and with the boy not much more literate than I, she sounded confident and sure. Now, however, she circles back to the desk, to the documents that lay there. In the dim light of dawn, she holds them close, as if to find meaning beyond the words and numbers printed there.

I am no help with this kind of toil, and yet I will not leave her, even as my own sleep is disturbed by her murmurings. I could hunt at this hour, when the night-loving creatures begin to retire and their daytime counterparts wake, but I do not. Although the girl is too agitated for my comfort, she readies herself for some action, to enact some plan, and I would be here when she makes her move.

'I don't . . .' She stops and shakes her head. Day has dawned, its flat light revealing the fatigue in her face. 'Unless . . .' She bites her lip and reaches for another page, then stops and looks up. It would appear that she is looking at me, recumbent on the windowsill. Only I know her sight is not acute enough to discern my own cool gaze, the angle of my whiskers signaling my interest and concern. No, she is lost in the light behind me, and perhaps in the illusion it creates of a glow, my guard hairs illuminated by the rising sun. She is seeing something that does not exist in the brightening grey sky or the buildings beyond. From the slight shift in her mouth, a gentling around her eyes, I would believe she sees hope.

I would also, at this juncture, advise her to rest. The events of the previous day were tiring, and the boy's brief visit has upset her. But as she begins to gather up her papers once more, I jump from the sill to wait by the door. I cannot ascertain what she intends, but I will aid her, if I can.

Indeed, I have specific fears. This girl has learned to survive in this city, but she is not of it, and in some deep inner core still reacts to other prompts. The promise she has made to Gravitch, for example, likely holds more weight for her than it would another street waif seeking favor. As she descends the building's stairs, treading carefully not to wake the alcove sleeper, I see this in her, and, as I dash by her as she pushes open the front door I experience a strange confusion. It is not practical, this side of her, bound up as it is in the past and a code that does not apply to the life she now leads. And yet, it stirs me and I feel the faint tug of memory. This, as well as her intellectual capacity, is why I chose her. It is why, in a large part, I give her my allegiance now.

But if the girl is planning to make good on her offer to Gravitch, going to offer her skills to find this missing item the boy spoke of, it will not be now. She has turned off the avenue and is heading once more toward the workhouse, toward the sick-sweet smell of putrefaction. But the morning is growing warm with the first real heat of spring, and the night's puddles are fragrant with fresher lures than one rotten rat. Part of me wishes to go off. She has her routine, waiting and watching. And I am an animal, with hungers of my own.

Only there is something off about this visit. Surely, the girl no longer seeks information. She has found her friend, conversed with him only hours before. And so I turn away from the fresh, moist scent of a new trail to watch as she slumps back against the alley wall. As she waits for the men to be released, and for the visitor who will join her there.

# TWENTY-SIX

'Gina?' she calls, questing. The yard is empty; the men not yet released for their daily exercise, if they will be today at all. The rodent corpse nearly ash. But the woman is already there. She starts at the sound of her name. 'I'm glad you're here,' says Care. 'I think I've found something. Something about your boy.'

The girl speaks softly, her voice intended for the woman alone. I, of course, hear every word, but her caution does not ease my mind. The woman is surprised to see her, and this should serve as warning. This woman has made deals of her own, and not only with her body, in order to survive. I watch her blink and color, and I wait for Care to notice this as well. She did not expect the girl to meet her here today, despite her request of the night before. She had expected some other fate to befall the girl and has not the wit to dissemble now.

'My Billy?' she asks, even as Care nods in confirmation.

'I think so.' Care pauses. 'Only, I'm not sure – and I might need your help. You ever go into Gravitch's factory?'

'The shop?' The woman seems confused. 'All the time.'

'Onto the factory floor, I mean.'

'Where the machines are? Nah. It's not allowed.' She looks away. Bothered. 'The office is better. There's a sofa, and it's warm.'

Care lets that pass, but my fur starts to rise as I realize what she's after. 'So you don't ever see the workers?' A low growl begins in my chest, and I must force myself to stay calm. To listen.

'The workers?' Gina forces a laugh. 'You're kidding, right? They don't have any coin.'

Care nods, and presses on. 'I think – I'm not sure, but have you ever asked if Gravitch has your boy? Has him working there?'

'No,' Gina shakes off the idea. 'He's just a kid, and Gravy

wouldn't. He knows how much I miss him, and he – we spend time together. Besides, Dingo would have . . .' Her voice trails off.

'Would have what?' Care pushes, perhaps too much. 'Tell me about Dingo, Gina.'

A nod. This woman is accustomed to direct commands. 'I told you he was different. Dingo was nice to me, and he – he found something,' she says. 'Something that's been missing for, like, years. Said he could use it. Could help me find my Billy.'

'I think I know what it was.' Care reaches into her bag. Extracts a single sheet, one of the bunch she took from the hovel. 'Could it have been this – a page like this?'

The woman reaches for it. Stares, shrugs.

'It's a list.' Care explains. 'I know it's not names, but see?' She points at some markings. 'This first number – it's got to be code for a place. A business. And these?' Her finger moves. 'I've seen these. They're case numbers. Maybe the numbers of the boys who've been taken. Who've been sent away.'

The woman looks up. The page she holds trembles. 'You mean – my Billy?'

Care nods. 'Maybe,' she says. 'That's why I wanted to talk to you. Do you think you could get into the factory? Get me onto the floor?'

'Dunno.' The woman's voice has gone soft. 'It'd be – it might be dangerous.' She is holding the page with both hands now, gently. As if it were her child. 'Can I keep this?'

Care hesitates as the woman waits, longing. 'Sure,' she says. 'For now. And you'll let me know?'

'I'll let you know,' she says.

# TWENTY-SEVEN

I don't like this plan. For once, at least, that woman spoke the truth. But Care is so focused on her friend, on Tick, that she doesn't realize the danger, doesn't recognize that truth. The woman wants her son, more than anything. That means she will do anything to get him back. Will trade anything, or anyone. It's bad enough the girl has put herself at the mercy of that man. Gravitch is a brute, a fan of casual cruelty and braggadocio. A creature of an even more brutal master, if I am right. Indeed, it is her honor, her pledge, that makes her more vulnerable still. Those such as Gravitch view such integrity as a weakness, fealty to an oath a sign of simple-mindedness or worse. Those such as Gina see her honor only for what it may fetch in trade.

It matters not. When I allied myself to this girl it was a better considered deal than the one she has made, and I do not regret it, although it may yet prove my end. And so as she heads down toward the harbor, down to the appointment she has promised to keep, I trot alongside. This time, I make sure she sees me in the brightening morning light.

'Blackie!' Her face and voice both evince joy, and in that I am rewarded.

'I wish I could send you back,' she says a moment later, as we pause just shy of an intersection. She is going about the boss's business, this girl, and in broad daylight. Still, old habits die hard and I am glad to see her take her time. Witness her scoping out the avenue – the traffic vehicular and human – before she would cross.

'You can't come in where I'm going.' Sadness has crept into her voice. With, I dare to believe, a trace of comprehension. 'It's not safe.' A little laugh. 'I know, it's not the greatest place for me either. But Tick . . .' She pauses. Stares out at the street. 'I don't know why I talk to you like this, Blackie. Maybe it's just that there's nobody else, but I almost feel you understand me.'

I stare up into her face, hoping the intensity of my gaze will transmit my understanding – my empathy. But my fur obscures any subtle changes in my features. Even were my face like hers, eloquent even in silence, my thickened coat, its midnight color, would hinder her ability to read anything in it. Even, that is, if she expected to find a response there.

She does not, nor does she wait. Instead, she turns back toward the open street and, gauging her moment, breaks out, trudging quickly and with purpose across the thoroughfare. At this time of day, the commerce of the city is in full swing. This far down by the harbor, that means labor of a rougher sort – the muscle that loads and unloads the goods that flow to and from this city, conveyed via ship and truck and otherwise, and those who feed upon them.

It is one of the latter, a vendor of fried meats by the smell, who takes note of me.

'Hey, watch out!' He jumps back as I dart from the shade of the corner to the shadow beneath his cart. 'That's nasty!'

A head appears sideways, eyes blinking, and I hiss.

'Yo, Bob!' He retreats, although not for long. 'Bob,' I hear. 'You got that hook still? Can I use it?'

I am gone before he returns, foolish man. The visitors he does not see have already made a home in the underside of his carriage. As well as helping themselves to his store of rolls, they have gnawed holes in the tubes that shuttle hot oil this way and that.

At least the mild fervor has distracted any attention from the girl. She has grown, it is clear to see, even in the weeks we have known each other. Her long strides reveal a flash of skin at her ankle, and although hunger keeps her slim, there is something about her movement that speaks more of a woman than a child. That hair, now divided by a widening strip of dark brown, does not help, announcing her presence even when she would stay unnoticed. I do not understand the urge behind that, I confess, but at this moment I am beset by other concerns.

The traffic alone is bad enough. For me to remain unnoticed, or at least unremarked, I must make my way by stages – moving from cover to cover – a journey that is slow at best and at times like this, dangerous. The truck I shelter beneath starts up with a growl; the clear path to the next gutter is suddenly obscured by feet, which depart only in time for another vehicle to drive through.

If I were not aware of her destination, I might have lost the girl. Her scent is nearly overwhelmed here by the heavier musk of men and their quarrels, not to mention all their ripe and rotten wares. Beneath it all, the deep, rich breath of the harbor intoxicates me. It is thick with life, in all its stages, while the building ahead exudes a strange, unhealthy stench – some alchemy of oil and steam. It is with some effort that I force myself forward, racing to catch the girl even as she openly crosses the street and treads upon the flagstones toward that squat brick building.

The grey door is open, as she steps into the alley. The rumble loud. An unstopping growl, it is near deafening, and I feel my ears flatten as we approach. Even Care seems to recoil, although she gathers herself and addresses whoever it is who has opened the portal.

And then it closes, latching with a click, muffling the noise within, and I realize I have begun to breathe again. 'No.' She shakes her head as she mouths the word. She has seen me, here, beside the step. But the reprieve that I have hoped for is not to be. With another click and a wheeze that grants warning enough for me to sink into the shadow of the alley's edge, the door opens again and although I cannot make out the voices as the growl esculates, I can see a hand beckon. The girl steps up and proceeds within, and the door closes once more, behind her.

For a moment, I am perplexed, unsure of how to follow. Unlike others of its vintage, this building appears to be secure, its brick kept dry and hard by the stone beneath, if not the vigilance of those who occupy it. There are no rat holes, no broken windows here. Unless—

I race around to the rear, to the street. To where the metal barrier now hangs closed. Except – yes – it is as the boy has said. One side does not hang true. A breach has been left where a truck has backed too close. Although I do not give much credence to any of the boy's statements, I am grateful to find in this some truth. Despairing of the time already lost, I lunge into the void.

And lose myself. It is not the dark – for the space I find myself in is not truly dark, low lights hum and buzz above. It is the noise that befuddles me, a bestial roar, constant and deafening, clattering and growling all about me, that oppresses and deranges all my senses.

I cannot hear. I cannot see or move, it seems, the noise is such. Only the thought of the girl, alone and unguarded elsewhere, reaches me in my panic. Ears flat, I run, aware as I do of feet and of the close and fetid smell of unwashed bodies. Voices ring out, adding to the confusion, but I ignore them, intent as I am on moving, as fast as I am able, through this building. Past this terror. I barrel into a doorway, jarring the unlatched barrier into opening, and I am through. The noise, the beast contained behind me. A hallway – then an antechamber – and at one end, the girl.

'In here.' I catch the words as the doorman waves Care into a room. He closes the door behind her, leaving me in that foyer. I crouch and back against the wall. He may be a fool, and an unobservant one, but surely the presence of a large black feline will catch his eye at some point. And the exit to the alley is closed.

'You came.' Gravitch. His voice as clear as if he stood behind me. My ears twitch and then I find it, the source my sound-fogged mind had failed to perceive. Loose siding, dyed to look like wood, and sloppily hung, grants space for me to poke my head through. This building may be built of brick, but its interior walls are flimsy as cardboard. No wonder then that the fiendish growl pulsates through this place. With an undignified squirm, I find myself looking at the legs of a desk and then Care's feet, in those threadbare sneakers. The floor is bare. The patterns of dust reveal where regular shapes – papers, perhaps – once covered it. The voice comes from behind that desk.

'Good girl,' he says. From his voice, I can tell he smiles. It is not a pleasant smile by far. 'And you'll do my errands, won't you?'

'I'm an investigator—' begins Care.

He cuts her off. 'Yeah, yeah,' he says. 'But what use have I for an investigator? I want something, Georgie here can get it for me.'

I had missed the presence of a third man. A grunt of assent places him closer to the door.

'I was hoping—' Care again, trying.

'Yeah, yeah, I know.' Gravitch sounds troubled, as if Care's request bothers him. 'You want your little friend. But he's a good worker.'

Silence. Now that I have some shelter, and have perhaps become more accustomed to the infernal thrumming, I can hear her breathing. She is holding it steady, but there is effort involved. She is anxious, I can tell, and also, I suspect, curious. Why did this man summon her, if he had no use for her?

'Sir?' One syllable, phrased as a question. It is the smart response.

'Oh, get her out of here.' Shifting and creaks: the third man had been seated, as well. And though I cannot see who stands to escort her out, I am able to mark her passage into the antechamber. Peering from behind the loose siding, I see the confusion on her face. The hurt.

'Come on, girly.' The doorman takes her upper arm, and she pulls free. It is a pointless gesture and makes him chuckle, but it serves the same purpose as grooming does for me. She steps toward the door with a better sense of herself, despite the distressing meeting, and I begin to back out, intent on following.

'Hang on.' I duck down just in time, back behind the siding. Gravitch has emerged from his sanctum, as well, and is heading toward the outer door. He grabs it and holds it open as Care descends the stairs.

She stops and looks up at him, and I can see the question on her face.

He steps down beside her and would close the door behind him. Unnoticed, I slip through just in time.

'There is something you could do for me.' He speaks in his usual suggestive tone, but he is nervous. He works the matchstick in his mouth with the same rapidity as his eyes twitch back and forth, surveying the alley. 'Nothing important, you know. Just so I know you're up to the job.'

Care waits, her head tilted. To the man, she probably appears subservient – his newest slave awaiting orders. I, however, experience a slight swell of optimism. It's the tilt – an angle I vaguely suspect the girl has picked up from me. She is alert, her posture tells me. Observant of more than the greasy man's words.

'Call it a token,' Gravitch says. 'Nothing big. Just a – well, a certain file. Something that got mislaid. If you can find it for me, well, then, maybe we can talk about some real work. And then . . .' He takes the matchstick from his mouth and twirls it between his fingers. He looks around once more. The hubbub is muted out here, now that the door is closed, but still he drops his voice as he describes a set of figures. A particular heading that would distinguish this trifle, this token. He pulls his billfold from his pocket and peels off a note and then another.

'Just a private job,' he says. And then he lumbers back inside.

# TWENTY-EIGHT

The street has grown quieter while we were inside. The deliveries have been made, and those with a trade are now engaged in it. Still, Care walks slowly after Gravitch leaves her. So slowly that at first I fear she plans to remain. To insist on visiting the boy or viewing his working conditions. But despite her pace, she continues on as if returning to the office. Only after a few minutes does she stop and step quickly behind a low and crumbling wall.

The sun is at its zenith; the mists of earlier have burned off, dispelling as well any shadows that would conceal me. Still, I follow her lead and find myself in a refuse tip, ripe with rot.

'Blackie, here!' she calls to me, and I turn to see her crouched by the wall's edge. I had paused, intrigued by a scent. Not the moldering fish head that perfumes this snug passage, but the traces of those who have examined it before me, both my kind and others. The winter has been hard and made scavengers of many of us, I realize as I turn. More incentive for the girl to continue her quest.

She is clearly on the hunt. Although she has beckoned me, her focus is now given over to the street. Watching, I now understand why she strode so openly. Once again by her side, I am also made aware of what that last interaction cost her. The sweat drying on her is slightly rancid from the antipathy she did her best to cloak with dignity and poise. I lean in, enjoying the warmth of her as well as that of the sunlight. I close my eyes to better savor her distinct smells. I am proud of her, although I do not know—

I sit up straight, all thoughts of rest banished.

'Shh.' She puts a hand out, as if to quiet me. Indeed, I believe she would smooth down the fur that rises along my ruff and back. I stare up at her astounded by my blindness. By hers. She does not turn.

I would warn her. Would stop her, before she proceeds further down this desperate path. But how?

She's chewing her lip again. Habit, I now know. But by such habits are we undone. I watch the blood bloom by her fraying lip. See her tongue dab at it in an unconscious response, much as I would groom or . . . or . . .

Gravitch with his matchsticks. I had thought that we were safe. For surely, Care has sensed what I have. That the man is withholding information from his colleagues, from his betters. That his supposedly 'trivial' errand is, in fact, the reason that he entertained the girl's offer in the first place.

Yes, she must. She is no fool, this girl, although burdened not only by her inferior senses and lack of experience but also by the unfortunate sentiment that binds her to that boy. She would see through the ploy in the office. Her apparent dismissal, and his subsequent summons, minor though he wanted it to appear. Even more than the money – the casual peeling off of bills – his eyes gave him away, darting like a nervous prey animal's at every sound. That and his own execrable habit: gnawing on wood and sulfur as if such bitter sustenance could soothe his nagging fears.

It is that habit, though, which I did not account for. Which I in my foolish pride did not consider. Hidebound, I am, in ways I cannot even begin to fathom. No, worse than hidebound: *fur bound.* Illiterate as any beast. But how could I not see?

The papers. Those pages Care has fussed over, which she grabbed from the warehouse and out of which she plucked one to give to that woman. They are what this Gravitch seeks. The reason for his belabored ruse, all to reach the girl.

But not, as I had thought, merely to evade his colleagues – those supposed employees who may, in fact, answer to another, higher up – for private gain or enterprise. There is a darker purpose as well. He has been in that warehouse – the place of records, of documents. I knew him by his habit: the bitter trace of sulfur, the gnawed upon stick of wood. Whatever it is he wants to hide, the carnage there was part of it as well.

Does she sense this? Can she perceive just how duplicitous her erstwhile client is? I look up at her, face intent and waiting, and I do not know what I fear. That she does not know, and I, in this mute and bestial form, cannot find the means to tell her. Or that she does, and risks it all, desperate to save the boy.

The girl is cautious, and for that I am grateful. I have time enough to track – and devour – a large beetle before she ventures forth again. When she does, she remains circumspect, keeping close to the buildings that line these streets and pausing whenever an overhang or the remnant of a stoop offers shelter to scrutinize both the path she has tread and the way ahead. Not that she follows one road. No, in an echo of that six-legged morsel, she jogs thither and yon, although I sense that her wanderings are neither so heedless nor so random, and soon I recognize her intent. An open square, once paved with cobblestones. Narrow streets, and the faint, sweet smell of ink.

When she comes upon a ruined building, its bricks still stained by smoke, I begin to understand. And as she descends a set of broken stairs to an unmarked basement door, I am mindful of the reason for her to take heed. As she closes the heavy door behind her, I make my own way in, slipping past the rag that covers the open window and leaping soundlessly to the floor.

'Ms Wright.' The man behind the desk sounds pleased, though his voice remains even. 'Please, have a seat.' He has been working, the gas lamp on the surface before him giving off a steady whisper of a glow. He pushes up the magnifier, blinking as his eyes return to a more normal size, and rubs them. From this motion, as well as the ink on his hands, I surmise he has worked through the night.

'I'm sorry to disturb you.' The girl approaches. She is holding her bag against her side, as if it were suddenly more precious. 'I need your help again.'

He nods, as if this were expected. 'I will do what I can.' His voice is sad. 'For your service, as well as for your old man's.'

'Thank you.' The girl grasps the bag more tightly as she approaches, and the crabbed man draws back his hands. It is reflex, nothing more. She sees this too. 'I'd like you to – I need you to keep something for me. A document.'

'You – you trust me?' His eyes open wider, although his tone is still soft. 'Trust my security here?'

'Any man can be undone by violence,' says the girl, and in

her words, I hear an echo of another voice. Her mentor's. 'But I was not followed here, and none know what I carry.' She licks her lips. She is venturing into territory that unnerves her. 'In fact, I've been hired to discover these, or something very much like them, and I need a place – I need these documents to be secure while I explore the case. No one knows I have them,' she promises, before he can object.

'All right.' He nods and sits up straight, as if to pull courage from his posture. 'Let's see them.'

She reaches into her bag then, removing the papers from her desk – all but the page she gave the woman, and I wonder. There was no lie in her voice. Dissembling does not come naturally to her, and when she twists the truth it costs her, tightening her breath in ways she cannot yet control. Perhaps she does not consider what the surrender of that one document may mean, what knowledge that woman may have gleaned from it – or to what purposes of her own she, a creature of commerce far more coarse than any Care has known, may choose to apply it.

'These—' He catches himself. Beyond all else, he will remain true to his code. But the eyes, red and rimmed with bags like bruises, convey the questions his voice will not. She holds her silence, watching him, and as they remain locked in each other's silence, I approach. The girl has done this man a good turn, but this world breeds grudges more than grace and I have other means of ascertaining truths.

The cuff of his trouser is frayed. It smells of dirt and ink, the warm and waxy smell of candles and the cleaner one of gas. But there is more, even beyond the overlay of fear worn by all prey creatures in this world. His scent, I realize now, is familiar because it is reminiscent of the girl. Either the tools of his trade – the writing implements, the ink, the reams of paper, much of it scraped clean for reuse – or some other more elusive linkage have imprinted themselves on his skin.

'Care,' he says at last. He speaks her name as if he knows her. 'These pages . . .' He pauses and looks down at them. He shakes his head. He will not ask. 'This is what those men were looking for. The night they wrecked my place.'

# TWENTY-NINE

I am not a reader, of papers or of minds. And so I cannot attest as to what happens next in that low room, with these two humans. I do know that the girl hesitates, not out of doubt of the man, but of the circumstance. I hear the question in her voice as she starts to ask, and the answer as she stops herself. She trusts this man, or at least his veracity in this one area. Instead, she looks at the papers once more, her eyes roaming the pages as her teeth worry her bottom lip.

For the length of several breaths, she stands, her brow furrowed in thought. The man waits, as well, studying her with a face that reflects his pain and an inner dialogue of his own. Finally, she nods once, as if a decision has been made. She holds the papers out to the man once more.

'If you will, I'd still like you to keep these for me,' she says. 'If you'll undertake the risk.'

'The risk isn't on me,' he says, his voice soft. There is an understanding between these two, an agreement that I do not fully understand. 'He's looking for these. You know that.'

'I do.' Her lips draw back in a toothy grin. It's an odd look for her, a gesture more of my realm than of hers, conveying more threat than pleasure, and he knows it, starting back ever so slightly. 'And it explains a lot.'

He takes them, then, and places them on his desk. 'I'll keep these,' he says, in formal agreement to the request she has made.

They do not shake hands. They do not speak of terms or security, or when she may return to reclaim the documents she leaves. Instead, with one more nod, Care turns to go.

'Wait!' He calls to her as she reaches for that heavy, ineffectual door. He rises from his seat as she pauses, as she turns. 'I have – just . . . wait.'

She does, the certitude of moments appearing to crumble as her brows knit in confusion. He sidles over to the wall, which under his hands reveals itself to be not as solid as it had appeared.

Care's gasp reveals that she has been taken unawares by this rudimentary ruse, the false front of the brick, although my ears could have told her of the scrabblings in that wall, of the faint whistle as the wind was filtered through.

But it is not surprise that causes her to turn, to face the still closed door rather than the monkish man who has removed the hollowed brick. And it is my turn to be schooled, as my own preconceptions crumble. She has not been caught out by the man's ruse, but by his confidence. A keeper has little but his secrets, and this man has paid dearly to retain them. Now he shares them freely and without fear. Her turning away is more than a courtesy then. It is a sign of respect, a means of indicating that she will honor the trust he now so freely gives.

I have no such compunction and observe with interest the doings of the little man. He removes a pouch from within the wall. Canvas or some other heavy cloth, its dun surface shiny and pliant with frequent handling. Holding it close, he turns to peer over his shoulder. Reflex, I believe, as a slight flush creeps into his face. Embarrassment at doubting the girl after he has breached the space between them. He blinks, the trace of tears bright in his weak eyes, and pulls out the documents within. These are folded and as he moves them, they give out whiffs of their origins – the sweat of different hands. Of ink and oil. Of blood. Some of these, their dust suggests, are of great vintage, a trust held even as their purpose was abandoned or their owner gone. I smell no mold. The keeper knows his trade.

Finally, he removes two pages. On one, I see the scrawl of a pen, the ink cheap and faded even more than the age of the paper merits. The other appears to be of better quality, and yet it is not this one he lingers over. In fact, after what seems a tortured moment, he shoves the second back into the sack and hurriedly replaces them both in the wall. It is a moment's work to fit the hollowed brick back in its niche, a light touch of his fingers resettles the dust on the ancient mortar, the source of that faintly earthy smell.

'Here,' he calls to her, his signal for her to turn. She does, and he extends his hand, offering the remaining, faded page. 'Please,' he says. 'You should have this.'

She steps forward, the question in her eyes.

'It was entrusted to me,' he says. 'By your father.'

'My—' She chokes on the word. She shakes her head.

'I told you I knew him,' says the scribe. 'I could not help him, I'm afraid. But I did hold onto this.' He nods toward the page, which she reaches for as gingerly as if it were a small, live thing. 'I believe I've been holding it for you.'

# THIRTY

I do not understand this girl. I have never seen her act like this. She is tough, she is resourceful. But when she leaves the basement office, she dashes for the corner, with no regard to who may see, and stands there, in the full sun, as she pores over the paper in her hand.

It has importance. I understand, and she must gather what meaning she can from it before she folds it once more and tucks it in her bag. But it acts on her like poison, like a drug. Or, no, an infected wound, that she will worry at even as it sickens and unsettles her. For after staring at it, she wanders like a day-blind mole, crossing streets and alleys with no more care than any panicked creature, seeking a hideaway. Seeking safety.

I follow, of course, keeping her in sight. My hearing and every guard hair on my body alert for the inevitable predator such aimless wandering will draw. The day has grown bright, those early clouds have burned off and the mud of these lots, of these gutters, is fragrant with the heat. There are few creatures out at this hour, a bright and unforgiving time, and those drying pools have left even weaker prey than she stranded and defenseless. Still, I do not like this inattentive wandering, the soft sounds of sorrow that she makes no effort to conceal. I do not like them, and I am powerless to prevent them, and so I follow, on my guard.

I am not surprised when she returns to the office. Like any wounded beast, she seeks the comfort of her lair. And as I slip in behind her, waiting until the outer door has nearly swung shut before I dash inside, I am gratified to see her glance my way. To see the flash of recognition, through her grief.

I do not like how she drags herself up the stairs, unconcerned with who might hear the scraping of her shoes on the worn steps. My superior senses have already told me we are alone – the fragrant occupant of the building's foyer has taken advantage of the day's warmth to seek nourishment or, more likely, oblivion from the charity of a passerby. But her lack of caution, her disregard for all her training concerns me, as much as the soft mewling noises she makes as she throws herself upon the torn and battered couch.

'Dad,' I hear her say, her face buried in a cushion that has surrendered most of its plush stuffing. 'Daddy.'

I sniff at her, trying to discern the source of her pain. With my forepaws on the sofa, I can reach up to where she lies curled, back toward me. Her shoulders heave as she weeps into the battered upholstery, and I take in her sweat and her dismay from the arc of her backbone, from the way her thin sides rise and tremble. I have never experienced a bout like this. Not with this girl. Not, I believe, ever, and it disturbs me in ways I cannot explain. Some of it is the vulnerability, that thin back left unguarded in this unlocked and insecure room. Some of it is the raw nature of the emotion, unrestrained by thought or caution. And some, I slowly realize as I leap soundlessly to take my place beside the crying girl, is something deeper. More ephemeral and yet no less real.

I love this girl, this Care, and she is crying. And so I stretch my long furred body beside hers, leaning in to comfort her with softness and warmth. She does not acknowledge me, although I know she must feel my presence. Feel the heat and texture of my fur. She does not speak, nor turn. Not even as the sobbing fades and gives way to quieter sounds, the exhalations of slumber, of exhaustion and despair. And still I lie beside her, unwilling to seek refreshment or relief. I am giving her nothing that she needs. Not my wisdom. Not any of the skills or aptitudes that I would have her learn. Not anything of value, beyond my animal warmth. I lay beside her and listen to her breathe. I have never felt so helpless or alone.

*There are three of them, these men. They stand tall above me, in the sun. The light behind their backs obscures their faces, but I know their expressions to be cruel. They stand like bars before the sun, like monoliths. Like death, and even as I peer up at them, I know this is the end. They will kill me, as they have killed others. I have no recourse, but still I watch them, recording what I can of their posture. Of their clothing. Scent*

*is not yet so vital to me that I can capture their essence this
way. Instead, I peer up at them, desperate to see them. To see
once more their faces.*

'Blackie.' A soft voice wakes me to shadows grown long. In
the fading light, the girl's green eyes are nearly obscured by
swollen, reddened flesh. 'Good boy,' she says, and strokes my
fur.

I am unaccountably gratified, and accept the caress with a
purr. Her hand is warm against my body. It makes a welcome
change from the memory of that dream. I was awaiting less
gentle hands then. I was awaiting death.

'You're getting quite domesticated,' she says, the lilt in her
voice indicating amusement, though her face remains sad. Well,
let it be. If I may lighten her burden by the sacrifice of my
dignity, I am willing. But even as she rises and I follow, to arch
my back and stretch, I wonder at the chronology of that dream,
its sequence of events. Those men – that memory – were cruel
by force of habit and profession. I was not their only victim,
nor was I theirs by accident. They had laid a trap for me, much
as others would for any small creature in the pursuit of meat
or fur. I had meddled in their affairs, pursuing the profession
to which I had introduced the girl, and they had responded to
protect their interests. Although the details remain murky, of
this I am sure. They laid a trap and executed it. And as the girl
pulls that paper from inside her shirt, I am forced to consider
the nature of such traps and such cruelty, to consider what such
men could do to one thin and lonely girl.

As much as I dislike the strange lassitude that has taken over
the girl, I approve less of what she does next. Not that she
washes her face and hands. Despite her pleasing natural scent,
I do not feel like this girl – like any human – keeps to the
standards of cleanliness that I embrace. Nor that she goes
through her meager store of clothes, donning an old shirt above
her thin one. It is when she shrugs her way into that old overcoat, pulling up the torn sleeve to cover her arm, when she piles
the few remaining apples, the rest of that dry cheese and the
few crackers she has left into her bag, that I know we are
heading out for the night, if not for good.

I watch her preparations with growing unease, an emotion I

attempt to communicate by twining around her ankles. If I could only stop her for a moment, if we could only converse . . . Rarely have I felt so hindered by this mute and bestial form. 'What is it, Blackie?' Her voice interrupts me. I have begun to bathe, a default and useless reaction to my overwhelming frustration. 'You know something's going on, don't you?'

I stare up at her, willing her to see beyond the reflective surface of my eyes. To see my concern, to see my soul. I open my mouth. I would speak to her. I would speak.

'Meh,' I say, one small syllable that slips by my fangs like a frightened mouse. 'Meh,' I say again. To intend so much, and to have control over so little . . .

She smiles, and for that I am grateful. It is the first time since we left the scribe's basement that I have seen anything other than tears or fierce concentration on her face, so young and so pale. To my confusion, she reaches down, her hands closing around my sides, and lifts me, retreating to the sofa, where she deposits me on her lap.

'I don't know what it is with you, Blackie,' she says. Her voice has gone soft, her mind on something other than her words, as she stares down at me, one hand smoothing my somewhat ruffled fur. 'Maybe it's just that you pick up on my mood. I mean, you can't . . .'

She pauses, then reaches into her bag, retrieving the document that has caused her so much pain. 'It's from my father, Blackie. He was a good man no matter what anybody says.'

I reach up to sniff the letter she holds, and she lets me, holding it still as the black leather of my nose runs along its edge. She says nothing as I work my way along it, my eyes closing as I concentrate on its rich offerings. First, there is her hand. Her sweat and tears both stained this page, softening the old paper further. Warming it, as well, which has released some older scents. The brick dust of the keeper's safe, dry and crumbling: an earthy aroma that recalls its long-ago origins in mud and clay. The hand of the keeper, stained with ink and with the powdery smell of age. And is there something more?

I open my mouth slightly, seeking the faintest traces. A breath of someone older still and dear to this girl, this Care. The scent of someone gone. A trace of that other paper, the

one the mole man chose to replace. I lean in, taking in the air.
Hoping to taste.

'No!' My eyes open as the girl jerks back, nearly unsettling
me. She is examining the page, where, I see, two small holes
now mar the corner. I have bitten it, in my reverie. I did not
mean it harm. No matter, the damage has been done. As the
girl folds the page back up, I see her eyes well up once more.
I stare at her, mouth open. Dumb as any beast. Surely, she must
see my contrition. Surely, she must forgive.

'Oh, Blackie.' She speaks as if she does, only the words serve
to distance us. They illustrate the gulf I cannot cross. 'You can't
help it, can you? As much as I might wish otherwise, you're
just a cat.'

I turn away. It is too much, and so I jump to the floor to
nurse my disappointment and despair. To await her judgment.
Her dismissal. I belong down here, another useless beast.

But her voice is soft and even, once the sniffling has stopped.
It speaks not of my incompetence but of something other.
Something older. She is reading to me, it dawns on me. Sharing
that which I could not take in on my own.

I close my eyes to better grasp the substance of what she
says and, more, the voice I hear behind hers,

*We live in evil times,* Care begins.

*When I was placed here, to serve out my time sorting
and filing records, I thought myself lucky. Here, I
believed, I would finally be able to trace the misstate-
ments and errors that led to us losing our home and I
my livelihood. What I found was worse by far. Our lives
had not been ruined by a mistake, but by a pernicious
system devoted to disowning small shareholders like
me, devoted, instead, to imprisoning us for our labor
and our land. The system was bigger than my small
family, bigger than me.*

*I should have stopped there. I realize that now. As a
father, I should have considered how my actions could
hurt my family. But, as a father, I also felt a moral
imperative to behave as I have tried to teach my daughter
to. At any rate, I fear it is too late now and that my*

*questions have made me a target of retribution. I have one
play left, however, and on it may rest my fate, as well as
the fate of countless other poor souls. If all goes well, I
will be in touch. If not, please look after Martha and our
dear Carrie. I cannot thank you enough, Q. It helps to
know that although this city seems particularly cold right
now, those I love most have friends who will care for them.
Friends who will see them right.*

She is quiet after this, as contemplative as a cat, if only she
knew it. And I, too, am at peace. She does not seem to hold
my sins against me. This is likely due to her charity, to my
being deemed a low creature, incapable of reason. Perhaps she
has even forgotten my trespass, as she rouses and resumes her
preparations. As she approaches the door, she turns as if to wait
for me. As if, perhaps, to consult.

'I don't know if you want to come with me,' she says, a half
smile playing on her lips. 'I understand you're loyal. But this
– well, this might be dangerous.'

I stand, tail erect, to signify my readiness, and I believe
she recognizes this, as with a nod she turns and sets out down
the hall. I do not require her consent. I am an adult, older far
than she, and would follow whether she would or not. But there
is something pleasant in trotting by her side, even as I consider
where we may be headed. For I do not trust this mood of hers,
this current easy mirth. It follows too closely on her sadness
and is underlain by something darker – a sense of danger or of
fatalism. One advantage of my current state is that I can more
easily detect the undercurrents in her voice. For all its lightness,
and for all her easy smiles, there is tension working on her
now. She is not afraid, and that may be what scares me most.
Instead, she is determined. Along with the fruit and cheese, she
has packed her knife.

She does not hesitate once we hit the street and leads a
swift pace in the growing dark. And as we leave our failing
commercial district for other, more benighted streets, I recognize
our path. It is as I've feared. She heads once more to that
place of records and of death. The Dunstan, as she's called it.
Where more than paper has been laid to rest.

To her credit, she moves with stealth. Any concern I may have had earlier about her concentration is dispelled. The dusk has not yet settled on the city, but she finds the shadows. She moves between them, treading as soundlessly as one of her kind can. When we pass a uniform on his beat, she eludes him with no effort, her pace undiminished as she mirrors his movements with her own.

Only once she has reached the hulking brick monstrosity does she pause. She raises her face up to its iron gate, and for a moment, I see what this journey has cost her. Her father – the writer of that letter – spent his last days in here. And though I would rather her be wary of another death, more recent and in closer proximity, I find myself wanting to press against her. To comfort her.

I hold back. This girl knows I am here, and just as I must let her ponder her plans, so too must I. She will have entrance; that is clear. The challenge before me is how to aid her, and to secure her safe passage, once her errand here is done.

# THIRTY-ONE

This time, I am prepared. The hellish klaxon will not catch me unawares. Will not shock me into senselessness, as it did once before. The girl beside me prepares as well. As we make our way around the side of the building, she pauses, ducking down behind an outcropping of trash. And when I see her cover her own ears, I steel myself. Somewhat removed from its direct blast, when that hideous noise lets loose, it does not this time overwhelm me with its cry of death and horror. And yet, it pins my ears flat, and I must exert all my self-control to refrain from bolting. As it is, my claws extend to clutch at the pitted stones beneath me, and, cowering, my eyes see naught. That I do not run, that I retain some semblance of myself – my dignity – is a victory of sorts. This form, with all its heightened senses – is not entirely bereft of discipline. Is not devoid of all control, even when faced with such hideous volume. Yes, I pant as the echoes die, revealing the thudding footsteps of the workers who flee – no, I realize – who are herded at the behest of that fiendish sound. But as I look up, alert and ready, the girl smiles down at me, and I am amply recompensed.

It is not yet dark as we once again approach the building, and the city is humming. Nocturnal life of all sorts has begun to stir, from the sickly raccoon whom we disturb as she rooted through the day's trash, to the young hustler who will do his own version of the same, as he summons the strength for another night on the game. He eyes the girl as she passes, dismissing her as a client – and then as possible competition as she moves swiftly past.

Only when we return to the Dunstan's gate does she stop moving, holding herself back as the shadows reach and fade into the dark. She's counting; I can hear it under her breath, and soon I see why. Above, in the windows, a figure passes from one to the next. A watchman, probably, as the building appears to have emptied of its other occupants, he makes his way from one window to the next and then, after an interval, reappears on the floor above. And she begins once again to count.

Once I have discerned the reason for her watchful murmurs, I begin my own calculations. That the girl intends to enter, to conduct some kind of clandestine inquiry, is clear from her actions. What my role can be is less so. First, I must attain a means of access: if the girl plans on once again climbing through a window, I will need a different entry, as I do not believe she will now accept or allow any attempts to accompany her.

I follow her around to the alley. The bin has been replaced with another of the same stout build, and once more she drags the heavy thing over to the closest window. Only then do I make my move. I sensed water nearby, slow-moving but alive, when we were here before, and the soft earth of decay around it. It is the work of minutes to find its source: a drain from some gutter that has long gone unrepaired. As my superior senses have indicated, the disrepair has led to rot, and that in turn has opened a pathway for creatures smaller than myself to make ingress, scraping and gnawing at the softened brick and sandy mortar. I can smell them here, those burrowers, and were circumstances other, I would hold back, waiting until habit and hunger accustomed them to my own scent. Then I would feast. But now is not the time for such prudence, nor is it my own need that drives me. Instead, I dive in, feeling the damp mortar give way further to my own claws, even as I push my way through the rotted brickwork.

The walls press dangerously close. I do not like enclosed spaces. As does any creature of sense, I fear the trap. The cage. And as I push further, I am aware at all time of my whiskers brushing against the damp walls. Through them, I sense the patterings of the original architects of this entry, scattering in fear as they pick up signs of my approach. Through my whiskers I am made aware of other movements, farther away. That guard whose slow and measured tread has not changed, and some-where, closer still, the louder scrape and scramble of the girl. The window jamb is wood, not brick, and she works it with her knife. Through the wall around me, I hear the click of the latch giving way.

As she wriggles and kicks her way inside, a dribble of clay dust descends on me. I flick my ears in irritation and feel them brush the top of this passage. This place is close, and I need to be through it, both for my own ease and to catch up with the girl. She has won her way, though with less grace than I would have hoped. Despite the growing urgency, I pause and listen. A moment passes. My heart beats. I hear no change in the night guard's measured tread. She has not been detected.

As she lowers herself to the floor, my breath catches in my throat. The close confines have begun to take their toll. I have grown glossier in recent weeks, but I am not young. I feel the stiffness in my leg as I claw the softened brick and push myself forward. The dampness has gathered here. This far inside the structure, it neither drains nor evaporates. I feel it seep into my fur. The air is thick with rot, with the wet and the droppings that collect between my pads. I taste their musk on my tongue, for I am panting with the effort. With the pressure of the building bearing down. Above me, a rumble – the girl is walking – and more mortar falls, damp pebbles on my back. I start as they hit me, surprised at the sudden touch, and slip, the leather of my paws gaining no traction in the slime. I clamber up – and slip again, as the clay dissolves beneath me, falls around me, filling the very air. I breathe in mud. I taste it. My tongue grows clogged and dulled. I cannot see, but still I hear. All around me, the scrapings of curious creatures. They come to see their foe brought low. They wait, and they will feast.

My eyes are closing, and my chin comes down to rest upon my paws. Such is the nature of life, and I cannot resist. I have lived long. I have been pulled from danger before. I have—

'No!' A voice breaks through, faint but clear – to me, at least. A syllable spoken aloud when stealth was the goal. Is she in trouble? Has she been caught? I sigh, my head, which bobbed up at that sound, begins to dip again. This fight is beyond me now. I have done what I could.

'Friends who will care for them.' The voice is not one I recognize. It echoes through my mind, even as I drift. 'Friends who will see them right.'

'It can't—' Care's voice, the girl's, and right nearby. I see no light, no exit. My eyes are blind here in this airless dark.

But still, I rouse myself. I kick. I push, my whiskers pressed too close, the clay against the wet fur on my brow. And, with one more surge, I am through, the last cheap patch of mortar collapsing out to reveal a room. And air, and standing by a cabinet, the girl, alone.

I take a breath, what feels like the first in a very long time. The creeping terror of that passage, and my concern for the girl, begin to fade, replaced by relief at my release. And then, as is my wont, I sit, twisting to groom the foul wet earth from my fur. Only as I do, I realize I have indeed been blind. For as she stands, gazing into an open drawer, she does not realize what else her voice has summoned.

There is a shadow in the doorway that is not cast by the opened door, nor by the cabinets inside. It is still, but not still enough. I have seen it move, even as I twisted back to clean my fur. Waiting for its moment. The guard is watching.

# THIRTY-TWO

I do not spring with claws extended. I refrain from the howl and hiss. These are not the tactics of a hunter intent on flushing out his quarry. Nor, I confess, would they be wise for any prey animals intent on living. For such are we now, and so I remain still and quiet, waiting for a moment of vulnerability. Anticipating the point in time when I may best effect the girl's escape.

He is watching her. Now that I have spied him, standing in the darkness of the hall, his strategy is clear. Lurking in the shadow of the hall, he believes he has her trapped. Indeed, I see no other door. And so he waits.

He must, it occurs to me, be curious as to her motive. Buildings like these are made to contain people more usually than to keep them out. It cannot be common for someone to break into such a fortress of thick and enduring brick. The girl's age, and her slight figure, must add to the confusion. She is no streetwalker, seeking a quiet place to ply her trade, nor a desperate street rat, looking for an easy score. Now that I am aware of his presence, I can hear his breathing, its slight unhealthy rasp. It has speeded, even as he stands there, apparently at ease. He is curious, maybe even a little afraid.

'And more?' The girl has removed a sheet of paper from the drawer, the file that held it lies flat upon its peers. She is speaking to herself, so taken by what she reads that she has forgotten where she is. Forgotten caution. With no interruption to remind her, she peruses further, pulling one and yet another page from within the file.

She stuffs them in her bag, and I hunker down. This is when the confrontation will take place. This is what the watcher has been waiting for. She will be trapped and taken. Documents from this place will be found upon her person, incriminating her. Sealing her fate.

I do not waste my time wondering what her punishment

will be. We have seen what violence may be perpetrated on
the vulnerable, what forms it takes. It matters not, for I will
not let it happen. Even as she maneuvers the papers within
her bag, even as she pulls it up onto her shoulder, I crouch
in waiting. I ready myself. Hindquarters twitching, all my
stiffness, any soreness is forgotten now. I will leap on the
intruder. I will howl and bite, and with all the commotion I
can muster, I will buy her the time she needs to evade him.
The time to escape.

I am a coiled spring. I am—

She turns, and I blink up in surprise. From her sudden movement – the way she holds herself now, breath itself at bay – I
know she is on the alert. Some movement has broken through
her ill-considered absorption. Can it be that I have betrayed
myself? That after my ordeal, I have lost the capacity for silent
motion – the mastery of stealth?

Daring a subtle shift, I move my ears and pick up, yes, that
hoarse intake of breath. It is not I who have betrayed myself,
it is the guard. The girl has heard him in the doorway, although
surely she sees him not.

'Who's there?' Her question, soft and low, is barely voiced.
And yet I hear the sudden gasp of a response. 'Who is it?'

I watch her with wonder. Surely, she must know what manner
of man is waiting. She saw the watchman. Timed his passage.
Is this some play that I have not foreseen? I resume my pose
and ready for the leap.

Footfall. Heavy, booted. A man. I gauge distance, gauge his
height as he steps into the doorway and pauses. He is big, this
man, with shoulders that nearly touch the frame. And although
his clothes hang on him, hang from the arm that holds the heavy
light, I do not doubt his strength.

I will have one chance with this man. He is tall, but I will
launch myself up at his face, with all my strength. If I can reach
it, I can hold him. He will tear at me, pull me from him by my
fur and my limbs, but in that struggle, I will draw him from
the doorway. I will win her egress. Win her freedom no matter
what the price.

'Are you an inmate?'

My ear flicks back. She is still talking, her voice still soft and low. It is a strategem I had not considered. Distraction, maybe, or a lure of sorts to reel him in.

'You can't—' His voice as rough as that breath and, even at this distance, foul. He has a sickness. The air rots within him, and I feel myself relax. This man is large, no doubt, but he will be unable to pursue her. I understand now his hollowed frame, the slow and measured pace with which he made his rounds.

'What are you doing here?'

'My father was an inmate,' she says in response. He shakes his head, his query still unanswered. 'He also wasn't strong,' she says, her voice hesitant as she chooses her words. She, too, must sense the sickness in this man, or see it. Now that he has stepped into the room, the faint light from the window rakes the gouges in his face. The hollows beneath his eyes are dark as mud.

One false move, and I will aim for those eyes, as deep set as rodent holes. I will make him blanch. I lean back, readying for the spring.

But it is she who steps forward, one hand outstretched. 'He worked here, too,' she says. Her palm is up, as if she would take his hand. Or, no, the heavy flashlight that hangs still by his side. 'His sentence was for debt.'

Another step, and my fur rises. She is too close. She is within his grasp and, worse, now stands between me and the hulking guard. My ears go back as I take in the changing scene. My angle for attack, and hers.

'I found the files he was working on,' she now says. 'The accounts he was in charge of. Work release, they call them.'

She chuckles, an odd, sad sound in this darkened space. Her voice, though soft, is clear, its warmth at odds with the cavernous room. Even the small beasts within the walls take heed of it. I hear them settle, their frenzied scrabbling pause.

I look at her, then, and see her as he must. The moonlight shows her youth. Shows as well, the strange half-smile that plays about her chapped lips. 'Work release,' she says again.

And then I hear the oddest sound of all. A sigh – or, no – another rasping breath. A wheeze. The guard is laughing, too. His thin shoulders heave up with the effort, as if they have shared a joke. But then he doubles over, coughing. The flashlight hits the floor, and I turn to her. This is her moment. Her chance to run, to leave this place. I race toward her as she begins to move – and freeze, as she wraps her thin arms around the big man and helps him to sit against the wall.

# THIRTY-THREE

'Poor old Dingo, he never did have any luck.' The guard – 'call me Terry' – shrugs, those big shoulders jerking his scarecrow jacket up against the wall. 'Maybe he got greedy.'

He and the girl have been talking for a while now, their voices low and urgent. She has told him of her mission. Of the death of the man she was set to find. I have retreated to the shadows to watch. Care saw me race forward, and she knows where I sit, but the man seems oblivious. His illness may have dimmed his vision, I realize. Or else he has become accustomed to the scurrying of creatures in this, his nighttime realm, and no more considers their progress than he would a mote of dust.

'No.' The girl shakes her head, her face grim. 'This had nothing to do with luck.'

The guard sighs. Despite his size, he is weaker than the girl and more fatigued. 'I saw him, what? A week – maybe ten nights ago. He said he was going to be leaving town. That he was leaving with a lady friend. Some gal and her kid. Said he had his papers.'

'Papers?' She picks up on the word. Terry nods.

'Said they were his ticket out.' He rubs his cheeks, rough hands rasping on the bristle. 'Parole, I figured. Least at first. I wished him luck.'

'But they weren't, were they?'

He shakes his head this time, the gesture sad and slow. 'He'd hit the jackpot, Dingo did. He found the lost papers. The ones we're supposed to look for.'

'Found them?' The girl chews it over. Her fingers twitch at the bag on her side. Eager to be sorting through the papers within. 'He didn't get them here?'

'Never came in.' Another demurral. 'I asked. It was one of those rainy nights, you know. But he said this place creeped him out. That he was meeting somebody. I thought it was an odd place for a meet. I told him to bang on the door after, even if he didn't want to come in. I had something warm brewing. But he didn't. We had some good times, me and Dingo.'

Care is listening, as am I. If she could, she would tilt her ears forward as I do, the better to catch the nuances of voice. I believe she must gather what I do, however. That the man is losing himself in a memory of times that in retrospect appear golden. He must have been healthier then, as he describes working the trucks. Loading and unloading with muscles not yet ravaged by disease.

'He and I, we used to crash in that shack of his.' His lips twitch at the memory. 'We got paid in coin, most weeks. We'd get some drink. We had some times.'

'The shack.' Care watches his face. I do, as well, but although her voice has summoned him back to the present, the smile lingers. The recollection is an agreeable one. 'That's where I found the papers.'

Terry shrugs in acquiescence. 'He'd take them there, sure. It was our place. That's not where he found them, though.' A cough bends him double, wracking his body with a sharp bark that sets my ears back. The girl doesn't stir, however. She only waits for him to sit back up. To wipe his mouth on his sleeve. I can smell the blood flecked there. If she sees it, she does not comment. Instead, she asks again.

'You sure?' Care is doubling back. 'Do you know where they'd been?'

The man only shakes his head, his voice silenced by another cough. It matters not. He has already told her about the pages. That the files she has so recently perused were rifled long ago, the most salient of their contents removed. Accounts of job placement – work release – for inmates sent into private service. Of deals made between private industry and the state. Those accountings – the 'count' the boy spoke of – were removed years ago. But although their intended use was thwarted, the documents were never returned. Never refiled after that one, long-ago theft – when a foolhardy whistleblower sought to make a difference. They have instead become the stuff of legend.

I confess to having doubts at the way she handled the interrogation. True, once this guard – this Terry – collapsed, sick and in apparent despair, she seemed to have the upper hand. His vulnerability and her kindness created a dynamic unlike any I recall. Still, the man is a liar – a convicted felon, as demonstrated by his placement here, a trustee working in this hall of records.

What I can confirm, I have. That the man has not been outside is apparent. His ancient work boots have paper-thin soles, but the signs of wear on the toes and ankles are all dusty, the cuts in the leather dry. Nor do his clothes reveal any sign of the outside, no trace of earth or dampness, or of any other living thing. Instead, he smells only of decay. The odor of this building, of paper and crumbling brick. And of his own rotting lungs, which surely imprison him more securely than any legal sentence could.

'I knew,' he says, with a calm that may have betokened only his shortness of breath, though the way the girl nods, I am drawn to wonder if she sees in it more. 'I saw him, out there. Waiting.'

'Out there?' She looks at him, the question in her eyes.

'Yeah. In the alley. Dingo never came in,' says the guard. 'I knew he was playing a sharp card,' he shrugs. 'Hell, I'd have helped him, if he asked. I almost did, that night.'

He stares off into the middle distance again. Were his eyes as sharp as mine, I would think he was seeing the small scrabblers in the wall. Mice and centipedes, as busy in their lives as he once was in his.

'For old time's sake,' he adds, and then he turns to her. 'It wasn't Dingo's fault I got pinched, you know. It was this.' He brings one hand to his chest. 'I got too slow. Granted,' he smiles now, at the memory. 'We were doing the boss's work.

'Sometimes, I wonder about that.' His voice goes soft again. 'Why that night. Why me. I know I wasn't as good an earner as I used to be. I know there were complaints. At any rate, it wasn't Dingo's fault. He was a good egg.' He turns, once again facing the dark.

'Anyway, he made his bid.' The big head sinks low, heavy with a grief that is also audible in his voice. 'I knew when I heard the news. I knew that was it.'

He straightens up and turns toward her, renewed vigor in his voice. 'That's why I say I'm lucky to have this job. I'm lucky to be here at all.'

# THIRTY-FOUR

B y the time the guard leads her to the back door, the girl has peppered him with questions. She has asked him about Dingo, his friend. About his habits and his duties for the man they both have served. She has asked, as well, about the guard's life – about his failing health. About the risks he had to take, just to keep up. About the bust that seemed so well timed to remove the team's least efficient member, tie him up for whatever years remained. She hasn't asked about the justice of such a sentence. Her own family has suffered under the draconian laws, I gather. Besides, she has picked up that this man may not be the best judge of his own life.

'I'll bring these back,' she says, as he chooses one oversized key from the ring he carries. She holds the remainder of the file, as scant as it may be. 'I don't want you to get in trouble.'

For a moment, I believe he is going to respond. He is quiet, but the walk downstairs has started him coughing again, and the effort he expends even now has wearied him. But then the moment passes, and he remains silent, even as he leans on the metal door, turning the key just so with a practiced hand.

'No rush,' he says quietly, as he pulls the door open. She looks up at him, then, another question forming. But he only shakes his head and smiles, and as if this were answer enough she nods and steps out into the night.

I follow, grateful not to have to attempt that damp passage again. I do not fear death, but I have tasks to complete. I wait, as is my wont, for the moment when the portal has begun to close before racing through, the better to elude pursuit. But as I do, I catch the scent – the bitter bit of sulfur. The matchstick.

I freeze in the doorway, whiskers up.

'Wait,' the guard calls, leaning on the door. I use the pause to nose the trestle, where – yes – I find that unburned match.

'Watch out for your friend here,' the man says. 'Some of the boys – well, they can get rough.'

I would bristle at that, were I not otherwise engaged. I am not a pet, nor do I ever want to be a burden to this Care, this girl. But it serves its purpose. The girl reaches for me and, doing so, sees what I have found.

'Gina,' she says, as the door latches behind us. 'I've got to warn her.'

She shoves the matchstick into her bag and heads for the street. It is full dark now. Even the moon has sunk, and she does not see as I race alongside her, as she runs toward the docks.

# THIRTY-FIVE

' f it isn't the gutter rat.' The barkeep looks up with a smile
full of malice. 'Getting a taste for the fare around here?
Looking for a more profitable trade?'

Care has burst through the wooden door and stands blinking
in the low light of the ramshackle bar. Custom is thin tonight.
Two drinkers whose odor I recognize. I doubt they've moved
much since we were last here. A pair of toughs who smell of
the factory – sweat and dust. They're the ones the barkeep is
performing for. They've turned to size the girl up. One of them
starts to stand.

'I'm looking for Gina.' The girl holds her ground. Stares at
the man, who sinks back onto his stool. Turns to take in his
companion. 'You know her. Big girl. Blonde.'

'Yeah, yeah.' The second man nods, more intent on his drink
than on any recreation the barman might suggest. 'Good ol'
Gina. Not seen her tonight.'

'Dirty Gina, huh?' The barman could be talking to himself.
'She's a friendly type. Likes to chat.'

Care waits, then pulls out a coin. She can't have many left
– those bills from Gravitch are too large and too conspicuous
for such use – but she places it on the rough bar. The man
scoops it up and leans in. 'Gina says she needs to meet,' he
says. Even from my low place, I can smell his breath. 'Says
she found out something about Dingo. Something you need to
know. Says she'll wait for you in the alley by Gravy's place.
Says you'll know where.'

I don't like it one bit. But I am a dumb beast, unable to
make my displeasure felt, as Care turns to leave. She doesn't
see the vagrant in the corner, whose tattered garb shifted with
more than the breeze as she blew in. The rag woman, who
shakes her head, a movement so small that I doubt most would
notice. But I have and I do what I must, ducking in front of
the girl to trip her as she turns to go.

'Blackie!' Her foot catches me beneath the ribs, and I go flying. 'Oh, I'm sorry.' Ignoring the cruel laughter of the men, she falls to her knees as if to cradle me. But I dart away as if in fear – sheltering by the rag woman's side. My move was deliberate, although it will not seem so to those observing. But I find myself taken by surprise. The creature beneath those rags is not clean. Far from it, and yet she doesn't reek of the rotgut the barkeep serves. Nor are the eyes that glance down at me clouded by more than age. She's been watching the exchange from deep in the shadows, the realization dawns on me. Gathering intelligence, as well as husbanding the warmth from the fire, as close as she's tolerated.

'Blackie?' Care's voice is limp with hurt as she regards us, wide-eyed, and slowly steps forward.

'Good kitty.' A hand as hard as horn rests gently on my back. Her voice, however, is soft. An old lady talking to a cat. 'He wanted us to meet,' she says, apparently to me.

'Watch it, Aisha,' one of the drunks called. 'People already say you're a witch.'

'You've got a smart cat,' says the ragged woman, ignoring him. 'He knows who he can trust.' Her voice, already low, drops to a whisper. 'And who he can't.'

I doubt if the men notice the girl's reaction. The way her head jerks up, startled. She catches herself quickly. Turns back toward me, and then to the door.

'Have it your way,' she says. Her voice is a little too loud, and my ears flick back. But I hold my place as she rises to leave.

After Care steps out of the bar, that flimsy door flapping behind her, the rag woman leans on the wall. Manages to stand. She waits until the men at the bar are distracted, laughing over their whiskey about some poor fool they ripped off. Somebody who got beat down. When she slips out of the shack, the door barely moves, and that's when I follow. Care is waiting, hands on her hips as she peers up and down the street.

'She knew, you know.' The rag woman has shuffled close, her voice little more than a whisper. Care doesn't turn, and I wonder if she hears. 'She knew,' says the woman again. 'Should have, anyway.'

'Knew what?' The girl turns to face her, skepticism writ on her pursed mouth. 'And how do you know?'

'I saw her.' The woman attempts to stand up straight. 'Saw her when they dropped her off. Dingo helped her.'

This gets Care's attention, but she's smart. She waits, and I wait with her.

'Dingo cleaned up,' says the woman. 'After they were done with her.' A strange rattling comes from beneath her layers. She is laughing, a sad sound.

Care doesn't respond. There is no response to make.

'He didn't like it, what they did. Knew what he'd found though, didn't he?' the woman concludes. 'She should've too, once they had her on the floor. Only, why would she risk it? They owed her, once they'd had their fun.'

She starts to move away, back to the bar and her corner of warmth, and Care watches her go. 'Wait,' she says, before the woman reaches the door. She runs over to her and digs in her pocket. A hand appears, as grey as those rags, and Care places a small coin in it. It is, I suspect, the last of her store. 'It's not much, but if I can help you in any way,' she says. 'I find things. Find people.'

The hand with the coin disappears in the rags, but the woman lingers, looking her over with those filmy eyes. 'Looking for people,' she says, her voice a low whisper. 'Sometimes you find trouble instead.'

# THIRTY-SIX

The rag woman's words should be warning enough. Should send the girl fleeing from this city, this life. But she is on a mission, her chapped lips set tight, and nothing about Gravitch's lair – no hellish odors, no growling beast – will hinder her passage through the waterfront.

She takes what caution she can, I am gratified to note. Pausing by the fire escape, she eyes the building, with its unnatural thrum, and approaches the alley indirectly, skirting the open stone in front. Illuminated by that far streetlight, the passage appears empty, save for a car parked back on the street, its windows dark. The only movement comes from a trash heap, a new deposit near the alley's end. Some activity, too large for the predations of a rat, shifts the rubbish as we watch, and a groan issues forth.

'Gina?' The girl calls and slowly begins her approach. Beneath the sulfurous yellow light the trash ripples. The building beside us hums. 'Are you there?'

Another groan, and I strike a pose before her that is unmistakable in its focus and attention. Staring at the trash heap, I begin to advance, low to the ground in a hunting stance. That gets Care's attention, and she follows until she, too, hears the pitiful sound. Until she finds the woman, her face bloody and almost unrecognizable were it not for the familiar effusion of sweat and cheap scent, of male funk and usage.

'Gina?' Care hangs back, reminding me once again that she lacks my acuity of smell. 'Is that you?'

She is a quick study, however, and as soon as she recognizes the woman – the matted gore has not entirely obscured the bleached blonde of her hair – she reaches toward her, pulling her from the filth where she has, apparently, been thrown.

'What happened?' She steadies the woman, ignoring the rubbish that sticks to her still.

'You got my message.' Gina reaches to brush herself off and

almost topples over. As Care reaches for her again, she pulls away. 'I'm okay,' she says again, anger doing as much as anything to help her regain her balance.

'Is this . . .' Care pauses. I can see how she struggles to find the words. 'Were you hurt because of me?'

A laugh. 'As if,' she says, wiping her mouth. Her hand comes away smeared with blood. 'Gravy and the boys always did like it rough. Only, I should have known, shouldn't I? After what you gave me.'

'After . . .' Care's teeth worry at her lip, biting back the rebuke she would make. 'Gina, did you show that paper to someone?' she asks at last, the effort to keep her voice even makes it flat.

Gina shrugs, wiping her face with her forearm. 'I thought, maybe, there was more on the page than you told me. I thought, maybe, there was something I could use.'

'It was just a list of numbers – the case numbers of boys who'd been remanded to work release – and one that might have been code for a shop or a—'

Gina doesn't answer, and the girl exhales, the full force of what has happened hitting her.

'You couldn't—' She catches herself. Works to keep her voice level. 'You got someone to read it to you. To read it for you.'

'I had to know.' The woman stares off into the street, refusing to meet Care's eyes.

'Who did you ask?' Care's voice is low, but she cannot hide the tremor.

'Just—' The woman shrugs. 'Just Stinger. He's the best of them, after Dingo. At least, I thought he was.'

Care's breathing speeds up. I can almost hear her thinking. Strategizing.

'And then I had to tell them. Tell him.' The woman before us says, although the question has not been asked. Her voice tightens up into a whine. 'He made me send for you. You get that, right?'

Care would respond – would question her further, I believe. Only at the moment the door of the car at the alley's end opens, and Gravitch steps out. He is followed by two men. The smaller, with a face like a hatchet, has a knife.

Care's head whips around, her eyes confirming what my ears have already told me. The alley door behind us has opened, and we are not alone. There are other men – Gravitch's men – coming in from the front of the building as well. We are trapped. I feel my fur start to rise. I will not survive this fight, but I will not run. Not if I can buy her time.

'Mr Gravitch.' I do not expect this. She walks up to the little man. She has courage, this girl. She will bluff. 'We need to talk.'

'You and me? Our business is over.' The matchstick moves as his eyes dart. His men are in place, and he turns to go. 'She's yours,' Gravy starts to walk away. 'Just – clean up my office after. Will you?'

'Wait,' says Care. Her voice reveals no fear. 'I've got something to say first. And these gentlemen will want to hear it. That is, if they want to know what really happened to Dingo.'

'What happened to Dingo?' Gravy forces a laugh. It sounds like a bark. 'You killed him, my girl. You're the one who found him, didn't you? Gina told us all about it. How you had the papers – the ones your old man stole. Dingo figured it out and tried to get 'em from you and you stuck him. He was a good boy, wasn't he?'

Gravitch turns to his men, who nod and rumble in agreement.

'The papers . . .' Care falls silent. Her bluff gone. 'My father,' she says. Gravitch laughs again. He nods to his men, who begin to move in.

'We sent your boy for you. Let him go. Thought you might share your findings with him. But you were too smart for that.' Gravy's voice is rough with bravado. Loud enough to carry. He's still speaking as he turns to go. 'Smart like a gutter rat – a gutter rat with a knife.'

'But I wasn't.' Care speaks again as she takes a step toward Gravitch. 'It was you Dingo was going to meet over by the Dunstan. I've just come from there. Old Terry told me all about it.'

'What are you talking—' Gravitch turns back.

She doesn't let him finish. 'You tried to clean up but you can't get rid of all the traces of a body, the signs that someone fell there.' Her voice speeds up, getting louder, as the men pause to listen. 'You hid his body in the trash bin. Left him there for days, and then pretended he was out on a job. Washed the alley down after. Your car, too, probably. But you didn't have your boys with you, did you? You weren't careful enough. Working at night, in secret. You left things. A tag from the factory floor,' she says, her hand reaching into her bag. 'Or something more damning.'

All eyes are on her as she gropes. She blanches, and I freeze in my tracks. The bag. The match. It must have fallen, lost through the hole I kicked in my nightmare frenzy. Lost along with what else, I can only guess. A low growl begins deep in my chest. This will be it. The final battle.

But the light is bad. The men not as observant as I, nor do they know the girl as well. And she is quick. In lieu of the matchstick she would present, she draws forth a handful of papers. The pages she has retrieved from the Dunstan, as well the remainder of the file from the hovel, too bulky to have fallen through the tear.

'These papers,' she says, as if that were her purpose all along. 'The ones you hired me to find. Hired me in private, when you realized Dingo didn't bring them to the meet. Why else would I have brought them with me tonight?'

A low rumble begins, and the big man, the one from the car, reaches for her. She winces, but he only grabs her bag from her shoulder. Rifles through it.

'No knife here, boss.' He throws the bag to the ground. I crouch, ready to pounce. But there was doubt in his voice, and she seizes on it. She shakes the papers in her hands.

'Sure, I showed one page to Gina,' she says. 'I didn't realize you wanted to keep them secret. But now what Terry said makes sense. You told Dingo you wanted to make these safe,' she repeats, for the better understanding of the men around her. 'Put them back in the files, where they were supposed to be.'

'You were covering for yourself,' says a low voice. The scar-faced man. 'You and your sloppy ways.'

The big man opens his mouth, then closes it. He, too, waits for an explanation.

'But why Dingo?' his colleague asks instead, the sharp features of his face growing soft and muddled in his confusion. They are all watching, waiting, when Gina throws herself against Gravitch.

'You knew!' She pounds her fists against his chest. He reaches for her wrists and holds them. Looking over at his flunkies, he waits for their laughter. But they stand still, their faces impassive. 'You killed Dingo because he was trying to help me.' She is sobbing now, her voice choked by tears. 'Trying to help me find my boy.'

'No.' Care's voice is low, but the surprise of it causes the men to turn. Even Gina quiets. 'No, he had him killed because he was scared.'

Gravitch lets go of one of Gina's wrists. He reaches toward Care as if he would hold her still. Make her stop. 'Now, girly, cut your nonsense.' His voice is low and full of threat.

'He knew from the start, Gina.' Care steps forward, away from Gravitch. Toward the woman who now cries quietly. 'Even when he hired me to look for Dingo. It was all a cover up.'

The woman sniffs and wipes her face. Gravitch has dropped her other hand, and she retreats to the rubbish pile. Retrieves her bag, soiled and torn. But I am the only creature watching her now. All eyes are on Care.

'Dingo wasn't threatening to blackmail Gravitch with the authorities.' Care is thinking. I doubt the others notice how her brow furrows. That mistake – the loss of the matchstick – has given her a moment to consider. And as Gravitch sputters, as he tries to formulate his excuses, the final connection comes clear.

'That logo – on the truck. I know it. It's a big business. Bigger than Gravitch's little shop here. But it was Gravitch's fault those papers were out there. He was charged with security, with cleaning up. And he botched it.'

The logo! Of course – the looming mountains. Only not mountains . . . but a man. A third man. I lash my tail, infuriated at my own ignorance. If I could only read . . . If I could only remember. It took the girl – a child – to piece things together. Everything I suspected, everything I feared. She puzzled it out, with the aid of the little mole man – Quirty – and the memory of another, older case. A whistleblower who tried to expose the exploitation and failed. An old man who went up against an implacable foe.

*You can't . . . no.* I blink as her words come back to me. As

I hear her calling me, as a truck backed into view, its logo clear to one who could read. *You can't know*, she said. And I did not. If only I could have remembered.

'When Dingo came to him, Gravitch set him up.' Care is speaking as if what she says is common knowledge. As if it were as obvious as the marks on that paper are to her. 'Had the poor fool meet him at the Dunstan. Probably told him that they would bring those files back in together. Put them back where they came from. All along, he was going to pretend Dingo had taken them. That they'd been in the files, in the Dunstan, for years.'

'You don't know he didn't.' Gravitch's voice has some of its old bravado back. Some of its growl. 'Your good old Dingo couldn't be trusted.'

'No.' Care is calm. Certain. 'Not once he saw what you had. Maybe these were the final straw. The way you treated Gina. How you hurt her and kept stringing her along about her boy. How you treated everyone, once they'd given you all they had. It all must have added up. But he didn't steal these papers. He wouldn't have gotten old Terry in trouble.

'He got those papers from your office. Maybe they started on your desk, but they weren't secured and when – well, when Dingo helped clean up after your party with Gina, he ended up taking them. It took him a while to realize what he'd found. Most of your crew can't read, you've seen to that, but he could – a bit. Enough so that he realized he could finally help Gina out. You'd have to let her go. Give up her boy, with what he had. You see, Dingo knew you were responsible for security, all those years ago. You should have returned these papers to the Dunstan years before. Only – what? – did you get lazy? Or did you think you could use them for leverage? A bargaining chip with the big boss?'

Gravitch recoils as if he's been struck. Only the presence of the other men – his former henchmen – seems to keep him upright.

'What about Dingo then?' the hatchet-faced man asks.

'You killed Dingo,' says the big man, and his colleagues join in, their voices angry.

The little man draws closer to Gravitch, his hand cradling

his blade's handle. 'We only work for you because the big boss says so.' His voice is cool. Appraising. 'Dingo, too.'

Voices start to rise as the men crowd around. Only Care stands back – Care and Gina, who is blinking, mouth open. She appears to be in shock.

'You were supposed to take care of that.' The voices grow louder and more angry. 'That's why he gave you the shop – the right to run the kids . . .'

Only Care among them can hear the blowsy woman speak. Only Care and I, whose ears are sensitive to such soft sounds.

'He said he was going to help me,' Gina says, her voice barely above a whisper. 'If I took his favor – if I put up with the pain . . . He was going to find my boy, when all the time . . .'

She reaches into her bag, as if for a tissue. As if for the flask. What she pulls out, however, is the blade. Smaller than the one the hatchet-faced man carries, but still sharp. And while the men are circling, she pushes her way in without hesitation. Without any fear left.

A shriek cuts the night. The iron tang of blood fills the air, and the men fall silent. One steps aside, and Gina staggers out. Her hand, now empty, is bright red, bloodied to the wrist.

Care staggers back, unsteady, as if she herself had dealt that blow. Reaches behind herself for the wall, where I too wait, watching. Before us, the men crowd closer again, silent now. From their midst the fading cries – whimpers, really – of the dying man.

'Please.' His voice has lost its command. 'Help me.'

'Help you?' It's the smaller of his henchmen. The one with the knife. 'Like you helped Dingo?'

'Care.' An urgent whisper, close behind us, causes the girl to turn. It is the boy, peering around the edge of the building. He waves for her to join him. To exit the alley. Despite its source, it is good counsel, and I follow closely, hugging the wall.

'In here,' I hear him say. They have turned the corner, while I have chanced a last glance back. The men have converged, waiting. The death cry, when it comes, is faint but unmistakable. Before it can fade away, the boy's words sink in, and I race after them.

The car, beneath the streetlight, is running now. The driver has stepped out. But the boy crouches by the bay door, where the crumpled metal has pulled free. He motions toward the opening. Toward the dark within. He reaches for her hand, as I jump between them. Place myself in front of the girl, before her feet.

'What?' She blinks, still in shock from the violence she has witnessed. From that which she has escaped.

*Don't trust him!* I stare into her eyes, willing her to understand. Willing her to remember what Gravitch implied, only minutes before. *You cannot trust this boy.*

'Care, come on!' He grabs her hand. Pulls it. 'We can hide.' And in that moment, she nods ever so slightly, and begins to draw away. She has heard me. She understands. She will turn away. Only she doesn't.

'I have to.' Her whisper a mere breath, meant only for my ears. 'Please,' she says. And she disappears inside.

# THIRTY-SEVEN

The noise is deafening. Even with my ears flat, I can barely stand it. Can barely make myself follow, for follow I do – slipping through the breach after the girl – into the place of madness and despair. As before, the space is dim. Poorly lit, but not dark. Close, as well, and thick with steam and oil and the fug of unwashed bodies. But it is the noise that oppresses me, more than any lack of illumination. A din loud enough to banish reason, to blind my senses and turn my acuity against me. The horrible roar besets me, compels me to run, as I did once before, through this hellish room. To escape the clamor, the nightmare of sound.

Only I cannot. Even as I battle against the onslaught, I remain aware of the girl and the boy by her side. They cower against the wall, where I join them, panting. As panicked as any beast, but bound by love.

'Blackie.' A hand reaches out, and I glance up. Even in this near dark, she must see the whites around my eyes, the terror that makes me tremble so. Her voice, as much as the gentle hand she lays upon my back, calms me, somewhat, although my ears stay flat against my head. I would gather reason back. Would be alert, unsure as I am about this boy's next move. About the workings of the trap, for trap it must be.

And then the light diminishes further, and I understand. The triangular breach is blocked, as by a shadow or – no – a large creature. Something is pushing through. I hear panting that is not my own, the low sounds of distress adding to the maddening clatter around me. And then it is through. I blink up as it rises, towering above us, a silhouette against the dark, as terrifying as any nightmare.

I am frozen. But I must not— I cannot be. For surely, this creature – this hunter – will not stay still for long. One step, another, and arms reach out. I stare up willing myself to see, and to my amazement, I perceive that it is unbalanced. Indeed, it flails, arms outstretched in this close space. And in that moment, I catch my breath.

It is blind in this room, I realize, the lack of light even more pronounced to one newly arrived from the alley outside, from the streetlight's yellow glare. Here, then, is my moment, before the predator adjusts. Before it – he – can see. I will my quaking limbs to serve me. I cannot spring. I can barely lift my belly off the floor, but I approach the creature. Slowly, slowly, and then reach out – my claws extended – and bat.

'Ah!' A high-pitched voice, more squeak than shout. I bat again, slapping at the intruder with lightning speed. And bat once more.

It works. The monster retreats, thrashing at the air. It hits the wall with a dull thud, and suddenly the noises all converge.

'Care!' It is the boy, shouting, as a booming, grinding sound adds to the clamor.

'Tick!' Through my panic, I see the girl as she reaches for the boy. The light is growing, the noise becoming louder and yet less intense as the horrible echoes fade as – yes! – the metal gate is rising, triggered by the intruder's frightened thrashing. By Gina, for it is she, who has pushed her way in, the blood still wet on her hands – and on the control switch her flailing arm has hit.

Able once again to breathe – to see – I survey the scene. The space we are in is a workroom. A factory of sorts, lined by huffing metal giants. Their breath reeks of oily steam, as their giant jaws clamp down with a hiss. Before us, smaller beasts, whose furious metal teeth clatter endlessly, pulling spools of garish thread through row upon row of cheap woven stuff. Only, one by one, they begin to slow, to fail. To fall silent as the children – for it is children who stand by each mechanical beast – pause in their labors. They blink in the dirty yellow light of that streetlight, as the machines – not beasts, I realize as my own pulse calms – grumble to a halt. As Gina staggers forward, mouth open, to take in the hellish scene.

From somewhere in the back, a small voice calls, 'Ma?'

# THIRTY-EIGHT

'**G**ravitch should've dumped Dingo's body in the harbor. Kept to his story that he'd gone missing, and he'd have been fine.' The girl worries over the problem like a kitten with a mouse as she sews, her bag before her on the desk. 'Why didn't he? Was it only 'cause people were asking for him? Or was there something else going on?'

We are sitting in the office. Our office, once again. With one of Gravitch's bills, she has purchased food and eaten. She has slept, at length, on the sofa, while I kept watch by her side. Now she works to patch the old carryall with a piece of bartered denim. Her stitches are fine, the patch will hold. She should be at peace. Rested, but she cannot let go of the dead. Her eyes are hot, and I cannot help but wonder at her innocence.

As a girl, as a newcomer in a dangerous field, she must have seemed an obvious patsy. Expendable and easy to play, a pawn that would help Gravitch lay to rest the issue of the missing Dingo, of the missing papers, which his own greed and carelessness had put at risk. For these reasons alone, Gravitch would have set her up. Would have used her.

But she will not let her questions lie, and frets at them as her needle works its way through the cloth. Does she wonder, then, at the accusations Gravitch made? Does she realize that there would be other reasons for the man to set her up? As she has repaired her bag, she has also pieced together that he served another. Does she not realize that she had thwarted the big boss once before – that her father had set all of this in motion?

'He tried to frame me,' she says. It is a conclusion she has reached before, but it gives her no peace. 'Tried to draw me in, using Tick. If he could only get me into the system or under his control – and he almost did.'

Gina is gone. Disappeared that night with one small, pale boy in tow. The others scattered into the night. After some deliberation, the girl turned the papers over to Miss Adele, but not the children themselves. No word of them, or where they may be hiding. She'd learned. Besides, she had promised the boy, Tick. He still works at the factory, for it operates still, commerce being the one constant in this city. Spends his days sewing shoddy goods for the export market. But he comes out to the office each night. He sleeps until first light. He's paid little enough, but it is something. The new overseer, an older man past his fighting days, keeps the machines running, but he's less greedy, Tick says.

'More important,' says the boy, 'he's obedient. He knows his place.'

Our place, for now, is here. The lease had been renegotiated. I watched with some concern when the girl visited Quirty. When he talked about setting up a shell company of his own and reapplying for the space. Strangely, there was no fuss about the application, which Gravitch's remaining bill enabled. Nor any about the anonymous tenant at will. It was almost as if someone believed the girl was owed. As if she had done a favor for those in power, for a certain faceless corporation. Or perhaps, that someday she will.

This bothers me in ways I cannot explain. Much like my inability to read, or the memory of another paper – a document of higher quality – that a small man pondered and then hid away again. There is so much that I, a cat, cannot express. It does not get easier, but at times like this, as the girl talks through her thoughts, I find I can bear it. That I want to comfort her. To share the great wisdom of beasts, which is to live in the moment. To appreciate the calm that is now. We are warm. We have fed. And so I sit and watch the girl.

The knock wakes me, as tentative as it is.

'Yes?' Care looks up from her bag. The patch is almost secure, and it is with a sigh of regret that she puts the needle down. It's the apple seller, from the market. She stands in the doorway and blinks, unaccustomed, I believe, to being indoors.

'Aisha sent me,' she says. Stepping forward, she unwraps a rag and shakes out three small coins. 'One of my boys ran off. I'm hoping you can find him?'

'I can try.' Care stands and goes to greet her. 'Please, have a seat.'